# THE HIJACKING OF CASSIE PETERS

## Mary Stanley

NEW ISLAND

THE HIJACKING OF CASSIE PETERS
First published 2012 by
New Island
2 Brookside
Dundrum Road
Dublin 14

www.newisland.ie

P/B ISBN 978-1-84840-124-2
ePub ISBN 978-1-84840-179-2
mobi ISBN 978-1-84840-180-8

Cover design by Nina Lyons
Typeset by Mariel Deegan
Printed by ScandBook AB

New Island received financial assistance from
The Arts Council (An Comhairle Ealaíon), Dublin, Ireland.

10 9 8 7 6 5 4 3 2 1

*For Eugen and Herta Higel*

**Also by Mary Stanley:**

*Retreat*

*Missing*

*Revenge*

*Searching for Home*

*The Lost Garden*

*The Umbrella Tree*


In the Open Door adult literacy series:

*An Angel at my Back*

*Bruno, Peanut and Me*

**Praise for Mary Stanley:**

*Retreat*

'Mary Stanley's atmospheric novels tend to draw you in from the first page and haunt you long after you have turned the last... This book is beautifully written, achingly poignant, dark-edged but tempered with humour' – *Irish Independent*

'A deeply satisfying, reflective read... Lively conversation and richly varied settings' – *Evening Herald*

'A fresh new voice in Irish Writing' – *Irish World*

'The pages turn with ease' – *Observer*

'Warm, and even at its darkest, never entirely black. An engrossing read... Lively conversation and richly varied settings' – *Irish Sunday Independent*

*Missing*

'*MISSING* is a perceptive and poignant novel exploring the ramifications of loss and abandonment with compassion and a wry, perfectly pitched wit... This is a book about the need to communicate openly and honestly with those we love and the possible consequences of our failure to do so. Stanley writes with a lightness of touch reminiscent of Jonathan Coe – both explore life's darknesses with a gentle humour which encourages understanding of our frailties and fears' – *The Big Issue in the North*

'A gripping and mesmerising novel, which twists and turns at every opportunity... Skilfully written with bursts of humour, Stanley weaves a compelling web of deception and intrigue' – *Glasgow Evening Times*

'Mary Stanley creates a fascinating story that is full of intrigue with disturbing and dark moments' – *Sunday World*

'Touching, intriguing and often humorous' – *Sunday Business Post*

'Stanley's writing is alive – witty, moving and engrossing... The characters of the three girls are richly portrayed' – *The Sunday Times*, Malta

## Revenge

'[T]his is a woman [who] once she's embarked on something, who moves into top gear and, well, stays there' – *Sunday Tribune*

'A gripping story that is both detective novel and psychological thriller... The characters are likeable, funny and real. A great read' – *The Irish Times*

'Compelling' – *Sunderland Echo*

'Moving and darkly funny' – *Bella*

'A wonderfully written book' – *Herald Sun* (Melbourne)

'A compulsively different read... This imaginatively and stunningly written novel... is warm and poignant... Thought provoking and compassionate, the tale is as strong as its characters and once again Stanley has proved herself as a spellbinding author' – *Irish World*

## Searching for Home

'Settle down to a deeply satisfying, reflective read' – *Evening Herald*

'Stanley lures you in with a big event, then drags you through the dark recesses of memory, usually through a child's eyes, until you emerge blinking and perhaps laughing at the end' – *Daily Ireland*

'Stanley effectively develops the theme of displacement in a well-written novel that will grip you to the very last page' – *Ireland on Sunday*

'This novel is one of the best books I have read this year' – *The Irish World*

'A gripping read' – *Belfast Newsletter*

'Poignant and perceptive' – *Eastbourne and District Advertiser*

'In the fashion of the best page turners, this keeps you guessing until the very end' – *Buzz*

### The Lost Garden

'A beautifully crafted story by a very gifted writer' – *Sunday World Magazine*

'... had me laughing out loud' – *Ireland on Sunday*

'Stanley's sensitive and heartfelt writing shines through in *The Lost Garden*' – *Belfast Newsletter Special Supplement*

'A clever novel. A charming read' – *Nottingham Evening Post*

'A compelling, suspenseful story... complex and elegantly written' – *Sunday Independent*

# THE HARLOT'S HOUSE

We caught the tread of dancing feet,
We loitered down the moonlit street,
And stopped beneath the harlot's house.

Inside, above the din and fray,
We heard the loud musicians play
The 'Treues Liebes Herz' of Strauss.

Like strange mechanical grotesques,
Making fantastic arabesques,
The shadows raced across the blind.

We watched the ghostly dancers spin
To sound of horn and violin,
Like black leaves wheeling in the wind.

Like wire-pulled automatons,
Slim silhouetted skeletons
Went sidling through the slow quadrille,

Then took each other by the hand,
And danced a stately saraband;
Their laughter echoed thin and shrill.

Sometimes a clockwork puppet pressed
A phantom lover to her breast,
Sometimes they seemed to try to sing.

Sometimes a horrible marionette
Came out, and smoked its cigarette
Upon the steps like a live thing.

Then, turning to my love, I said,
'The dead are dancing with the dead,
The dust is whirling with the dust.'

But she - she heard the violin,
And left my side, and entered in:
Love passed into the house of lust.

Then suddenly the tune went false,
The dancers wearied of the waltz,
The shadows ceased to wheel and whirl.

And down the long and silent street,
The dawn, with silver-sandalled feet,
Crept like a frightened girl.

*Oscar Wilde 1854-1900*

# CASSIE'S TALE

My clothes were sticking to me when I arrived at the airport. I looked around. No sign of my mother at first, but then I saw her. She was in the middle of farewells. I kept well out of sight.

I found the toilets and joined a queue. Then I washed my face and hands and hauled my rucksack onto my back before joining another queue for checking in. I dropped my rucksack again on the floor. My mother joined me as my passport was being checked. She looked tired. She smiled at me, but it felt forced. She drank coffee and I drank water as we waited for our flight to be called. There is time, I thought, time to talk and to understand. No rush. I had waited this long; a few more hours or whatever it took, it did not matter.

My mother and I sat in the front row on the plane back to England with a spare seat between us. I had the aisle seat, and she the window. There were several empty seats on the plane. It hurtled down the runway and lifted off, and we saw the Acropolis beneath us as we turned and flew above the Aegean. I was eighteen years old that day. I remember that, and I remember wondering if she would remember. Goodbye, Greece, I thought.

We did not fly to London.

The hijackers moved up the plane and one sat between my mother and me. One broke into the cockpit. Two addressed the plane. Addressed? They screamed. They shouted. There was no time to understand. My hijacker put a gun to my head and told them that I would die.

The Minotaur had found me.

Commotion, confusion, terror, the brain incapable of following what was happening. Senses heightened and then dulled. The pounding of blood in the ears distorting the words that were being spoken. Wherever he moved, I moved too, like a strange and bedraggled attachment, a puppet pulled by his manipulative fingers. I saw my mother's face, white beneath her newly acquired tan. The plane changed direction and we headed away from our northern destination. Panic. Fear. Terror. *Terror*. Same word in English and in German. I had not known the meaning of the word terror. I thought it meant fear. But it is deeper. It goes into your bones, absorbed into the body until it is all that there is, the pounding of the heart and the sweating of the hands and laboured breathing.

They took our passports, sorted them into nationalities, called out names to see who was who. They were excited by having two Americans and one German – me – on the plane. Many English. My mother now had a British passport. Many Greek. An Irishman. They liked him for some reason. Why oh why had I changed my passport? It had been easier to get a German one like Papa's when he was updating his. I wished I had made the effort to contact the Irish Embassy in Germany and renew my passport as an Irish citizen. It had seemed to be too much trouble at the time.

We landed in Addis Ababa. I had no notion of time. My internal watch had stopped. Time kept clogging and then going backwards and some-times forwards. The immediate present was excruciating. Strung up and crucified as a puppet in the Minotaur's pantomime was not a role I knew how to play. But to turn back time and change this moment into a different one; how far back do I have to go to do that? How far back to change the course of history or destiny? Or to put it forward to the ending of this, and then what is there? Is that worse? Can that be worse than this? Is it pos-sible that this is the moment to cherish, that this is a moment while there is still hope and I should be holding it as a treasure? To be on this cross, crucified as a puppet in the Minotaur's pantomime is the best role the moment can offer, and I must play the role and bear this. I would change this for anything, but I have no choice.

Everything is coming back, and it is unbearable to bear in my mind. I couldn't hold it in my mind when it was happening. Now I am baring the unbearable.

I remember being hauled to the open door and used as a screen as the Minotaur held the gun to my temple while he shouted down instructions. There was a television camera, soldiers, armoured vehicles, and the ice cold barrel of the gun on my brow.

I would have screamed, only I had no idea how to scream, how to utter a noise.

I tried to shift my weight slightly. 'Fuck up,' my hijacker shouted into my ear. Fuck up? Fuck off, shut up? Who knew what he meant? I closed my eyes as the heat washed over me. What a stupid way to die, I thought. Panic unending in the air as the plane was eventually refuelled and, horrifyingly, we took off again.

And then, somehow, that moment passed. Airborne again, Pegasus took us on a new route.

We were given water. 'Sip it slowly,' my mother said. I did what she told me. The good daughter now, obedient, hopeful that she could fix this terrible development. The hijackers were more relaxed when the plane was off the ground. The toilets stank and were filthy. The gun was transferred to my mother's head when I went down that long aisle. Faces gazed at me as though I might have some answer as to why my hijacker had chosen me. The Minotaur and I were interlocked.

We flew and landed, each time the shouting and the increased fear. I was the perpetual shield in the open doorway. My bowels turning to water. We flew again. Their demands were simple. They wanted prisoners released from a prison. I didn't understand. Where was the prison? What had the prisoners to do with us? We were the prisoners. The value of my life came down to an exchange that I knew would never happen.

Papa had said just that, some time ago when a plane was hijacked in an effort to release the Baader Meinhof gang. Papa said then as we watched the television, 'There will be no exchange. They cannot comply with the demands as it will open up a whole new wave of terror.'

I wished he had told these men that. Why did they think that this would work?

But you live with hope – that is the one thing I learned on that flight. Down in the bottom of Pandora's box there was one thing left. In the midst of the despair and the horror and what I could see as being the only possible ending to this, I still felt a tiny flicker of hope. I told myself a thousand times during those seemingly endless flights to clear my mind, to clean it, to absolve myself of things, but I could not focus on any of those things. I thought of the sea and the dance of the waves and laughing as we played on the sand. I thought of a rock we used to swim to and clamber upon and how thrillingly and refreshingly cold the water was on a hot, hot summer's day long, long, long ago.

As my hope waned, I thought of my sisters and I hoped that Mer would find Ali and see that she was all right. I hoped that my sisters would have long and fulfilling lives. I hoped that I would not disappear into the unknown without them knowing where I ended up or what had happened to me.

I hoped that I would see them among the stars.

I thought of Papa, and wished that he would find someone to love him as he deserved to be loved. And Opa and Oma, my German grandparents, down on the farm with the tomatoes ripening in the sun. The walnuts growing on the trees. The snip snip snip of the green grass in summer. And then my mind would go back to the sea and how cold and refreshing... and then I was back in the present, over and over again, with the heat, and the stench and the smell of fear wafting through the plane.

No country wanted us to land. I wondered if we could stay up there, forever circling around the African continent, seeking a runway that would allow us space.

When I slept, just fitful dozing, I dreamed of things that had not happened but seemed so real. I dreamed in English as I had done as a little girl. Once, I dreamed I was back on the beach with Mer and Bernd. In my dream they had two little children, a boy and a girl, and I was playing with them. We made sandcastles. I helped them gather shells and tiny bits of sea-washed broken glass, brightly coloured until they dried in the sun, and we decorated the castles.

If I ever got off this plane, that is where I would go next. I would get on a train and then a boat and I would find my way back to Ireland, to Seapoint, and I would wash my feet in the sea, I would cleanse my soul and I would stay long after twilight, long into the night and I would sit and watch the stars falling into Howth across the water.

When I was a little girl, Seapoint, beautiful Seapoint, I remember, long ago. My sister Ali, she sometimes scared me. We were living in our house overlooking the sea, full of childhood hopes and dreams. Lying in bed waiting for sleep, waiting for the bedtime story. I remember Ali whispering to me in the dark.

'Half man, half bull, he lived in the labyrinth. He was called the Minotaur. He ate girls and boys.'

'Where is he now?' I asked.

'He's still in the labyrinth,' she said. 'He's always hungry.'

'Where is the labyrinth?'

'It's in the palace grounds of King Minos on the island of Crete. He howls with hunger and they bring him food... the girls and boys.'

'When you started the story, you said he lived in the labyrinth,' I said. I thought I had caught her. 'Not lives; lived,' I repeated.

'I meant *lives*. He lives in the labyrinth.' Ali was relentless.

I wasn't sure if I wanted the story to continue, but surely any bedtime story was better than none. I wished that Mer had brought me up to bed.

Ali usually told me fairy tales, unpleasant ones about dark forests and witches and ovens and birds eating the breadcrumbs that would have guided the children home. Sometimes the stories had happy endings. Sometimes not. It was Mer who told me stories from classical mythology, but they were full of interesting images, pictures of gods and goddesses, rolling pastures and skies full of constellations. We were named after the stars: Ali, Mer and Cassie, short names taken from long names.

I said to Ali,' I think I want to go to sleep now.' I didn't like her diversification into Mer's world of ancient Greece.

'But the Minotaur…'

I put my thumb in my mouth, I rolled on my side and closed my eyes.

'He's out there,' Ali said. 'He's waiting in the dark for the girls and boys.'

'I'm asleep,' I said.

I could hear her footsteps moving across the room away from my bed.

'He's waiting,' she said, as she went out onto the landing and pulled the door half closed behind her.

I waited until I heard her footsteps descend the stairs, and then I slipped out of bed and crossed the room. I peeped out carefully. There was a stillness upstairs in the house. On silent feet I went to Mer's room and opened the door quietly. Mer was sitting on her old, battered sofa in front of the window in the dark. I ran across and curled up beside her. We sat and gazed out across the sea to Howth in the distance. The window was slightly open, and the smell of the sea was in the air.

Mer ran her fingers through my tousled, knotted curls, and I leaned in against her. It was safe there, watching the stars and hearing the sound of the waves on the rocks below.

I remember saying, 'I wish you'd tell me a story, Mer.'

'Once upon a time…' Mer began. She always began her stories like that. I smiled and put my thumb in my mouth.

'Once upon a time…'

Sitting on the plane beside my mother during the hijacking, I had the feeling I was caught in the labyrinth and that there was no way out.

# CHAPTER ONE

Time goes back ten years to when Cassie Peters was only eight years old. It was a Friday night late in the summer of 1972. Karl Peters came home from work to find a letter addressed to him in his wife's childish handwriting lying on the hall table. He had slit it open with the paper-knife that was kept in the drawer beneath, while he called hello into the surprisingly quiet house. Pulling out the single sheet of paper, he read the contents quickly, and then, as the words penetrated his mind, he read it again. He folded it neatly back into the envelope before going upstairs and throwing up in the bathroom.

He washed his face and cleaned his teeth and then proceeded to the bedroom, where he stood and stared into the mirror on his wife's dressing-table.

In that moment he saw an ageing man. The mirror reflected nothing he recognised. His usually tanned skin seemed pale, his eyes dull. The few silver streaks appearing on either side of his head now seemed white. He shook his head and tried to re-create the man he had been when he had walked into his home some fifteen minutes earlier.

He turned and opened his wife's half-empty wardrobe. He shook his head in disbelief, went and sat at the dressing-table and looked at the few remaining items on it. Miriam had left behind some jars of cream, a pretty box that one of the girls had decorated for her tissues, a comb with a stray blonde hair. He had the desire to smash his fist into the mirror. Instead, he removed the envelope from his pocket and reread the letter. He was about to tear it up when it occurred to him that he might need it. In the same moment, he realised that he was able to think again and he put the letter in a drawer in the tallboy where he kept his folded clothing. He buried it beneath some handkerchiefs. Back in the bathroom, he washed his face again and dried it carefully.

Returning to the bedroom, he stood at the window and looked across the bay. The tide was out. Down below on the beach he could see people still swimming in the warm summer's evening, but his eyes were drawn to the horizon, to Howth and the distant flashing of the lighthouse and a ship, long since disappeared, bearing his departed wife away.

'God damn it,' he uttered aloud. 'And damn her, too.' In his mind, he added, 'Damn me too for being such a fool.' He straightened his shoulders and, turning, he walked towards the door and down the stairs to find his daughters.

They were in the kitchen, and their voices drew him towards them. He was dreading what was ahead but knew there was no avoiding it. They must come first. He would find a way to deal with his emotions later. As he put his hand on the brass doorknob he braced himself for what was ahead. His feelings of betrayal, humiliation, anger and loss were put on hold.

They were laughing as he came into the kitchen. He looked at them for one last moment before he was about to change their lives forever. All three looked happy in that instant. Ali was sitting on a chair, giving instructions. She had just turned sixteen, and her dark hair was tied back, her brown eyes checking what the others were doing. Mer, aged twelve, was slicing bread and concentrating on the sawing movement of the knife. Like her older sister, her hair was tied up. She was not beautiful as Ali was, but she had a gentle prettiness and softness to her face. Cassie, the youngest at eight, with a spray of blonde curls, was clattering at the cutlery drawer and counting out knives and forks. Count one fewer of each, he thought, as their smiling faces turned to him. Cassie dropped the cutlery and came to throw herself into his arms. He swept her up and kissed her.

'Hello girls,' he said, amazed that his voice sounded normal. His face apparently did not appear normal because, as Mer came over to him to kiss him, Ali looked at him carefully from her seat on the red kitchen chair. Her eyes seemed to narrow, and he had the feeling that she knew there was something amiss.

'Dinner's ready,' Mer said, pushing back a wisp of her hair that had slipped from its rubber band. 'Well, almost ready,' she added. She was the cautious one, always qualifying what she said, always careful not to get things wrong. She kissed him as he swung Cassie back to the floor.

'Where's Miriam?' Ali asked. 'Did you get the letter she left in the hall?' On their mother's insistence the girls called her by her first name. For a moment he wondered if his wife had disliked being defined by a generic maternal name. Her insistence on being addressed as Miriam had always slightly puzzled him.

'Yes, yes,' he said. 'I got it. A drink first...'

'But where is she?' Cassie asked.

'I'll tell you in a minute, girls,' he said. 'Let's have a drink first and then dinner. What will you have?'

'A gin and tonic for me,' Cassie said with a giggle.

'A gin and tonic for *me*,' he said, 'but lemonade for you I think. In ten years' time I will consider giving you a gin and tonic. You will be eighteen then. Hmm. No, I think you may have to wait until you're thirty,' he added, trying to make his voice sound light.

Ali got up off her chair, and still not saying anything she went and got glasses, lemonade and tonic from the fridge. Karl poured himself a gin while Mer got ice-cubes. They took their drinks up to the drawing-room, where the girls sat in the bay window on the green velvet cushions. He stood in front of them, his eyes drawn once again towards the horizon. From here he could see neither the Martello tower below nor the evening swimmers, but the sun shone down from behind the house, its rays catching the oak tree at the end of the front garden with the dried-out grass around its roots. The hedges needed cutting, he thought.

'Where's Miriam?' Cassie asked.

He drew his eyes away from the overgrown hedges and back to the three expectant faces.

'Your mother has had to go away for a while,' he heard himself saying. Whatever he might say to Ali and Mer, he suddenly felt it could not be said to Cassie. How could you tell such a thing to an eight-year-old? Or a twelve-year-old? He looked at Mer and could not help thinking that she looked no older than Cassie. How could he hurt any of them, he wondered?

He tried reminding himself that he was not the one who was wounding them, but nonetheless it was the words he was uttering that were going to hurt them. Whatever words he chose made him the messenger, and maybe they would blame him. He shook his head, trying to stop his thoughts. He had to be strong because they would look to him for guidance.

'When is she coming back?' Cassie asked.

'I'm not sure at the moment,' he said, and even as he said it he wondered if it was the right thing to say. Maybe it would be better to just destroy them all in a few short words than to give them hope that would never be realised.

'Is she all right?' Mer asked.

'Yes,' he said, trying to keep any sardonic tone out of his voice. She was more all right than any one of them was likely to be for a long while.

He saw Mer's hand reach for Ali's, and he knew that he was going to have to be more honest with the older two.

'Where has she gone?' Ali asked.

'She had to go to England,' he said.

'Cassie,' Ali said. 'Why don't you go and put the cutlery on the table? We'll eat in the garden I think. It's such a nice, warm evening. Will you put everything on the garden table and we'll join you in a minute?'

'But I want to stay,' Cassie objected.

'I'll go with you,' Mer said, giving Ali's hand a squeeze. Their eyes met and Ali nodded. Karl knew that they had their own forms of communication, and that Mer was clearing the path for him to talk freely to Ali. In a way he wished she had not, because it brought closer the moment of clarification.

'C'mon, Cassie,' Mer said.

Cassie, over-energetic as ever, hopped on one foot all the way across the room and out the door. As they left, Mer looked back and smiled. It was such a sweet, kind and gentle smile that he had the desire again to smash his fist into something. He realised that he almost needed physical pain in order to feel something stronger than the emotional pain he was enduring and was about to inflict. He was not a man given to violence, and yet he had this need, never felt before but now twice in one evening. He felt shocked by his emotions.

She closed the door on her way out, and he turned back to Ali.

'She's gone, hasn't she?' Ali asked. Her voice was dull. Her face was calm. She closed her eyes.

'Yes,' he said.

'Do you know why?' she asked.

He hesitated.

'Did she explain in the letter?' she persisted.

He must hide the letter somewhere better, he thought. Maybe he would bring it into work. The children must never see it. Plenty of locked drawers in his office, and even as those thoughts came to him he realised that he could not go back to work. How could he face them all?

He waited until Ali opened her eyes again, and then he went and sat beside her on the window-seat.

'I could lie and try and protect you and say she's coming back,' he said, 'but in the end it will come out. You're sixteen and you are the most sensible sixteen-year-old a father could ask for, and I need your help to protect the others.' His voice sounded calm, and he wondered how that could be. 'Mer will probably have to know; it will put too great a burden on you if you don't share it with someone, and in the end she will find out anyway. But Cassie is too young; too young to understand, too young to handle it.'

His voice trailed off. He felt that he too was incapable of understanding it. How could Miriam go and leave their three children, whom she professed to love in her own particular way, and the home they had created and the dreams they had shared? How could she leave him to raise these three girls with all their needs and hopes? How could she abandon them just like that, so calmly, so cruelly on a late Friday afternoon in August? He must be strong, he thought. He must not wilt in front of Ali. She needed his strength and his logic. She did not need to see him having an emotional meltdown.

'Do you think she'll be back?' Ali asked.

'No,' he said. 'I don't.'

'Was there a row?' she asked.

'No. We never rowed. Maybe that's part of the problem.'

'I don't quite see how she could leave Mer and Cassie,' she said thoughtfully.

'And you,' he said, disliking the fact that Ali had not included herself in her comment, and then realising that he did not include himself in his thoughts about this either. His concern was for the children, even though he knew he should be concerned for himself as well, but he felt there would be time to think about that later. First he needed to get Ali to a safe place in her mind.

'Things happen,' he said carefully.

He needed to explain to her in some kind of terms that she might understand, though how she could understand he could not imagine, as he himself could not. He found himself searching for words to give her some kind of meaning. What could he possibly say? What if he said that everything is repeated over and over, often in different ways, in different combinations, but there is nothing new; that in some ways he felt their mother was repeating a pattern learned in her own childhood. Her father ran off with some woman when she was only eight years old. She survived his absence, and often said that it was much better that he left, and, while she missed him, she was in fact happier. She may have transferred that to Cassie in particular as she was only eight. How could he say such a thing?

He heard himself saying, 'I don't think she has been happy in quite a while. I think she just felt it was the right time to leave.' It was the best he could do.

'There is no right time to leave,' Ali objected.

'I know. I agree. But I'm trying to understand too. Your mother often said that she and her mother were better off without her father, that the tension in the house and the endless arguments were so destructive that, once they had picked up the pieces, the situation was better for them.'

'But there were no arguments,' Ali said. She paused. 'Maybe there was a bit of tension,' she added as she considered the situation.

'Were you aware of tension?' he asked. He had always hoped that Miriam and he had managed to protect the children from the undercurrents within their home.

'Yes… no… I don't know. I sometimes thought… but then I would think who really knows what is going on between adults…? You sort of think they know it all and are in charge.'

'We will get through this,' he said. 'At this moment I can't think further than today. Like you, I'm trying to digest the fact that we need to…' he struggled for a word. 'Regroup, I suppose.' But he saw the mother as the foundation within the family structure, and he wondered how he was going to regroup them when he had no idea what he was supposed to do. He thought of a friend in a different department in his university, whose wife had been killed in a car crash, and he remembered the man saying, 'I simply do not know what to do. I don't know how to mother. Sometimes I even wonder if I know how to father… and now I have to play both roles, and I don't seem to be able to find the script.'

But he had survived. That man and his two sons had moved to England and restructured their lives. He too must find a way. They should eat, he thought, and then maybe a walk or something. What do you do with three daughters and no mother? He went over to Ali, noting the whiteness of her face and the pain in it. 'We will get through this,' he said again. 'Let's go and have supper.' Supper was not a word he usually used, and it sounded strange to his ears. They had dinner in the evening, but he could not bring himself to use that word, probably, he thought, because it would not feel like dinner if Miriam was not there. In his mind he could hear her voice calling, 'Dinner, girls. Wash your hands, hurry up.' He could not use her words; they grated, as though she had created a language of her own. He had not earned the right to use it.

They ate at the garden table behind the conservatory at the back of the house. Cassie kept referring to her mother. 'I wonder where Miriam is now,' she said. He tried to ignore the repeated question. 'She has gone away for a while,' Ali said. 'She needed a rest.'

Everyone needs a rest, he thought, though some of us aren't quite that goddamn selfish. Some of us have a notion of responsibility and feel the obligation to do what we are supposed to do. He realised that anger was coming to the fore and shock was receding, if only briefly.

After dinner, he left the girls to clear up and he took the newspaper down to the end of the front garden where a solitary deckchair stood in the farthest corner. It was the last corner the sun reached, and the eight-foot wall surrounding the garden protected it from any sea breeze. He sat there with the newspaper open, but his eyes would not take in the words. '*One word of truth will outweigh the whole world,*' said Aleksandr Solzhenitsyn in a quotation in the paper. What on earth did he mean? Not even the date in the paper made any sense to him. 1972. Solzhenitsyn's Nobel Prize acceptance speech from two years earlier was finally published. Where had the years gone? Where had this year gone? It was late August already. He looked back down the months and realised that the shock factor was there because he had not had any forewarning of Miriam's departure.

Perhaps he should have, but he had not. He had thought the issue with Elsa, their goddamned au pair, that had occurred the previous year had been laid to rest, and with that thought came the slow realisation that maybe, not yet, but maybe sometime in the future, he would see that Miriam's departure might be better than her staying and real bitterness entering their marriage.

He knew that he was not perfect, but then who was? Certainly no one he knew. When his children were born they had seemed perfect for quite a while. Ali was such a good and calm baby but had been none too pleased when, at the age of four, Mer had arrived. Mer's perfections were short lived as she became ill at just a few months old, and the stress attached to her illness had affected them all. Ali had grown beyond her four years at that time. Her jealousy towards her baby sister had faded, and instincts to do with loving and caring had emerged as she held Mer's tiny hand and whispered into her ear. He had come into the room once and heard the whisper, urgent and forceful, 'be well, baby, be well,' and he had been moved almost to tears at little Ali and her prayer.

When Mer had part of the flesh on her upper left arm removed, and she lay in a cot in the hospital with drips and machines attached to her while he and Miriam had stood beside her, afraid to touch her for fear of disturbing anything that might be keeping her alive, he had wept. Miriam put her arms around him and held him as he cried into her hair. They had kept each other going then, one lifting the other when one felt darkness and doom beyond bearing. Their strength had alternated and they had balanced each other. He had thought then, despite the terrible illness that Mer was enduring, that they were lucky: lucky in their love for each other and for their two little girls, lucky that Mer survived, because survive she did against all odds, and lucky that when they brought Mer home, Ali, once so jealous, now became her baby sister's guardian.

He had felt lucky because of the bond that had formed between Ali and Mer during those two long years of sickness and fear, and he had correctly felt that if Mer survived, the sisters' strength together would carry them through childhood and, for all he knew, through life itself. He had an adopted sister, Anneke, but there was no particular bond. Yes, they cared for each other, but he did not see or hear from her from one end of the year to the other. Miriam had no siblings and, coming from a broken family, he had always understood from her how much she wanted this family to work. Or so he had thought. His feelings of luck extended to that too, encompassing her need to have this family, and the good fortune continued when Cassie was born.

He thought of a conversation he and Miriam had the previous week. He had been offered a lucrative position in his old university in Germany, the kind of chair that he doubted he would ever acquire in Dublin, and he had tried discussing it with Miriam. He had received a phone call from an old friend asking if he would be interested. He had come home feeling excited and hopeful, full of the phone conversation he had with his friend. That was soon dashed. 'Selfish,' Miriam said to him. 'It's always what *you* want.'

He wanted to say to her, 'Please, please would you just consider this opportunity?' But in the face of her evident annoyance he had dropped the subject, unable to face the confrontation. It had been an honour to have been asked, a dream he had dared not think about let alone share. Her annoyance was palpable, even after he changed the subject and told himself that sometimes just to be asked had to be enough.

He lifted his head in disgust from the unread newspaper to see the three girls sitting on the front steps, which were long since in shadow. He pulled himself together and got up from the deckchair. Maybe she was right and he was selfish. He had taken this hour for himself to sit in the deckchair, pretending to read, just so he would not have to handle the girls and their emotions.

'Isn't it bedtime, Cassie?' he called as he folded the paper and walked briskly back towards the house.

'Do I have to go to bed?' she asked with a yawn.

'You do,' he said. 'Tomorrow is another day.'

And it would be another day. On that summer night of August 1972, he would work out what to do with three daughters and a motherless household.

# CASSIE'S TALE

I am Cassie, born by chance, born to dance and sing and shout, born to please, on a trapeze, just give me a squeeze. There is a rhyme for every vowel, be it howl, or bowel, or growl. There is a song that I will sing. There is a song...

But I can't remember the words. I can't find the first or the second or the third word. I can't remember the lines. All the links in my life are slipping away. I remember some things though. Some things are very clear, the sound of the waves on the rocks, the lights twinkling on Howth Head across the bay, the dull, insistent boom of the foghorn on November nights, the warmth of Ali and Mer's bodies as we slept curled up together in one of our beds when we were little girls. Who knows which bed any more? I don't. Sometimes a star fell from the sky and disappeared in the infinity beyond our tiny planet. There were times, as a child, when our planet seemed so very large, with a depth and endlessness that was inaccessible.

Now it does not seem large enough. Now there is nowhere to hide.

I remember a day, one day, my mother Miriam... an ordinary day; a day when I still had a mother, when I was just a little girl, but she left on that day, and she didn't come back. She was gone and it was all so wrong. I sat in my bath that night and played with the soap and I didn't get my hair wet because Ali said not to and I was going to be so very good, and the better I was, the better the chance that Mum, Mum, Mum, not a word she liked, would return to the house by the sea to be with me. I had heard Ali whisper to Mer, she's gone, she's gone and she's not coming back. I wanted my mum that night so long ago; I wanted to put my head against her chest and hear her heart beating and smell her perfume.

Her perfume was gone. A small wisp of scent remained in the comb she had left on her dressing-table, but not enough to persist for long. Open her wardrobe doors and I could feel her presence in her absence, the remaining clothes on hangers hanging on a rail, not on her. Their hanging shapelessness was one more reminder of her going and leaving us. Going, going, gone. I listened at doors, I heard strange things but none made sense, not then, not now. Ali so pale and withdrawn. Her face set like a mask. Dark hair pulled back tightly. Her mouth a straight line that night in her beautiful face. Mer trying so hard to be a big sister, she in the middle of three, once the fourth oldest in our house, now the third. I, once the fifth, now the fourth. Sequences change. The unexpected. The unwanted.

Mer tucked me into bed that night, so long ago, and took out a book to read me a story. Once upon a time. Once upon a time.

'Once upon a time there was a girl called Pandora. In Ancient Greece she was the first female on earth, created by Zeus, the god of all gods. He gave her a jar and told her not to open it.'

'Why? Why could she not open it?'

'Because inside were all the evils in the world, and they had to be kept safely tucked away in that jar. Then, one day, Pandora opened it, and out they flew, sorrow, cruelty, illness, disease, all the awful things that Zeus had hidden in the jar.'

'What happened then?'

'Pandora was so frightened that she quickly put the lid back on the jar, and she did not see that there was one thing left in the bottom. And that one thing was hope...'

'Did she go away because of me?' I asked Mer as she put away the book.

She shook her head, biting back tears. If we all cried all the tears that were in us where would the tears go? Where do all the bits of us go that we lose? The hairs that come out in hairbrushes and combs, the trimmed or broken nails from our fingers, the snot from our noses, the skin that we shed? Where are all the things that once were us but are now gone?

All gone. All wrong. Long gone. All wrong. Nothing is right, bright, take flight. Oh, no, oh no, not a flight, not this flight. Sleep now, my mother whispers. Sleep. Yes, I had found my mother. But for what?

Hope, of all the evils in the jar, hope, left inside is the greatest evil of them all.

# CHAPTER TWO

That August night in 1972, after Cassie was tucked into bed, Mer went to her own room.

Like her parents, she had a front room with a large bay window with its view to the east overlooking the sea, where the lights on Howth Head across the bay now twinkled in the dusk. Her room was sparsely furnished with a single bed and a wardrobe on the bare, wooden floorboards. In front of the window sat an old, brown sofa upon which she spent a lot of time, sometimes alone, sometimes with her sisters. Down below, beyond the garden wall, across the railway line she could see the Martello tower, now just a shadow in the late summer evening's light. It was too dark to see if the tide was in or out, but she knew from the sound of the water that it was out but was turning. The summer tides were never high, and it would merely reach the rocks and barely cover them before turning back on its endless journey across the sands and out into the bay.

She put on her nightdress, went and sat on the sofa and tried to piece together the events of the day. Cassie had asked her if Miriam had gone away because of something Cassie had done. Mer had reassured her that was not the case, but like Cassie she feared she was the cause of her mother's sudden departure, and like Cassie she wanted assurance. She curled up in a ball and waited, hoping that Ali would come to her before going to bed. Ali had whispered that Miriam was gone for good.

She thought back over the years, trying to understand what had happened. She remembered Cassie's birth in August 1964 and the excitement attached, she sitting on a hard bench in a room in the hospital, holding Ali's hand, waiting for their father to return from some room upstairs.

She remembered a moment when she felt something changing, an indiscernible puff of air, and she had turned to Ali and said, 'Did you feel that?' and Ali, who had hitherto been sitting silently gazing out the window, turned to her and whispered, 'Yes.' At that moment a light in the corridor, or maybe in the car park, was turned on, and Mer had felt that a light had been turned on in the world. And the pair of them side by side on that hard, wooden seat, totally oblivious to the panting and sweating and screaming in the delivery room, had looked at each other, startled. 'He's born,' Ali had said, and Mer had nodded.

But it was a baby girl who was born, not the expected boy child that their parents had been truly convinced was joining them. A new name was sought, and the baby was called Cassie, another star to add to their constellation: Alcyone, Merope and Cassiopeia, conceived with love, born with hope, named after the stars, bound inextricably for life.

Mer was excited beyond belief by the arrival of this baby sister, someone she could hug and hold and play with just as she had learned from Ali. Their lives had changed completely that night. It had been the biggest change that she could remember, but now, she realised, things were changing all over again, only this time there was no sense of hope.

She got up and fetched a photograph album that was under her bed. Her flashes of childhood memory were always enhanced by photographs, and she was the keeper of the albums. It was she who opened the packets of photographs when they collected them from the local chemist; she who sorted them, selecting which ones would be put in an album; she who carefully stuck them onto the pages using tiny, sticky corners to hold them in place.

She opened the album now and flicked through the pages to the photograph of Ali, Cassie and herself on the day after their sister's birth. Ali was sitting in a chair by their mother's hospital bed, cradling Cassie in her arms and staring crossly at the camera with Mer hovering beside the arm of the chair grinning demonically. Because of the way she was semi-crouched, it was difficult to see that anything was wrong, and at that stage she was too young to understand that anything was really wrong. At four years old she just accepted the way things were.

Ali and she, at the time of that photo and of Cassie's birth, were eight and four years old respectively. Ali had been born in Germany, which was their father's country, and Mer had been born four years later in Ireland, their mother's country. Their first home in Dublin had been a small flat while they sought a house, and then the house where they now lived had come on the market and, using Miriam's money, her parents had bought it. Miriam wanted the children to call their father Karl, but it did not always sit easy with them. Cassie remember-ed him once saying to Miriam, 'I like them calling me Dad.' Miriam had seemed surprised.

Mer's early illness had brought her closer to Ali, although she did not remember that. Her father had told her. She and Ali had relied on each other's company and friendship. The au pair, Elsa, had arrived when Cassie was just a baby. It was Elsa who took most of the pictures with their mother's old but reliable Kodak camera.

Another photograph showed them in Dublin, now living in Seapoint, and Cassie was dancing at the sea. She was five years old and wearing a white dress, a woolly sweater and a sun-hat pulled down over her blonde curls despite the darkness of the sky, and she was barefoot. They were the only people on the beach, and Cassie was dancing what they called 'The Dance of the Waves.' It involved going as close to the water as possible and turning one's back to the sea, then following the instructions of the rulers, in this instance Ali and Mer, who yelled when the moment was right and the dancer had to hop on one foot as the waves, having pulled back, now crashed onto the pebbled beach. The rules of the game involved not getting wet feet.

Needless to say, when Ali and Mer were the rulers, Ali mistimed the instructions so that Cassie always lost, and Elsa scolded them endlessly as the dripping Cassie was walked back home.

There was a pecking order amongst them, friendships moved around, and whilst sometimes the three of them were best friends, there were other times when their meanness to each other outweighed everything. But when night fell, and they trailed off to bed, they were, more often than not, to be found in each other's beds, curled up together. This mostly happened in winter as the bedrooms had no heating, and their father had a fear of hot-water bottles ever since their mother had burned herself filling one some years earlier. 'I'm cold,' Cassie sometimes wailed when she was being sent to bed.

'Oh, you'll thank me in later years,' Dad said. 'It does no harm to be cold.' A strange comment, Mer often thought, when she considered the comfort of his parents' home in Germany. She loved going to visit her grandparents, especially in winter: there was a cosiness and warmth about her grandparents' farmhouse in their tiny German village that was lacking in her home.

The house was large and difficult to heat, small drafts coming through the edge of the window-frames, some of which rattled when the wind blew hard from the east. Condensation on the windows and rain on the inside window-ledge were the norm in winter, with tiny, wet puddles gathering on the sills. Years later, Mer realised that the reason why they swam late into November in the cold Irish Sea was because it was warmer in the water than in their bedrooms.

That August evening, though, was balmy after a hot, sunny day and she distracted herself from her thoughts as she looked down at the last shadow of the Martello tower and the lights on Howth Head, and she was glad it was summer. She dreaded the coming winter. The grey skies would darken the water, Howth would be invisible in the fog or rain, and she would long for the sun, long to be down on the beach, dancing with the waves.

The waves were always there. No matter where she was, the waves and their relentless movement were in her mind; the snake marks they left on the sand were embedded somewhere inside her. She knew that her sisters felt the same. Each of them at any time could tell what the water level was, or if the tide was going out or coming in. They would stand in the front garden behind the wall and listen, or, like Mer now, sit at her window and hear it and know the exact positioning of the water.

The tide had turned now, and was creeping back up the darkening beach, washing around the rocks. She wondered where Ali was and what she was doing.

She remembered then one of those summers, perhaps four or five years earlier, when they were down on the beach, Ali and she, not doing anything very much, a warm summer's day and the tide was coming in. Their mother called them and asked them to watch Cassie while she had a quick swim before lunch. Cassie was just a toddler then. Ali waved and called, 'We're coming!' Mer could see Cassie sitting on the rug beneath the tower, and she turned and started up over the pebbled beach to climb the steps.

A girl who had been swimming around them earlier came over and said, 'What happened to your arm?' Mer looked at her left arm, scarred, she knew, but *her* arm, the only left arm she had ever known. 'Dunno,' she said. 'It looks awful,' the girl said. 'Were you burned?'

'Leave her alone,' Ali said, pushing the girl away.

'I was only asking,' the girl said.

'It's all right,' Mer said.

'No, it's not,' Ali said. 'Now go away,' she said to the girl, and taking Mer by the hand she pulled her along the slipway to where Cassie was sitting on the rug, now munching the sandwiches, which had been left carefully wrapped in the picnic basket.

'She was only asking, Ali,' she said. She had no idea why Ali was behaving like that. Later, of course, she could see that her sister was being protective, but back then she did not know any of her history other than that they were privileged, though she did not know that word. She knew that there was something wonderful about life and how they lived it, and that every day was a joy.

Later that day she asked their mother about her arm.

'It's fine,' Miriam said, looking at it carefully. 'Why? How does it feel?'

'It feels like it always does,' she said. 'I just wondered.'

Her mother sighed. Mer had the feeling that they might have had this conversation before. 'You know how every year we go to the hospital and we see the doctor and we have your arm checked?' she said. 'You were ill when you were a baby, and they removed a little lump from the bone in your arm. That's why it's not quite the same as the other arm.'

'Will it grow?' Mer asked, looking at it.

'Your arm? Yes, It's growing,' she said. 'It's fine and that's all that matters.'

Yes, then she remembered. She also remembered that she tried not to remember because she didn't want to think about it. She had been told before. She was sick as a baby and that was why they didn't have Cassie until she was nearly five years old, and by then she was better.

'You're my special little one.' Her mother gave her a hug. She was the special one, Ali was the beauty, and Cassie was the baby.

'Do you love me, Miriam?' she asked.

'More than my life,' she said.

'But you love me the same as the others?' she persisted. She wanted to be just the same as the others.

'Yes, I love you all more than my life.'

'I was once the baby,' Mer said thoughtfully. 'Did you love me as the baby then?'

'No, I loved you as my little fighter.'

'But I don't fight,' she said puzzled.

'Not that kind of fighter,' her mother said. 'You battled against the odds – that makes you special and brave and my little fighter.'

Reassurances... Mer realised much later that she looked for them as a child, and suspected that she would continue to all her life. Reassurances that there is a place for each, that there is a purpose, sometimes only reflected in other people's eyes. She got those reassurances in abundance back then. She was a happy child, secure in the middle of two sisters, safe because Ali, strong and determined, paved the way for her and Cassie to follow. When she thought back to those early days, she remembered the sound of the waves crashing on the rocks at night, the taste of salt in the wind, the sky, either blue or murky with dark clouds that coloured the sea a dull grey, or late at night standing at the window looking out at the stars.

But when she now looked back on that childhood night, aged twelve, with her mother gone, Cassie bathed and tucked into bed, Ali and her father still downstairs talking, she could find nothing to give her reassurance. It was like a gaping hole, like the hole she imagined had once been in her arm when she was a baby, although that, with time, had healed to leave a puckered, livid scar.

Would time heal what she was now feeling? She could not imagine.

# CASSIE'S TALE

Cold at night, warm at night, huddled in bed, stretched in bed, socks on my feet, feet outside the covers.

It was Mer who used to come and climb in beside me. She held me close and whispered, 'You smell so nice, tiny baby Cassie.' She held me until I was warm, and I fell asleep safe in her arms. During the day she played with me. She pushed me in the pushchair until she was too tired, and then Elsa or Ali took over. She trailed along beside the pushchair, one hand holding mine and laughing at Ali's stories. I must have been two or three years old.

Ali mostly told what I now know are called fairy tales and urban myths, except they are not myths. They are all based on facts. Mer's stories were classical myths, also based on fact. Once upon a time there was Eve in the garden of Eden. Once upon a time there was Pandora, the first women on Earth. Once upon a time there were gods and nymphs and pastures. Once upon a time there were children who got lost or were locked in houses with raving murderers. Once upon a time the gods placed the nymphs in the skies for safety. Once upon a time the children were rescued.

Once upon a time they were not.

Once upon a time there was a happy family, three little girls, a mother and father... happy times... where did they go? The days were full of fun and work and play. There was love and happiness and then... hanging upside down in a tree watching the world from the wrong side up.

Or was it the right side? When the gods watched the world they watched from above.

Or below. There is a place below, in the darkness... I can see into the darkness. It is looking at me.

Once upon a time the wicked witch came and destroyed the happy family. In another story she would be Medusa, a monster, one of the

Gorgon sisters from classical mythology. Look into Medusa's eyes and you turn to stone. Her hair was hissing snakes. The waves leave marks like snakes on the beach.

Grandmother came with colourful scarves. She tried to restore the balance. Can you balance what is uneven?

In Strasbourg, outside the cathedral, there is a statue of Justice. She is blindfolded. In one hand she holds scales. In the other a sword. Is it safe to be blindfolded carrying a weapon? It is not even safe if you have seeing eyes. Inside the cathedral there are the wise and foolish virgins. They are not weighed. They have already been judged. The foolish are excluded.

No, that is wrong. The statue outside the cathedral is called Synagogue; she drops the Tables of the Law. She is blindfolded because she has not chosen the right religion. Blindfolded. So is Justice. What religion, what church, what deity...? Does it matter? Mankind needs a deity. The foolish are still excluded. Perhaps it is wise to be excluded.

The wolf ate the grandmother and the little girl came to visit her. 'What big eyes you have, Grandmother,' said the little girl. 'All the better to see you with,' said the wolf. The grandmother is in the background, she tries to help. She tries and tries.

The little girl cried, 'Wolf, wolf,' but no one believed her.

Is this my story? I don't remember. Once upon a time there were three little girls, sisters... they were named after the stars…

Or maybe that was another story.

# CHAPTER THREE

The night their mother disappeared, Ali hovered in the drawing-room, for once unsure what to do. Her choices appeared to be either to go up to Mer, who she knew would be huddled on her sofa in the bay window, uncertain about what Ali had whispered to her about Miriam having left, or to stay with her father, who had poured himself another drink and was standing by the fireplace, leaning on the mantelpiece in the drawing-room, gazing at the empty grate.

Since he had come in from the garden he had repeatedly said things like 'I must cut the hedges,' 'we need to get the chimney swept,' 'we ought to make a shopping list,' and she realised that he was worrying about the things that had always been organised by her mother.

'I'll try and make a list in the morning,' she said. 'Mer will help me. It won't be difficult, and if you drive us to the shops...'

He nodded his head, and she was unsure if he had even heard her. She wondered if she should go over to him or just leave him there nursing his glass. It all suddenly felt too much, and she wanted the comfort of her own bed and silence and maybe the possibility of putting it all together and somehow making it right, though how she or anyone could make things right now she could not imagine.

She had the feeling that there was no turning back the clock. There were only a few days before they returned to school, and suddenly the dreadful tedium of everything exhausted her; the endless repetitive routine from which there was no escape. The holidays were different because they were a bit more under her control, but term time meant rising at a specific time, dressing in a uniform, walking to school, sometimes taking the bus if it was raining, sitting for hours in a class-room that was invariably either too cold or too hot, the summer sun baking her beside her window-seat, the winter sun glaring in at a low angle making her write with one hand at the side of her face to protect her eyes. She had once tried sitting in a different place, but the lack of a window beside her had made her feel claustrophobic. Like her sisters, she needed space and light and air.

She had planned to go to a disco with some of her school friends the following evening, and now she wondered if she would be able to go, or if indeed she would even want to go. The way she felt right now, she wanted to clear her head and to be somewhere very silent, away from her father and his gin and tonic. He never drank heavily, or at least not to her knowledge, and she felt frightened seeing his somewhat glazed eyes.

Mer would want her to explain everything, but she had no idea how to explain it, nor did she want to. Cassie kept asking for their mother, but hopefully she was now asleep in her bed.

Sleep... yes, and if she, Ali, slept, then what? She would wake up and the whole day would begin all over again, a lopsided repetition of this day. The only difference would be that when she awoke she would know that her mother had gone and had left them and would not be back, instead of like today, not finding out until the evening. Was it better to know or not to know? She had been puzzled by the letter in the hall, her mother's scrawling handwriting with her father's name on it. Her mother had made them sandwiches that morning, as she so often did, and told them to stay down at the sea and to enjoy the sun. Ali had long since given up asking her mother to join them. She had no idea what her mother did all day alone in the house, as nothing seemed very different when the girls traipsed back up from the beach. Sometimes the breakfast dishes were washed, but mostly they were just as they had been left that morning.

She lingered in the doorway watching her father, and then, suddenly realising that she could not handle him, and that he appeared oblivious to her presence anyway, she slipped out of the room and started to climb the stairs. She sat on the top step and leaned her head against the white painted banisters, and memory came crashing through the numb feeling she had endured all evening.

She tried to pinpoint when the events she was recalling must have taken place. Mer in hospital, she thought. But not when she was a baby, much more recently; maybe two years earlier? No, it must be less. Was it only last year when Mer got ill again? She shuddered. She had been afraid then, really afraid.

She had felt constricted that summer, always being asked to mind her sisters, to take care of them, to look after them on the beach, her mother making excuses to go into town and telling Elsa to look after the house while Ali took the others down to the sea. She had wanted to flaunt herself in her new polka dot bikini, and indeed she had flaunted herself, but she felt curtailed as she was supposed to be watching both Mer and Cassie.

There was a particular day during that previous summer that now came back to haunt her.

'You go in for a swim,' she had said to Mer on that day a year earlier. 'Look, Cassie wants to swim. I'll sit here and watch you,' and she stretched out on her towel on the stone slipway at the edge. 'I can see you perfectly from here,' she said, closing her eyes behind her new dark-rimmed sunglasses.

'But you could come in and swim with us,' Mer objected.

'Not now,' she said, trying to keep the irritation from her voice. It seemed unkind to let Mer see her annoyance, Mer who cried at the drop of a hat about anything at all, but never about herself. Stoic little Mer, she thought, a pixie child with her skinny limbs and her huge eyes in her small face and the furrowed scar on her short arm with its hand somewhat smaller than her other.

'Come on, come on,' Cassie had called, and Mer had looked at her and smilingly shrugged and followed little Cassie down the steps and into the water.

Ali had watched them for a short while as they swam to the rock and climbed it and then jumped off. The tide was not yet high enough for them to dive off it, but they were both laughing and having fun, and she closed her eyes again before rolling over and looking to see where the boys were.

They were two brothers, she thought. She had seen them before, and the older one had grinned at her and she had felt a thrill of excitement and wanted him to look at her. It did not seem fair that she was always landed with her sisters. Why did she have a mother and an au pair if neither did what they were supposed to do? She stretched out on her back, pulling Cassie's towel under her head to give her a little comfort. The edges of the large, cut-stone slabs on which she was lying were digging into her and she feared they would leave marks on her skin. She stood up and adjusted her bikini slightly before sauntering down to the steps and into the sea, hoping that she looked as good as she felt. She was tall for her age, with long legs, slender hips, and her dark, straight hair cascading down her back. She shook it for effect, and then she slipped into the sea. She felt like a mermaid as she swam across to the rock they called the Hillier, named she knew not when nor why. Her long hair floated around her.

'Look at me, look at me,' Cassie called to her as she jumped from the top of the rock with her arms clasping her knees to her chest and crashing into the water. The boys had followed her into the sea.

'Be careful,' Mer called to Cassie. Mer was always worrying about something, but never about herself, Ali thought. She found that odd. Mer had reason enough to worry about herself, with her annual check-ups and that awful illness when she was born. But Mer seemed unmindful of all of that, worrying instead about her sisters and her school work and getting things right. She was always so tidy, her room spotless, unlike the others; Ali only tidied her things once a week and Cassie's clothes were always scattered on the floor – even more so of late as Elsa seemed to forget to pick them up or even to nag Cassie to do it.

Ali did not like Elsa. When she was younger, Elsa used to belittle her, or so she felt. She always sensed a lack of warmth from the au pair, but she knew from both Mer and Cassie that they felt differently. Maybe it was because she always had to take Elsa into account, and when they went out in the car Elsa always sat in the front while Ali would have liked that. She would have liked, as the oldest daughter, to be able to sit with her mother in the front, and have Mer and Cassie in the back; but instead she found herself squashed in the back, usually with Cassie kicking and complaining in the middle of the seat. There seemed to be no benefit to being the oldest child.

It really was only a year ago, she realised. It had seemed an ordinary day and then had become a nightmare. She remembered pausing at the end of the slipway before diving lightly into the water and thrusting forwards with her arms straight ahead of her and the quick, strong movement of her ankles propelling her into the gentle waves. She had swum to the Hillier and then turned and swum outwards. Then the boys were beside her when she emerged above the waves, grinning at her and bobbing up and down. She had gone farther out than she intended and she could see Mer, brown and skinny, on top of the Hillier waving at her. She trod water for a moment and one of the boys, the older one, the one she liked, said 'Hi.'

'Hi,' she said, and then felt awkward and began to swim back in. They kept apace. 'What's your name?' he asked.

'Ali,' she replied.

'A what?' he said.

'My name's Ali,' she said, wishing for the hundredth if not thousandth time in her life that her name was something simple like Ann or... well anything in fact other than what it was.

'I'm...,' he said.

She couldn't hear what name he said, and was too shy to ask him to repeat it.

For a brief moment she thought of pretending her name was short for Alison, but a vision of a future with this boy flashed into her mind, where they were standing at an altar and he was saying 'I take thee, Alison...' to the surprise of her parents, her siblings and friends.

'My name is short for Alcyone. It's just a name,' she said, trying to extend the conversation, such as it was. 'My father teaches Classics and he chose it.' Why not 'Diana'? she thought. Roman goddess of the hunt, so much more poetic. No one ever seemed to have heard of Alcyone. Even Artemis, Greek goddess of the hunt, would be preferable. She could have been called Art for short. She stopped her inner monologue realising she was being addressed.

'So who was she?'

'Oh she was the daughter of Aeolus, and she married the Morning Star.' She couldn't remember the name of the star in the moment.

'And what did she do?'

'Oh, this and that,' she said. She did not want to bore him with the story of how she and her Morning Star offended the gods and she drowned herself when Zeus killed her husband. There were so many stories about Alcyone, and she wished she had just said how she became one of the seven sisters, a cluster of stars in some constellation.

'And could she swim as well as you can?' he asked.

Now she was sorry she had not told the whole story. Suddenly, being named after a star seemed more appropriate and more appealing than actually marrying a star.

'Probably not,' she said with a laugh.

'Oh, modest as well,' he retorted.

She did not know if he was being witty or rude. She reached the Hillier and climbed the smooth side looking down at the faces in the water. Cassie with her blonde curls all wet and stuck to her head, no cap on her head as there was no Elsa or Miriam there to insist. Mer was grinning up at her, and the boy was pulling back now, distracted by something. Then, someone who had climbed up behind her said 'Are you going in?' She turned around and realised that there was a queue for the jump into the water. She said 'sorry,' and leapt in.

She remembered leaving the sea that day, drying herself with a towel and then lying on it again until Mer and Cassie were ready to go home. The boys had waved at her, and the one who had talked to her called, 'see you tomorrow.' She wished she had asked him to repeat his name.

When they had come back up from the sea that summer's day, Cassie had fallen on the narrow footpath and cut her knees. Ali had picked her up and given her a piggyback while Mer carried all the towels and Cassie's abandoned flip-flops, one of which had split when she had fallen. They were very old, cast down through each of the sisters, until, almost worn out, Cassie had inherited them. Ali realised that was probably why her little sister had fallen – the flip-flop had finally come apart as Cassie hopped her way up the road. She remembered thinking that it was one of the best things about being the eldest child, her clothes and shoes were always new, not the hand-me-downs her sisters sported. They staggered back to the house and up the driveway to the steps, Mer running ahead laden with the wet towels and calling for their mother. 'Miriam,' her voice echoed through the seemingly empty house. 'Miriam, where are you? Cassie has fallen.'

There was no reply, and Ali carried Cassie through to the kitchen, where she put her sitting on the table and filled the sink with hot water and went upstairs to find cotton wool to clean the nasty cuts and grazes on her sister's knees.

She met her mother on the landing. 'We were calling for you,' she said.

'I was resting,' her mother replied. 'What's wrong?'

'Cassie fell and cut her knees,' Ali said. Her mother looked slightly odd but she couldn't work out what it was that was making her different.

'Go back to her and I'll be down in a minute,' her mother said. 'There's bandages and antiseptic cream in the bathroom. I'll fetch what's needed.'

Ali turned and went down the stairs, and as she did so she thought she heard someone else upstairs and she turned back.

'I'll be down in a moment,' her mother repeated. 'Just go ahead. I can't leave you girls for five minutes...'

'It was more like five hours,' Ali said, in what she hoped was a reasonable tone of voice though she felt annoyed and put upon, even more than she had earlier. If there had been someone else upstairs they never emerged, but she had puzzled over the sound, which now seemed to encompass much more than it had then. Now in her mind it was not just a voice, but the creak of a floorboard, the opening of a window, the urgent whisper of a lover...

But on that sunny afternoon she had let it go and had gone back to the wailing Cassie in the kitchen. 'Miriam will be down in a second,' she said reassuringly, as she put a towel under Cassie's knees. 'Now stop crying because that isn't going to make it better.'

Cassie pulled down the sides of her mouth. 'But it hurts...' she said.

'Yes, I know it does, but howling like that really doesn't help.'

She remembered Mer hovering at Cassie's shoulder, stroking Cassie's hair, holding her hand, and then presumably their mother appeared and magically fixed everything because she could not remember anything else about that afternoon. Cassie's poor, cut knees became irrelevant because some time during that night Mer woke and something terrible had happened to her.

Ali had gone to bed thinking about the boys in the sea, their bodies, their swimming trunks, their dark hair, their skin tanned from the sun; skin like her skin, skin that took the sun, not pale skin like Cassie's, which always needed creams to protect it and a sun-hat, which she, more often than not, refused to wear. In the water their bodies moved like hers, assuredly and strongly. She had felt alive, and desire had coursed through her as she cut through the water.

The whole five-minute encounter had stayed with her to be mused over in bed later, to distract her from the humdrum ordinariness of her life, the caring for her sisters, being the good daughter. Thinking about the boys while lying in bed that night, unable to sleep, would be a pleasant distraction, lying in the dark wondering if they would be back at the sea the following day. But then Mer came into her room at about four in the morning making a horrible noise. Ali switched on the light and could see terror in her sister's face. She jumped up from the bed. 'What's wrong, Mer?', she asked. 'What's happened?' Mer groaned and mumbled something but Ali could not make out the words. 'Sit down,' Ali said, pushing her sister into a sitting position on the bed, and then running barefoot across the wooden floorboards to her parents' room.

'Quick, quick,' she said to them, shaking her mother awake. 'Come quickly. It's Mer...'

They were out of the bed in a flash and back with her across the landing to Mer, now curled up on her side in Ali's bed. 'She can't speak,' Ali said, pulling back in the doorway so that her parents could get to her sister.

'What's happened?' Cassie was now in the doorway, blonde curls tousled on her head, her limpid blue eyes all wide, dressed in baby-doll pyjamas with the buttons askew, and with plasters on her knees.

'Come back to bed,' Ali said, taking her little sister by the hand. 'Come, I'll tuck you in. Mer's not feeling well. Miriam and Dad will look after her. Come now.'

'I don't want to go back to bed,' Cassie wailed. 'My knees hurt.'

And then suddenly their father pushed past them and raced back to dress. 'Stay with Mer while we put on some clothes,' he said urgently to Ali. 'Quickly, Miriam. Get dressed.' Then her mother, who had been holding Mer in her arms and talking to her, called Ali. 'Hold her,' she said. 'Hold your sister.'

'What's happened?' Ali asked, sitting beside Mer and putting her arms around her.

'We don't know. We need to get her to the hospital. No time for an ambulance. Cassie, go downstairs and waken Elsa, quickly.' Elsa had a bedroom and bathroom downstairs off the kitchen. Cassie wailed, 'But my knees, they hurt, I can't go down the stairs quickly,' and Ali called Cassie over forcefully, but with more patience than she usually had for her youngest sister. 'Cassie, baby Cass, sit here and hold Mer's hand. I'll get Elsa. Come quickly. It's important that you sit with her. We'll all be right back.'

What a night. What a terrible night. Their father appeared carrying Mer in his arms down the stairs. Their mother looking for the car keys in the hall. Elsa, in a pink satin dressing-gown that Ali thought looked very like one of her mother's, picked up Cassie and carried her back to bed.

And then the car revved up in the garden and the wheels spun for a moment on the gravel and they were gone. When Cassie was settled and back asleep, Elsa joined Ali in the kitchen and made them hot cocoa. Neither said anything, although Ali wanted to ask if Mer was going to be all right, but the words stuck in her mouth much as Mer's words had stuck just a little earlier.

'So, what happened?' Elsa asked her.

'She appeared in my room. Something was wrong. She couldn't talk,' Ali said. 'Her mouth looked funny, swollen maybe. I don't know.'

'Perhaps she was stung by a wasp or a bee.'

'Will they get to the hospital in time?' Ali asked.

'No traffic at this time of night. They'll be there quickly enough.'

'Maybe we should have called an ambulance,' Ali said.

'Probably quicker in the car – no waiting for the ambulance to arrive; I'm sure that was their thinking,' Elsa said as the milk boiled, and she poured it onto the cocoa powder. 'Drink this and get back to bed,' she added.

'Miriam has a dressing-gown like yours,' Ali said.

'Does she?' Elsa appeared uninterested, but then she always appeared like that when talking to Ali. She was better at interacting with the other two.

'Yes, I think so. It has the same roses embroidered on it,' Ali said.

'Does it?' Elsa said.

'She embroidered them herself,' Ali said, looking closely at the robe. Her mother collected old bits of clothing and cut them up and appliquéd them onto t-shirts and skirts and shorts. It was probably her mother's only hobby. Ali hated when she embroidered or appliquéd something onto one of her garments and had banned her mother from touching her clothes some time earlier.

Elsa said nothing; she just sat there stirring her cocoa and gazing at the frothy milk on top. After a long moment's silence, she said, 'I'm going back to bed.'

'Shouldn't we wait until they get back?' Ali asked.

'They could be hours. Go and get some sleep,' and Elsa was gone with the pink dressing-gown swishing slightly as she went out the door.

Back upstairs that night, Ali put her cocoa on the table by her bed and went to check that Cassie was asleep. There was no sign of her in her own bed and she looked in her parents' room before going into Mer's. There was Cassie, asleep in Mer's bed with the pale moon casting a light through the bay windows. Cassie was lying on her back, with her arms splayed back on the pillow around her golden curls, as though open to the world.

She remembered how long and drawn out that night was. She could not sleep. She drank the cocoa and read for a while, just passing time and waiting for her parents to return.

Her father had come back on the following day, shadows around his eyes, his face drawn and tired. With relief in his voice he told them that Mer had come through surgery.

He brought Ali to the hospital to see her. Mer was drifting in and out of sleep.

'Not keen to waken up yet,' the doctor had said, and she, Ali, had crouched by Mer's bed in the hospital and whispered into her sister's ear. 'Time to waken, Mer, time to come back to us,' and then Mer's eyes had opened and for a moment she had had a feeling of pure achievement. She, Ali, had succeeded where the doctors had failed. Mer was awake.

'Look,' she had said, 'she's awake,' and in the same moment she had felt fear because her sister awake did not look quite as happy and calm as her sister asleep. As Mer struggled through to consciousness, her face seemed to change as her mouth opened, and Ali could see the stitches and she knew that she had dragged her sister from peace into pain. It had suddenly seemed to be a very cruel thing that she had done.

But it had worked out all right. She had come back from a dream world to reality, although Mer had said later that where she had been had seemed very real indeed. Then, some weeks later, just after Mer had come home from hospital, things in the home took a terrible turn. Miriam, and Ali realised she would not think of her as their mother again, had become very withdrawn. During the weeks that Mer was in hospital, Ali had found Miriam's behaviour very strange. She had been in high spirits before Mer became ill that time. It was summer, she remembered. Could it really only be a year ago? It seemed longer.

Just as there had seemed to be no benefit to being the eldest a year earlier, there seemed even less benefit now, as she sat on the top stair thinking about her father drinking himself into oblivion in the drawing-room, and Mer probably huddled on her battered old sofa staring at the sea clutching one of her photograph albums.

# CASSIE'S TALE

Fear in the house that night.

Sore knees.

Mer ill.

Dad and Miriam rushing through doors with Mer in their arms. When was this? Oh, yes, before Miriam disappeared. Alone, I slipped into Mer's room and into her bed, so clean and neat and tidy. How did she sleep so still? My bed was always in a mess. Once upon a time Elsa used to make it up all fresh and straight for me. Then she said I was old enough to do it myself. I always meant to do it. Pull the covers, plump the pillow, pick up the things from the floor.

But never time.

Not enough time.

Too many other things to do. Play with my dolls. Swim in the sea. Dance with the waves. Dance and jump and hop and skip. Love my skipping-rope. And the tyre hanging from the ropes in the trees in the garden. Swinging back and forth. Swinging upside down. Twirling round and round. Reaching high to touch the leaves on the branches.  Reaching high to touch the sky. Once I will see too much sky. It stretches endlessly across the desert sands. It stretches across the sea. I will look for the sea. I remember looking for the sea. I must not remember. I am lost in memory.

When I was a child... oh to be a child... so much to do. Sore knees that night, the day I fell walking back from the sea. Skin and blood and two cut knees. On the ground, then piggybacking on Ali's long and slender back. I think she was kind to me that day. Out of character. Broken flip-flops. No swinging in the tree that day or the next day. But maybe a swim. Miriam, *the hand that mocked, the heart that fed*. That is a quote from a poem. I've forgotten the poem. I was good at poetry in school. I liked it. German and English. Words that filled. Miriam said the sea water was good for healing cuts. Sleep too. She said sleep heals all ills. Sleep now.

The moon is watching me. Is that now? Or was that then? Pale silver sliver in the velvet sky. Sleep now. But that night Mer... make Mer well. I needed Mer then. I will need her over and over in a never-ending need that can never be filled. The dark hole of need... to haunt me all my life. Must not remember. Must let it go. Replace the mother with the sister. Find the mother again. Hold the mother. Find the sister.

Bring Mer back and let her tell me stories, whisper to me until I fall asleep.

Once upon a time, so Mer begins her stories. Oh, the nymphs safe in the sky; oh to be one of them.

No, no, you cannot be safe, not in the sky. There has come a day, this day, when I am on a plane. A plane bound for nowhere. There is nowhere, nowhere to be safe. Come back to me, Mer, hold my hand, tell me your stories. I will listen until I fall asleep. Once upon a time... the desert sands, the snakes, they writhe and writhe. I writhe in my bed. I writhe in my mind. I cannot find the link. I will not find the link. I must not find the link. Mer, Mer, tell me your stories. Murmur to me, murmur till it is a whisper, a wraith in my mind and I will hold tight to your words to lull me to sleep.

That was all I needed.

That was all I wanted.

Maybe that is all I want.

# CHAPTER FOUR

Mer, on her sofa in front of the window, twelve years old, the photograph album now abandoned on the scuffed, cushioned seat beside her, was also thinking about the previous year and trying to link it with the present. Just like Ali, her mind was jumping back and forth in time.

She only vaguely remembered the frantic drive to the hospital. Then there followed a period that was made up of blurred memory, fantasy mixed with reality, no particular sequence of events, the drifting of her soul. She had awoken that night with her tongue swollen, so much so that she could hardly speak, though her throat was clear and she could swallow. Still in her pyjamas, she was brought to hospital where X-rays were taken, tests were done, and she listened to words of assurance and promises that she would be just fine as the morphine was injected into her. She drifted in a world that alternated between sleep and waking, pain and no pain, overhearing conversations with no idea if she was being spoken to or if the conversations were between other people.

'We have removed the tumour from her tongue. I don't believe it's malignant, though we'll know for sure tomorrow. The operation was a success, now we must wait. The stitches will heal, she'll be fine.'

'But the other tumour, the one you found in the gland in her head?'

'It's benign,' the cold, calm voice said. 'It's a particular type of tumour; malignancy is not an issue. We cannot remove it because of where it is. The central nervous system goes through that gland, and to touch the tumour would probably result in paralysis.'

'So what do we do?' It was father's voice.

'She will live with it.'

'Is it growing?'

'Probably. We have to wait and see. It is too dangerous to operate.'

She could see her mother's face. Her eyes were red. She looked like she had been crying. Mer hoped everything was all right with Ali and Cassie because clearly her mother was upset.

'Sleep,' her father said to her. 'Just sleep, my angel. It's going to be all right.'

Then there was another voice telling her to sleep. She was in someone's arms. There was a drip in someone's arm and something inserted in someone's nose. She thought that maybe they were her arm and her nose but she was far away watching through a window. She could see a lady dressed in white holding a little girl; she was talking gently to her. 'Sleep is the best thing. It heals everything,' she said. Her face was kindly. She was wearing a white head-dress and her dress and shoes were white. 'Tell me a story,' the little girl said. Her tongue was swollen and sore. She could feel the stitches in it and she did not know if the lady could understand her.

'A long time ago,' the woman said, 'in an ancient world, where the grass was green and the sky was blue, there were seven sisters: Maia, Electra, Alcyone, Taygete, Asterope, Celaeno and Merope. Their father was Atlas who held up the sky, and Pleione was their mother. They played on the grass and drank from the babbling brooks. There was a hunter called Orion and he pursued these sisters. He chased them so relentlessly that Zeus, the god of all gods in that ancient world, took pity on them and he changed the girls into doves and put them up into the sky so they became stars. We call them the Pleiades and they are up there. You can see them tonight. Look.'

They looked out the window and she saw them shining down, safe in the heavens. 'One of them is missing, though,' the story continued. 'Merope is known as the lost star.'

Her name was Merope, though everyone called her Mer. 'Am I the lost star?' she asked, staring up at the sky.

'It is time to sleep,' the gentle voice continued. 'What is lost is always found.'

When she slept, she seemed to think she was up there among the stars. Sometimes when she woke she was still there, looking down at the children's ward with the curtains drawn around her bed and people hovering. Sometimes the lady dressed in white came and sat with her and told her stories of ancient times. Once she saw Ali; she was dressed in jeans with her hair tied up in a pony-tail. Mer thought that maybe she had been here before. Her face was really beautiful; her skin tanned by the summer sun, the clean, fresh whiteness of her t-shirt enhancing it. She hovered over the child in the bed, and then she was the child in the bed and Ali was gazing at her. 'You're getting better,' she said. 'You're going to wake up and then you'll be better. I just know it. You're going to get better.' Her voice was like an urgent whisper. 'Wake up, wake up.'

Mer always responded to her older sister.

'Getting better,' she whispered. Her mouth was dry and her tongue hard, stiff with stitches, and she clutched Ali's hand because she was afraid.

'She's awake,' Ali said triumphantly, but maybe there was fear in her voice too.

Then there was a doctor with a nurse, and she was given water to rinse her mouth and to spit into a little bowl. She let a little of the water go down her throat and she thought that must be how the seven sisters felt when they were drinking from the babbling brooks. She wondered if they were thirsty up in the skies and then she realised they had rain to drink, and the whole of the heavens within which to play.

She stayed over a month in hospital. Dozens of young doctors came in with her surgeon to see her every day. They hovered around her bed and admired how she was recovering, how the swelling was going down, how she could talk with all those stitches in her mouth. Once she looked in a mirror and she nearly screamed in fright when she saw her tongue. It looked like a shark's mouth with shark teeth imbedded in the tongue. She only looked the once because she was so frightened. But the doctors were right. The stitches slowly disappeared, the hard, spiky feeling in her mouth faded away, the bruising on her lips turned yellow and then was gone, and she began to feel more like herself.

'You look fine,' her mother said when she asked her if she looked like a shark.

'You look more like a trout,' Ali said with a grin. She knew then that she was getting better, because Ali would not tease her if she were still ill.

'A trout,' she grinned.

'She does not look like a trout,' her mother said sharply.

She did not look in the mirror again until the day she was leaving the hospital. Her mother helped her dress in clothes she had brought from home as she had been living in nightwear for those weeks. She had brought in a blue skirt and a thin, pale blue sweater that used to be

Ali's. The skirt didn't stay up on her waist and her mother tried to roll it so that it would hold, but even that didn't help. Ali took off the belt on her jeans and they used that instead.

'We'll get you new clothes,' her mother said. 'Things that fit you properly, don't worry.'

'You need to get some flesh on those bones,' the nurse said as she fussed around and helped her into a wheelchair to bring her out to the car.

'But I can walk,' Mer said.

'Hospital policy,' the nurse said.

'Can I push her?' Ali asked. Mer wasn't very keen on that idea as she recalled how, when they were younger, Ali put her doll in her doll's pram and pushed it down the front steps. Mer had stood at the top hoping that the pram would survive clattering down the steps and crossing the pebbled drive before landing on the grass. It did not. It crashed over as it hit the fourth step and her doll and her bedding ended in a heap on the stones. The doll survived with only a small dent in her head. The pram was never quite the same; one of the wheels was bent and the spokes buckled.

'You can push her to the end of the corridor,' the nurse said, 'but I'll take her from there.'

And so she went home and lay on the sofa in the drawing-room in front of the fire that had been lit so that she would be warm. She played board-games with Ali and Cassie, and had soup in the dining-room at lunchtime before going back and lying down again, and she longed for night so that she could lie in her own bed and listen to the sea.

'We have a surprise for you,' Dad said. It was evening and they were back around the dining table.

'A surprise? For me?' That sounded interesting. Surprises were kept for birthdays and Christmas. Her birthday was not until the spring, and Christmas was still ages away.

'Oma is coming to stay,' he said. Oma was her German grand-mother, her father's mother, a formidable woman with blonde hair piled on top of her head, perfect skin and the ability to change anything that she chose. All of the girls adored her.

'I invited her,' their mother said, unsolicited.

'But what about Opa? Is he coming too?'

'No, your grandfather has to stay and mind the farm.'

That her grandmother was coming was puzzling. Mer looked at Ali, who was pushing her chicken around her plate and scooping gravy onto it.

Mer knew that Miriam was not usually that keen on Oma staying with them. There had been an incident in the kitchen some years earlier when Oma had shown her mother the correct way to dry glasses so that they sparkled, or at least that was what Ali and she had concluded was the problem. After that, Oma had not been to visit, although they went at least once a year to stay with her and Opa. What she liked best about Oma was the fact that things moved along apace while she was around. Yes, she was uncommonly bossy, in Miriam's words, but really she was just very organised and things got done while she was with them. Plans were made, the zoo was visited, picnics took place up in the mountains in the Feather Beds; the Japanese Gardens were explored in depth; Powerscourt Gardens were visited; horses were ridden; the Sugar Loaf was climbed; trips happened.

She had heard her mother once saying to her father that she felt she had to jump to attention while Oma was around and her father had laughed. 'I know what you mean,' he said, turning what might have been a complaint into something witty and positive.

'When is she coming?' Mer asked.

'Tomorrow,' Dad said. 'I'll collect her from the airport after I finish up at work.'

She wondered why Oma was coming, why their mother had invited her, why Dad started to clear the plates. It was out of character. She yawned. She felt very tired.

'You haven't eaten much,' Dad said, looking at the bowl of soup, which was all she could still manage.

'Not hungry,' she said.

'Time for bed,' Miriam said to her. She was glad. She wanted the silence of her own room and the distant sound of the sea washing over the rocks. 'We'll clear the dishes,' Miriam said to Ali and Cassie. 'You bring her up,' she said to their father.

He made as though to lift her up. 'I can walk,' she said.

'Not tonight, Mer,' he said. 'Tonight I'm carrying you.' He swung her up into his arms and off they set with Ali's voice calling after her.

'I'll pop in to you before I go to bed,' she said.

Mer waved at them, and for some reason that became one of her memories, as though in a photograph. They were all standing at the table, Cassie was looking at a plate and picking a piece of chicken off it and putting it into her mouth. Ali was smiling at her. Miriam was looking at something in the distance – Mer did not know what. 'Good night,' she called.

She was almost asleep by the time they reached her room. She was too tired to take a proper look, but it seemed the same. Her bed was freshly made and the covers were turned back. The room, for once, was warm. The three-bar electric heater that was usually in her parents' room was plugged in and it was glowing in the dark. The old sofa was in front of the window. Her father placed her in the bed and pulled the covers over her.

'Leave the curtains open, Dad,' she said.

'All right,' he said. He had been about to close them.

'I can see the stars,' Mer said to him. 'Look, the Pleiades,' she said. 'I can see them clearly.'

'How do you know about the Pleiades?' he asked.

'The lady told me,' she said, but her eyes were already closing. He bent down and kissed her.

'Everything is going to be fine,' he said.

He was the kind of dad you could really trust, she thought. She knew everything would be all right.

# CASSIE'S TALE

Mer came home from hospital that day a long time ago, a year before our mother left us. I think she was already leaving but we didn't see her going. I didn't see her going. I didn't see it coming.

Mer came home, white face, hands all yellow and green, lips cracked and broken. Pain inside her mouth. She didn't say about the pain, but I could see it. If you look into people's eyes, you can see things. Sometimes things you don't want to see. Sometimes better not to look.

I was seven then.

She sipped water and soup. She played with me. She slept. I slipped into her room to look at her. Her little hand was tucked under her face. Her bigger hand was clutching the covers. The sky was clear and speckled with stars. I sat on her old sofa in front of the window and I looked out. If I could not see the shadow of Howth in the dark I would think the lights on it were just more stars falling into the sea. Maybe there was no shadow, just the shadow in my mind, etched in for eternity.

I would have liked to get into bed with her but they said not to disturb her. She needed to sleep and sleep, and eat and get strong again. Again? Was she strong to begin with? I am not so sure. Ali told me she had a terrible disease when she was a baby. They said that what happened to Mer that summer's night was not connected with that disease. But how can they know? If there were flaws and weaknesses in her veins maybe everything was connected and they just didn't know.

Dad told me a story that night. He found me sitting on Mer's sofa and he lifted me up and carried me to my own room and put me into bed. 'When Achilles was born they tried to make him immortal by dipping him in the River Styx, but he was held by his heel and that part of him which had not been submerged was never as strong as the rest of him.'

'What's immortal?'

'It's living forever.'

'But Dad, first it was Mer's arm, and then her mouth...'

'It is just a story,' Dad said to me, 'about a warrior named Achilles. Not about Mer.'

'But was she dipped in the river Styx? Was she held by the arm? Was her head kept out of the water? Can I jump into the river? Can we bring her back to the river and I will get into the water with her?'

'No,' he said. 'It's a river in mythology, from long ago; it bordered the Underworld.'

'What's the Underworld?' I was just trying to stop him leaving me. I wanted someone in the room with me. I knew what the Underworld was. Mer had told me. Or maybe that was later. Everything is so muddled. Someone, one of them, had told me that the Underworld was where the dead went, ferried down the River Styx by Charon, the ferryman, into the darkness where Hades ruled as god, lord of his eternal domain. The living put a coin in the mouth of the dead person to pay the ferryman for bringing the dead to the Underworld.

But that night I was so glad Mer was home. She had come back from her Underworld although she described it as the heavens above. Oh, heavens above, Miriam said. Was there a sign there, hidden in those words? Was there an inkling of impatience? I was too young. I missed the meaning. I did not understand nuances. I remember some of the words, but in a meaningless and meandering way. I remember an argument of sorts while Mer was in hospital. Dad asked Miriam to ask Elsa to give the house a good clean. About time too, Ali muttered. Miriam asked Elsa and Elsa looked at her and said, 'No.'

Dad looked up from his paper, and suddenly Ali and I were ushered from the room. Ali and I sat on Mer's sofa and looked out the window at Howth. 'What's happening, Ali?'

'I don't know.' The hall door slammed. The whole house shook.

But the night Mer came home we were a family again. A family again. But not for long.

Lose a mother, find a mother.

I found my mother much, much later. I thought I could recreate that family. As the beads of perpiration dripped down my face, and from under my arms, and my back sweated into the seat on the plane until it and I moulded into one entity, I still hoped for something. Until the Minotaur yanked me by my arm and the seat and I separated.

# CHAPTER FIVE

Mer remembered the day after she had come home from hospital. It was strange being home. She had become accustomed to the children's ward, to the warmth and caring, nurses and doctors fussing over her. It was strange to be dressed in clothes that suddenly no longer fitted, that were too big for her. There was something about the routine in the hospital that was comforting. There was some undercurrent in the home that she could not identify, and she was unsure if it was real or some figment of her imagination.

She woke early on the morning after returning from hospital, lying there for a moment wondering where she was and why she could not hear the clanking of the breakfast trolleys that had woken her over the previous few weeks. She could hear movement in the house, and realised that she had been left to sleep.

She trailed downstairs wondering what was happening. Elsa was away, having taken time off while Mer was in hospital, and Mer thought that was very odd. It was surely a time when her mother needed more help in the home.

She found Ali and Cassie in the kitchen arguing with Miriam. It transpired that their mother had requisitioned Ali and Cassie to help her clean and tidy during the day, and Mer would be left to read or doze on the sofa in the drawing-room. Normally, when someone came to stay, Ali and she shared a room for the period, but because she had been ill she was being left alone in her own room, and Ali and Cassie were doubling up in Cassie's room so that Oma could have Ali's. This meant that Cassie had to tidy her room so that Ali could get in the door, and there had been a row over the bunk-beds in Cassie's room as Ali wanted the top one and Cassie, who always slept on the bottom, suddenly said that she wanted the top one.

Mer took a glass of milk to the drawing-room and, placing it on the floor, she lay down on the sofa. She was already tired and the day had not yet begun. She could hear Ali and Cassie arguing.

'It's my room after all,' Cassie said to Ali, clearly feeling she had the upper hand through ownership.

'But you're the hostess,' Ali said, 'and just like I have given up my bed for Oma, you should be gracious and offer me the choice of beds.'

Mer thought that their father would have been proud of Ali had he been there, reason and diplomacy being two of his favourite attributes. Ali sounded very grown up. She had no idea how the argument was resolved as she suddenly fell asleep, and when she woke again they were all upstairs sorting out the bedrooms and she could hear shoes and books being thrown around and a Cassie tantrum taking place.

Their mother, whose nerves seemed exceptionally frayed, was shouting, 'You're all spoiled! All you think about is yourselves! You have far too many things...'

'You gave me my things, my toys, my clothes!' screamed Cassie who, clearly, was not enjoying tidying her room for Ali.

Despite the age of the house and the thickness of the walls, voices travelled far too clearly down the staircase, as did the sound of the slap that followed Cassie's outburst.

'How dare you!' their mother shouted. 'Your father and I do everything we can for you, and that is the response we get...'

'I hate you!' Cassie's voice seemed to come through the floorboards and reverberate around the drawing-room, where Mer lay huddled under her rug. A door slammed and she could hear the key turning in the bathroom lock.

'If you are not out of there in one minute,' their mother's voice coincided with her rattling the handle of the bathroom door, 'I am packing every single thing you own and giving everything away.'

Mer had no idea where all of this was coming from as their mother was the most relaxed person she knew, and their mother was the one to diffuse situations and to distract them from their girlish rows. She often said that she had been born too early, that she should have been a child of the sixties and she would have been a hippy and gone to Woodstock. She was good at reminding them of their good fortune, of their cups ever overflowing, and now she was shouting on the landing.

It was Ali who said, 'Miriam, let's make a cup of tea and see how Mer is. She might like some soup or something as she didn't have anything for breakfast.' It was Ali who brought their mother downstairs and escorted her to Mer in the drawing-room while she went to the kitchen to make something to drink. Their mother sat staring at the fireplace where the ashes from the previous day lay in a grey and dusty heap. Mer watched her, thinking how tired and drained she looked.

'Are you all right, Miriam?' she asked.

'Yes,' she said vaguely. 'It's just been a difficult time… Worrying… I'll be fine.'

'Because I was ill?' she asked.

'Not just that, no… Just things,' she said. 'Don't worry. I'm fine. A good night's sleep…' That was something she often said, regardless of the time of day. A panacea for all ailments, be it tiredness, sickness or general grumpiness. Mer wondered what was really going on. She had half thought that Ali would come to her during the night for a chat, but she had slept so heavily that nothing could have woken her, whether she had visited or not. She had no doubt there was something going on in their home that had not been there before she had gone to hospital.

She was glad when Oma arrived. She swept in with their father in the early evening, a swirl of elegance and bright scarves, one on her head, another around her neck, as tall as their father and just as glamorous. It was always difficult to equate her with the grandmother she knew from Germany, a hard-working woman who helped on the farm and bottled tiny cucumbers and baked the most wonderful cakes.

She looked at them all as they stood in the hall. 'It seems so long since I saw you all,' she said, greeting them.

'Miriam,' she said to their mother, giving her a perfunctory hug and whispering something into her ear. Then she turned her attention to the girls, a kiss for each and then a special hug for Mer. 'How are you, Merope?' she asked as she led her into the drawing-room and to a chair and settled her on her knee. Mer felt that she was too old to be sitting on her grandmother's knee but it was nice to be the centre of her attention. When she focused on something, in that instance Mer, the object of her attention became the most important thing in the world.

'How is your mouth?' Oma asked her. Mer opened it like a horse for her to examine.

'Doing brilliantly, Oma,' she lisped. Her tongue was still a little odd, and she knew that her grandmother would have no idea that she had looked like a shark a mere few days earlier.

'Wonderful,' she said, looking carefully. 'You have lovely teeth,' she said to her.

'No, they're my stitches,' Mer said.

'No, I can hardly see the stitches,' she said. 'I really did mean your teeth. They sparkle, like teeth should.'

Should teeth sparkle? Mer had never thought of that before.

'Do I sparkle?' Cassie asked, coming up and sitting on the arm of the chair.

'You all sparkle,' Oma said. 'My lovely granddaughters. It's a joy for me, a delight to see you all again. I missed you.'

She spoke English just like their father did; flawless except for her occasional mispronunciation of the letter 'w' which mostly came out as a 'v', together with an odd and unusual turn of phrase. The rule was that they spoke German in Germany and she spoke English when she was with them in Dublin. Her English was very formal, learned with exactitude when her son had announced that he was marrying an Irish girl. She had taken herself off to classes for months on end, and forced herself to find time to read in English with a dictionary and notebook to hand.

'I'll have dinner ready in twenty minutes,' Miriam said. 'Perhaps you would get a drink for your mother, Karl.' Their father nodded.

'May I assist you in the kitchen?' Oma asked.

'No, no, thank you,' Miriam said quickly. Ali turned and glanced at Mer and each wondered what the other was thinking.

The atmosphere had changed markedly, and their mother rose to the role of hostess, at least for the time being. Their father poured sherry, and Mer went and sat on the rug before the fire, which was now lighting with smoky flames wisping up the chimney. Ali joined her and they sat, back to back, propping each other up. She could hear Cassie and her skipping-rope in the hall, and she wondered if the clicking sound would irritate their mother as everything seemed to have done during the day, but their mother seemed oblivious to it. Their father rested an elbow on the mantelpiece and Mer thought he looked sad.

She could see Oma out of the corner of her eye; she was looking at Karl and shaking her head slightly. He seemed to pull himself together, and he suddenly stood more upright with a more determined look on his face before gulping down his sherry. Behind his head, Mer could see the huge, gilt-edged mirror reflecting the room. Across from it was a painting of a marsh with seagulls flying and swooping. She often thought that a picture of the sea itself with seagulls would be better; the marsh distracted from the sky and the birds.

Dinner was the usual, soup for her as she still could not eat properly. She eyed the roast lamb and longed for some but knew she could not yet eat what she now saw as real food.

The three adults chatted and Ali, across the table, occasionally caught her eye. She felt that Ali too was aware of some undertone, a tension that was being hidden by manners and normal behaviour. Cassie was oblivious to that, but then she was only seven years old.

It was late by the time the meal was over and their father shooed them up to bed. He said that he would carry her, but Mer said no, she was able to go by herself. There were goodnight kisses and then Ali took Cassie's hand and the three of them trailed out of the room leaving their parents and grandmother to talk. Mer said goodnight to Cassie and Ali at the top of the stairs and headed for her room, leaving the door slightly ajar as she always did.

She must have slept for a bit and then woken to the sound of a door opening and a change in tempo in the house. She got out of bed and came out onto the landing to find Ali sitting with a rug wrapped around her on the top step of the stairs. She joined her, and silently Ali opened the rug and she slipped in under it beside her. She opened her mouth to ask her what was going on, but Ali put her finger to her lips and they sat in silence.

Oma's voice wafted up the stairs from the dining-room, the door having been left slightly ajar. 'I never heard anything like it, Karl.'

'Let me pour you some more wine,' they heard their father's voice, quieter and calmer.

'She tried to blackmail you? Tell me again what happened.'

'She was looking for money. She said she would expose the whole shambles of my life if I didn't pay up.'

'And you said?'

'I told her to get out. I told her I didn't care.'

'But you do care?'

'Of course I care. But if I paid her once, when would it stop? She would have leverage…'

'Well I do see that. But… Karl, I don't understand. Why did you ask me to come over?'

'It was Miriam's idea. Miriam felt… I don't know what she felt, actually. She just said that you being here would help.'

'What do you feel towards Miriam?'

'Probably what anyone would feel. Disgust. Betrayal. Anger. I don't know how she could have done this.'

'But you want the marriage to work? You want to stay with her? The children…' Oma's voice now sounded anxious.

'Of course. The children… what can I do?'

'Piece it back together. You can do it. At least she's gone. Are you concerned that she will come back?'

'No. I threatened her with the police. I refused to give her a reference. I told her to do her worst and I would contact her embassy and I would be pursuing her blackmailing attempts through the courts.'

Mer sat there horrified. Who were they talking about? She looked, panic stricken, at Ali who shook her head and mouthed *Elsa* at her. She felt a huge wave of relief, though she still did not understand what was going on.

'You need to forgive,' Oma said after a few moments of silence. Forgiveness and compromise are the basis of all marriages, and I should know. You two have it all, three beautiful children, a lovely home, a good life.'

They heard Miriam's footsteps coming back up the corridor from the kitchen. The dining-room door closed, and Ali and Mer sat there for another moment in total silence as they digested what they had overheard.

Mer wanted to cry. Something terrible was happening and she did not really understand. She did not know if Ali understood then or if comprehension came to her later. Ali stood up and whispered 'bed', and they both slipped back across the landing to Mer's room. Ali got into bed beside her. 'Adults,' she said. Mer did not know what she meant.

'What's happened?' she asked.

'Don't worry. Oma will sort it out.' Mer knew that she was right. She knew that if anyone could sort out whatever was happening it would be Oma.

She slept and dreamed about the stars, and when she woke in the morning she was alone in her bed, unsure if the night's events had been a nightmare. Unsure, that is, until she got up and dressed and came downstairs and heard that Elsa would not be returning, and that there would be no more au pairs.

'Au pairs come and go,' Oma said to her.

Later she heard her grandmother saying to Miriam something about a good school and a home with just two adults gives the best stability to children. Mer did not really understand what she meant.

And just like that, their lives changed. There was no return of the long-legged Elsa together with her nonchalant look and her increased disinterest in organising the girls. Once she had willingly packed school lunches and supervised homework, but that had changed, and she had increasingly challenged the girls, telling them to make their own sandwiches.

Mer remembered Ali saying to her mother, 'There isn't enough time in the mornings to make sandwiches. Isn't that why Elsa is here?'

And Miriam had shrugged and said, 'Well, Elsa says that you need to develop better organising skills; that it's part of growing up, and you could make your lunches on the previous evening so that you're not rushing in the mornings.'

'But she doesn't do anything any more,' Ali had said, 'she doesn't even make Cassie's bed.'

'She's very busy,' Miriam had replied.

'Doing what?' Ali asked.

'Don't be rude,' Miriam had said.

'I wasn't being rude. I was just asking what she does, as I can't see that she does anything at all.'

Their grandmother brought about change in their lives all right, just by being there. She stayed another week, helping the girls to get new routines up and running, sandwiches made the night before, and Ali and Cassie setting off to school on foot in those early autumn days. Then Oma left, returning to Germany with a swirl of her colourful scarves and a promise to see them soon. Mer stayed home for most of that term, reading the school books she would have been studying in class, and living off Ali and Cassie's stories of school and children getting up to mischief and the warfare of the playground, the primary school children separated from the older girls by a high, wire fence. 'When I'm in secondary school,' Cassie said, 'I'm going to throw stones over the fence at the little ones.'

'Throw stones at them?' Mer asked. 'Why?'

'Not at them. Not hard I mean. Just so that they will look at me, and I will wave at them.'

'When I get back to school I will wave at you,' Mer said.

'I miss you. I wish you were back,' Cassie said, flinging her school-bag onto the floor.

'When can I go back to school?' Mer asked their mother.

'When you're better,' Miriam replied.

If she and Ali had not heard some of the discussion that awful night she did not think they would have had any idea that something really serious had happened, and as time passed she was no longer sure if it had been serious. Their parents seemed fine and the tension in the house had disappeared. Perhaps their father was more attentive to their mother. He sat beside her more often. He pulled out her chair for her to sit when they had dinner. He brought her flowers. Once, looking down the stair-well late at night, Mer saw them standing in the hall holding each other. A silent moment like in a photograph, two people, he so handsome with tiny silver streaks in his dark hair, she so elegant with her fair hair cascading down her back, just standing with their arms around each other. She rejoiced in the passing of whatever had occurred.

***

'Miriam,' Mer said. Her mother was checking the contents of her handbag in preparation for taking her back to the hospital for an appointment. 'Yes, Mer,' she said as she rooted in the bottom of her bag and lifted out her keys.

'I painted a picture for the nurse who looked after me at night. Do you think we could go and give it to her while we are at the hospital?'

'If she's a night nurse,' Miriam said, 'she won't be there during the day. But we can always leave it for her. What's her name?'

'I don't know her name,' Mer said. 'I never asked her. I couldn't talk properly at the time. She's tall, and I think she's a nun because she had one of those huge white things on her head, like the nuns in our school used to have before they changed.'

'We'll find out her name when we get there,' Miriam said. 'Now, where's the picture?'

She ran upstairs to get it. Ali, Cassie and she all painted. Cassie was really talented in a way that Ali and she were not, but she was pleased with her painting. She had imagined that she was painting the Pleiades from the Milky Way. That way she had some light coming from the constellation where she had placed herself, and the stars were reflected lightly in the waves that were at the bottom of the picture.

'That's beautiful,' her mother said, taking it from her. 'I love the way you have the shadow of the Martello tower in the darkness.'

Mer wanted her to say that the stars looked perfect, but her mother didn't see the painting in the same way that Mer did. She had noticed that before. Ali, Cassie and she always understood what was the important feature in their paintings, but their parents often focused on some aspect that was trivial to them, and that they had only put into the painting to position it or to give it definition.

She put her painting in a large envelope, and they set off for the hospital. The consultant had his rooms in a building adjoining the main hospital, and they went through what was becoming a routine. Mer was prodded and poked. The sticks stuck down her throat made her think of ice pops, and she tried not to gag. There was a lot of nodding of heads and words of encouragement as she tried not to throw up. Her tongue, now completely healed, was admired, and she was patted on the head. Her mother was assured, yet again, that the problem had nothing to do with the tumour in her arm that she had as a baby.

'It is very simply a venous problem,' the doctor said. Mer thought back then that the word he was saying was 'Venus'.

She listened carefully when her mother asked him for further details, and it transpired that she had a flaw in her veins, a weakness that meant that the blood flowing in did not always flow out again. It was what had happened to her tongue, and apparently there were other pockets like that in her throat and head. She tuned out. There was talk of further operations, but the doctor seemed to be saying that this was something she was going to have to live with. Outside his window the traffic moved slowly, and down below a lorry was unloading supplies for the hospital. She wished they would hurry up. It seemed to her that there was not much to talk about if there was nothing he could do.

There was mention of a second opinion, and the doctor seemed to encourage her mother to obtain one. 'You've nothing to lose,' he said. 'And no one will be more pleased than me if I have not diagnosed this correctly, but I fear you will be wasting your money as I've consulted with colleagues here,' he gestured towards X-rays on his desk. 'We have all looked at these. I've even shared them with a colleague in London. It's an unusual situation and has attracted a lot of attention.'

In due course they left, with a further appointment being made for six months time. 'Things change, sometimes quite rapidly, in medicine, and in our understanding of illness and disease. We will keep on top of this,' he promised them. Her mother seemed despondent as they walked down the corridor and took the lift to the ground floor.

'My painting, Miriam,' Mer said. At first her mother did not appear to know what Mer was talking about, but then she nodded. 'Yes, yes of course. I had forgotten.'

They went to the main part of the hospital, and as they walked down the corridor Mer saw a picture on the end wall. 'Look,' she said in excitement. 'That's the nun, the one who sat with me at night.' There she was, dressed in white in this picture, with a huge, white head-dress on her head, and her hands joined. She was smiling ever so slightly.

'What a nice face she has,' her mother said, approaching the painting and reading the words beneath. Then she appeared to pull up short. 'I don't think this is your night nurse,' she said, as Mer too read the words beneath and saw to her disbelief that the nun had died the year after she, Mer, was born.

She felt a really strange cold shiver going through her as though her skin was lifting. 'Miriam,' she said. 'Miriam, it is, honestly it is. She sat with me at night. She told me about the stars...'

'It's probably the regalia on her head that is confusing you,' her mother said. 'There must be another nun who looks a bit like her.'

They proceeded to the children's ward where Mer had spent those weeks, and her mother asked the nurses, but they all said that there was no nun left in the hospital who dressed like that. 'It was the norm at one time,' one of the nurses said, 'but no nuns have dressed like that in some five or ten years I would say.'

Her mother enquired about who had looked after her at night during those weeks, but the nurses could not be sure. Some of them remembered Mer well and had indeed been on night duty at the time.

'It was probably the painkillers that made her hallucinate,' her mother was told. 'The nun you are talking about, the one in the portrait, was born in Ireland, she worked in England and founded a hospital or a sanctuary there, and then she came back here to Ireland. She worked here as a nursing sister until she died. She's considered a legend.'

Leaving the hospital, they stopped again at the painting and Mer looked up at the lady in white with her kind, gentle smile and she knew, she was absolutely sure, that it was she who had spoken with her that night.

'Well, it can't be,' her mother insisted as they left the hospital, Mer still carrying her painting in its large envelope. But it was. She was sure of it.

She thought about it endlessly, of course. She talked to Ali about it.

Ali sat and listened and then she said, 'Miriam thinks that maybe you saw her portrait the day you were brought into the hospital and that maybe the image of her stayed in your mind.' Mer realised then that her mother had been thinking about it too, and had found a logical explanation. 'There is a logical explanation for everything,' she always said.

Mer was not so sure. How could she have imagined the story of the stars for example? Her father had an explanation for that. He said that she and her sisters had their names from classical mythology. 'But Dad,' Mer said. 'You told us that Alcyone, Merope and Cassiopeia were stars in the skies; you never told me that Merope married Sisyphus or that Alcyone was turned into a kingfisher when she drowned herself. I know all of these things now. You never said that Merope is a lost star in the Pleiades.'

'You probably read those things somewhere,' he said. 'And I'm sure I told you different myths, but of course I don't remember which ones. There are a variety of different tales about each of the characters, and their names appear in many stories.' Yes, it was true there were many books of classical tales in the house, and that she read ceaselessly, but she did not remember reading that anywhere. 'Anyway, a nun is unlikely to tell you a story about a pre-Christian world,' he laughed.

'But she did, Dad,' Mer said.

'All peoples all through time have looked for gods, for explanations for life.'

'She told me. She said...' Mer's eyes closed.

'Sleep now,' her father said.

# CASSIE'S TALE

Something was wrong. They didn't tell the little sister. I smiled and simpered and looked for attention. Grandmother hugged me. 'There, there my little beauty,' she says. 'We'll go to the zoo and see the snakes.'

Biblical reference. Old story. Apple, tree, snake, man and woman. Hah. If only they knew.

*We're all going to the zoo tomorrow, we're going to stay all day.*

She packs us up, cardigans, anoraks, hand-me-down shoes.

Packed lunch in a basket with a bottle of lemonade and plastic cups, though far too cold that day with an easterly wind to eat outside looking at the lions. But we will. We will eat our sandwiches huddled on the stone wall. Pretence at normalcy. The lions will roar, and the tigers prowl. The giraffes will watch from above. In the reptile house the snakes are asleep, coiled together like children in their beds, until they move and uncoil. Away they slither in their glass cages. Away.

We stay all day.

Mer abandoned at home, tucked into her bed or curled in front of the fire. Zoo too cold that day for recovering patients. Mer all patience. Always.

Grandmother no patience with nonsense.

Miriam, no word for her. Not now.

Father, provider, supplier, Atlas who holds the roof over our heads.

Ali, the observer and the commander. Soon she will be in command. For a little. Until she makes the mistake of a lifetime.

No room for errors in a neat new copybook. Ali is the one who keeps her work so clean, tiny brackets close off any mistakes, a neat line through them. Mer copies her. I have my own style. Ink blotches, smears, the odd crumb that works its way into my essays. They sent me to school, what a fool. Oh what a terrible fool. There I will learn other things. How to be nasty, how to cheat and lie and pretend the crimes aren't mine. I will learn to pull hair to defend myself. I will use the nib of my pen in ways no one had foreseen. I will survive school.

Like Mer, I am a fighter. I will fight to the bitter end. Oh yes, the end. And it will be bitter.

Unlike Mer, I will lose my marbles.

We each had a bag of marbles. Beautiful coloured glass. Embedded deep in the clear outer glass are the colours, the oranges that twist into ochre, the greens that become aquamarine, the blue that is as dark as the midnight sky with shades of dawn on an eastern horizon.

I lost my marbles to Ali time and again. Then Mer won them back for me.

Time and again.

Some marbles are more difficult to recover. When they roll, the bright colours spin. They roll down the incline of the plane, mingled with the blood. There is no way to retrieve them.

# CHAPTER SIX

That alcohol-befuddled night in 1972, Karl's mind shifted back and forth between the events to do with Elsa the previous year and his wife's sudden disappearance now. He had been relieved when Elsa had gone and they had heard no more from her. It had puzzled him that she had left so quickly and that her blackmailing attempts had just been abandoned. For a long while afterwards, while he was attempting to be a better husband, he had still expected her to re-emerge. But she had not, and after a while he had dismissed her from his worries.

At four in the morning he started drinking black coffee and sat at the kitchen table with a pen and paper. As dawn broke, splintering light on the eastern horizon, and the birds began to sing, he went upstairs and found the letter he had hidden beneath his handkerchiefs and he read it again before slipping it into his wallet.

He sat on the bed and began writing a list. It started with what he saw as the priorities: his daughters, their schooling, his work. Beneath that he had written what he had to do: ideally change his employment, see if the job offer in Germany was still available, and if yes, move them there, find schools for the girls, deal with the house, find a new home... He was tired now, not just sleepy but tired to the core of his being.

When he slept he dreamed of Miriam as she was when he had first seen her, walking on the towpath along the Neckar River during his final year as an undergraduate in Germany. He was dressed in a white shirt and blue denim jeans, and had just left the boat-house to walk back to his rooms in town. She was standing with the sun beaming down on her staring at the water, dressed not unlike the way he was, but she seemed so young and beautiful in tight, white jeans and a loose shirt with the buttons open to the top of her breasts. He stopped to look at the oarsmen in the water, the sculls gliding smoothly as though of their own accord, the muscles of the men rhythmically flexing, the pull of the oars barely rippling the water.

He had bumped into her later in town as he hurried to an early evening lecture. She smiled at him then as though in recognition. He spoke to her and she had responded as though pleased to be addressed. She was on a year's exchange from her university in Ireland. They arranged to meet for a drink, and the drink had led to dinner and then to meetings at meals in the student canteen, and then to his bed. Secrets were shared in the nights, their pasts explored, his upbringing on the farm near the French border, her wealth and her broken home, her parents now deceased. The people they were becoming slowly emerged.

He told her of his plans to join the diplomatic service and the exams he would sit for that in the coming year. There followed his graduation, and then on a sunny afternoon he went down on one knee on that towpath where he had first seen her and their lives became inextricably interlocked forever. A quiet wedding, despite his mother's protestations, took place in the local town hall in his home village with just his parents, his sister and two witnesses. Miriam came unencumbered by family and seemed pleased to slip into his. Shortly after their marriage, he changed his plans and decided to go back into academia. Miriam protested.

'I don't think I'm cut out for diplomacy,' he said.

'But you promised. You said we would live abroad, we'd move from one country to the next, we'd see the world.'

'We'll travel anyway,' he said. 'But I really do want to go on studying and to teach, to stay in academia. I need to be true to myself.'

She did not like that he preferred studying, writing and teaching to the sociable world that she had imagined would be theirs. She had abandoned her studies when she married him, thinking that he would sail down the diplomatic route, and when that did not happen she hankered to return to Ireland. She got pregnant and Ali was born. She occupied herself caring for her baby, but constantly spoke of how she wished they could move back to Ireland. When Ali was three years old, Karl applied for a post in Trinity and they moved to Dublin.

They had eighteen years of marriage, three children, the ups and downs of life, but always Miriam at his side, his strength, his support, wife, mother... When he woke, memory destroyed the dream as he remembered some of what she had written in the letter she left for him. '*I need to be true to myself.*' He tried not to think about the hurtful words contained in her letter, words to do with his selfishness and his vanity, his need for personal fulfilment that ignored whatever needs she might have, cruel words that came as a total shock to him. Maybe she had thought that he would take that position in Germany, so recently offered, not realising he had put her wishes first.

Whatever hopes his dream that night might have woken in him died a quick death on the following morning. They had been blessed, he thought, and if she could not see that and did not want to remain, then he no longer wanted to try to lure her back. Like all marriages they had their ups and downs; he tried not to dwell on Elsa's blackmailing attempts, and Miriam weeping and begging him to take her back, to rekindle the love they once had. He had done it; he had complied and had done everything he could think of to restore harmony in their home. But it was not enough. Enough? Now he had had enough. He reached for the list he had made the previous night and ran his eyes down it.

Before showering and dressing he made several phone calls. The first was to Christian Waldfeld, the man who had phoned him offering him the chair in his old university. He was unsure if the phone would be answered on a Saturday morning, but it was, and the position was still available. 'Karl, I am delighted by your change of heart. I will need to confirm this with my colleagues on Monday, but that is merely a formality.'

Karl expressed his concerns about accommodation at such short notice, but was reassured again on that front. There was a house in the town that his predecessor had owned and lived in. The man in question had died. The house did not come with the job, but would be available for him as soon as he was ready, as the man's family was unsure what they wanted to do with it in the short term. The family would be glad to have it occupied and the rent would be reasonable.

His next phone call was to the head of his department – a call he dreaded as he was giving virtually no notice. 'I'm sorry to phone you at home on a Saturday morning, but I really need to talk to you. An opportunity has arisen,' he began. He explained the offer from Germany and how he had been considering it.

'I'm not that surprised,' she said. 'We'll be sorry to lose you, but I know that I would make the same choice. You have my full support.'

'Terms of notice…?' he hinted, still expecting some kind of argument.

'It is very sudden,' she said. 'When was the offer made?'

'Very recently. I thought at first it would be difficult for the children, but circumstances have changed.'

She was kind, if slightly prurient. 'Is everything all right, Karl? I see the appeal of the position, but the Karl Peters I know doesn't make such a move without a good reason…'

'We just feel it would be a good time to do this. I've considered it before, but there was really never an appropriate time.'

'Is Merope well?' she asked, remembering the health problems that his second child had.

'Yes, I'm glad to say that she is. Her last check-up was very positive. There were no changes. She is in good health.'

'Always a worry, I'm sure.'

'Positive thinking,' Karl said.

'Well, as I said, we will be sorry to lose you. There are six weeks until term begins here, although you will probably leave quite soon as the German semester starts earlier.'

'Yes. I will be in on Monday as usual, but I'll use it to clear things up and leave everything in order.'

'That sounds good. We can discuss further details of this then… paperwork, your semester plan, that sort of thing. Let's meet at, say, ten o'clock on Monday morning?'

He had intended his next phone call to be to his parents, but he decided to put it on hold. He could hear the girls getting up and he was anxious to appear to be in good form, conscious of the support they were going to need. He also needed to talk to them about his plans, aware too that they might not be so keen to move and to get away from this mess.

He put on his light summer bathrobe and slippers and brushed his hair. He peered in the mirror at his face and, like the previous day, he was slightly perturbed at what he saw. He did not see himself as a vain man; he was not given to thinking about lines on his forehead, or the changing colour of his hair. He was slim and tall and carried himself well, dressing slightly flamboyantly like his mother, enjoying a colourful tie and the feel of good quality fabric, and these were things that gave him pleasure. But as he looked in the mirror he could see frown lines clearly on his forehead, and tried to smooth them with his fingertips. His shoulders seemed slightly slumped, and he made the effort to stretch his neck and to put his shoulders back. 'Onwards,' he said out loud in an effort to give himself strength.

Miriam's words about vanity in his letter galled. They hovered as he turned from the mirror.

'Good morning,' he said, walking onto the landing as Cassie appeared rubbing her eyes and, seeing him, hurled herself into his arms. 'Good morning,' he said again, forcing himself to sound cheerful as he lifted her up. Turning, he saw Ali and Mer, both already dressed, standing at their bedroom doors as if uncertain. 'Let's go and get breakfast,' he said.

'We usually have bacon and eggs on a Saturday,' Mer said despondently.

'Well, that's what we'll have this morning,' he said as they went downstairs.

In the kitchen on the table was his empty glass from the previous evening, and the bottle of gin beside his dirty coffee cup.

'I drank a bit much last night,' he said. 'Sorry, girls. It won't happen again.'

'Do you have a headache, Dad?' Mer asked with concern.

'No, I got off lightly,' he said. 'Now, breakfast and we will talk.' Or rather, he thought, I will talk and hopefully you will listen.

'I can do the toast,' Cassie said. 'Let me do the toast.'

'What are the rules for toasting?' he asked.

'No metal objects to be stuck into the toaster when you are getting the toast out,' she quoted. The toaster was a new acquisition, and was a constant source of interest to Cassie, as hitherto they had toasted on the grill above the oven and she had been forbidden to touch it.

'Right, that's my girl. Now you are on toast duty.'

They made breakfast and brought it out to the garden table. The sun was shining and the morning was already warm. 'Excellent,' he said.

'What is excellent?' Ali asked. He realised that it was the first time she had spoken.

'A new day. A new start. I have plans.'

'Plans, Dad?' Mer said, her voice was uncertain but her face looked hopeful.

'Yes. A while ago I considered moving back to Germany for a year or so. Recently I was offered work, a position in my old university, something I've always wanted. I've decided to take it.'

'But what about us?' Mer said.

'What do you mean?'

'We can't live here alone. Or can we?' She seemed doubtful.

'No, my little silly one. I meant all of us – the four of us. We would go and live in Germany. You would go to school there. It would cement your knowledge of your second language – fluent and all as you all are. It would open your eyes to a different environment. It will be good for us all.'

He had thought that Ali would baulk at the suggestion, she who was that bit older, with close ties in school and about to go into her second last year before her final exams. But to his surprise it was she who said, 'Yes, yes. That's a wonderful idea.'

It was Cassie who said, 'I'm not going. I'm going into fourth class next week and I have my new school uniform and my books and I have new pens and I'm staying here.'

'All on your own?' Ali said. 'Great idea, Cassie. We'll send you a postcard.'

Mer, perhaps realising that it was settled, was looking a little hesitant, but she said to Cassie, 'Oh, Baby Cass, it will be such fun. We didn't have a holiday away this summer, but this will be like a holiday. A great big holiday. And there will be real snow in the winter and we can go skiing with Oma and Opa. And we'll get new schoolbooks and you can bring your pens.'

'Well, I think it's a great plan,' Ali said again. 'This way, we won't have to tell anyone that Miriam has walked out and left us all. I had decided to tell everyone she was dead.'

'She's not dead,' Cassie said. 'She's gone away and she'll be back. You said that she'd be back!' Her voice rose to a wail.

'She won't be back for a long time,' Karl said, glaring at Ali to try to constrain her. 'We'll talk later, Ali. I understand what you're saying, but now is the not the time.'

'Miriam had to go away,' Mer said to Cassie. 'That doesn't mean she doesn't love us. It just means she's not here at the moment.'

'But I want her here,' Cassie said.

'I know, Baby Cass,' Mer said. 'I know. Me too. But everything is going to be fine. Now, eat your eggs...'

'How can I eat my eggs when I only have one lump of egg?' Cassie said looking at the scrambled egg on her plate.

'If it were a fried egg,' Mer said, 'then I would have said, eat your egg. But these are scrambled eggs.' She was trying to keep Cassie distracted.

Karl got up and went inside to get more toast, leaving Mer to try to soothe Cassie. Ali followed him in. 'I hate her,' she said.

'Who do you hate?' he seemed surprised.

'Our so-called mother. Your wife. I hate her.'

He put his arms around her and she started to sob. 'I know,' he said. 'Trust me, I know. But it is going to be all right. Maybe not today, or tomorrow, but it will be all right. Just let me get us out of this... help me to get us out of this, and we will have a fresh start. I can't see it clearly yet, but I know this will help us all.'

'I know,' she said, pulling back and wiping her eyes with the back of her hand. 'But I still hate her. I wonder how I could ever have loved her.'

Karl got her a handkerchief from a pile of un-ironed laundry and handed it to her. In that moment he hated himself, too. He hated himself for falling in love with a girl dressed in white on a towpath long ago and bringing about this situation where he was alone with his three wonderful daughters. While he loved them with all his heart, he wished that he had never met Miriam because then the wounds she had inflicted could not hurt his beloved girls. He felt and hoped that a fresh start would make things easier for the girls, and for him too. There would be less explaining to do as no one would know them other than as a family of a father and three daughters. He was aware that there were ties of friendship that were going to be cut by this move, but reassured himself by thinking that, had he gone into the diplomatic service as planned, those ties would have been cut on a far more regular basis. It might have suited Miriam, but it would have been much more difficult for the girls.

'I love you,' he said.

'What if you leave us too?'

'Do you think I am the kind of man who would leave the most precious people in his life?' he asked.

'I didn't think she was the kind of mother who would leave... but then we can't have been that precious to her. What if something happens to you, Dad? What will happen to us? To Mer and little Cassie? What if I can't keep us all together? What if I can't be the parent...?'

'You aren't the parent,' he said. 'And nothing is going to happen to me.'

'But what if it did?' she was crying again.

'Listen to me. You have to be strong for the others, but the burden put on you stops right there. If anything happened to me, there is Oma and Opa and you know they would look after you. There is my sister, your aunt Anneke, and she would help. It's time we saw more of her anyway. We have family. We are lucky. We have each other, and nothing is going to happen to me. Now I need you to be strong for the others. Try not to worry. It is going to be all right. I'm your parent, and I'm responsible for you…'

'Not like Miriam, then,' she said.

'No, not like your mother. I'm going to raise the three of you to be responsible adults. We will all learn from what has happened, even if it is difficult to see that clearly now. We are Peters, you, Mer, Cassie and me. Strong, like rocks. We will care for each other as we have always done. I will not let you down. You will not let me down. You are already a young woman at sixteen…'

'I don't feel like a young woman,' Ali said. 'I feel like a baby who has been abandoned.'

'I'm not abandoning you. This family, this newly formed family of four will not abandon each other. We will support and love each other and will go out into the world with our heads held high.'

He told himself to listen to his own words and to learn from them. He knew that what he was saying was correct, but so much easier to say it to someone else than to himself. 'You are a strong, determined, intelligent girl. That is not going to change. We will all draw on our strengths and together we will get through this.'

He held her again and she hugged him.

'I love you, Dad,' she said.

'I love you too, Ali.' I love you all, he thought. The power of love would move this mountain, would pave a new pathway for them to follow, and suddenly he felt sure of that.

'Why did she leave us?' Ali asked. 'Why? Please tell me why.'

'I think…' he hesitated. To lie or not to lie? To say she needed time away, or to tell the truth? Which would he prefer? 'It's a long story,' he said.

'But Dad, why? Please tell me. Was there someone else?'

What would be easier for Ali to understand? What would be less painful? To lie, telling her there was no one and that her mother had left them for no one? Or the truth and to tell her that love for someone else had overtaken her and that she simply wanted a new life fulfilling her own needs and ignoring her family?

'Yes, there was someone else,' he said.

'I see,' Ali said. Then after a long silence, 'I suppose that at least explains it.'

# CASSIE'S TALE

I did not want to say goodbye. I felt like I was only beginning to say hello and all the doors were closing. Our bags were packed. An estate agent came for the keys to the house. I went one last time up to the attic where I had stored the toys and dolls we weren't bringing with us. I touched the cot where I had slept as a child, and my sisters before me, where my mother had laid me down and kissed me. I checked the boxes I had packed with my childhood and then I turned. I did not want to say goodbye but they were calling me, and I stomped down the winding stairs from the attic and looked one last time at my bedroom and I wanted to stay; to curl up in my own bed and to sleep and dream that everything was as it used to be before the order had been upended.

Did the nymphs carry regret when the gods placed them in the skies as stars for all eternity? Did they long to return for one last time to dance on the dew-clad grass and look up at the heavens from below? Or were they glad to go, glad not to be there when the god of the Underworld cleft the land and reached up to steal...

I would have liked to have found someone to blame, but when you don't understand all you do is cast around frantically. Had Miriam done a runner because she could not cope with Mer and her illness, because she could not bear Ali's bossiness, because our father was not the perfect husband, or was it because of me? All the trouble I had caused; not walking in a straight line, hopping across the pavement stones, skipping in the hallway on the brown tiles, always sliding down the banisters, whingeing at bedtime... had these things sent her over the edge and running out the door to Elsa to live in a houseboat near Camden Lock?

Yes, I had found the letter in Dad's wallet, angry letter, neatly folded, neat letter, angrily folded, the seams of it worn as if it had been read and read. I too read it and read it and then I put it back. I was too little to understand. Vanity. Selfishness. Self-fulfilment. I had no idea what these words meant. Other things too, but too difficult to understand, too difficult to remember.

Camden Lock – what kind of a place was that? It sounded like a prison somewhere. I imagined the houseboat; having no experience of one I conjured up an image of an old-fashioned caravan that I had seen in a picture, an Irish calendar hanging on the kitchen wall some time earlier. The roof was curved, the door was at the front, the driver and his passenger seated side by side. I removed the wheels and the horse, and I placed this strangely shaped home into water where it floated precariously with my mother and Elsa drifting in and out of the door. I did not want to say goodbye.

Ali's face was closed and hard, her mouth a straight line. Mer, so small with her short arm and her tiny hand, looked frightened all the time, but tried to smile whenever she saw me looking at her. Our father did not refer to the past. He spoke only of the future.

'Will we ever come back?' I asked Mer.

'I know we will,' she said.

I didn't know if she meant it or if she said it to please me. But she did say it with determination.

# CHAPTER SEVEN

There followed a hectic week of organisation, but Ali had seen to the packing and the putting away of items to be stored so that the bedrooms were left empty and clean. Her skills at organising had surpassed Karl's expectations. Her energy was relentless as she moved things along.

For his part, he had spent two days in his room in Trinity, sorting, tidying, leaving notes, and talking with the head of the department. Then he spent hours, if not days, on the telephone, arranging for the sale of his car, changing addresses with the bank, the stockbroker, the accountant and an estate agent to let the property. He was loathe to let it go immediately, and had no idea if he was even legally permitted to sell it. He suspected not, but he would find out later. Then he wrote letters to confirm the changes of address, and finally called his parents, a call that he had managed to postpone for four days.

His mother answered the phone, and he broke the news as quickly as he could. He was tired and he wanted to get through the conversation and get back to the minutiae of the move. His mother, of course, wanted details and explanations, but he just did not have the answers. 'She's gone,' he said. 'It's as simple as that.'

'Will she come back?'

'No. And I don't want her back. Not now. I did everything I could to save the marriage, but everything was just not enough for her. I am done with that,' he said.

'Shall I come over?' his mother asked.

'No. That's the second reason I'm phoning. We are moving to Germany, back to Tübingen at the end of the week. I was offered a position as head of the Classics department. I had turned it down because of Miriam, but it was still free and they have given it to me.'

'Where will you live? The children... school?'

'All arranged,' he said. 'My predecessor had a house in the town and we've been offered it, at least for this year while his family make decisions. I'm going to rent out the house here for the time being.'

'There must be something I can do to help you. This is an incredible burden; so much to do in such a short time. Are there enough beds and bedrooms in the house for the girls?'

It was the one thing Karl had not considered. 'I didn't think of that. I must check straight away.'

'Let me check that for you.'

'No, thank you. I have everything under control.'

'You say that as if you don't want my involvement or my help.'

'Not at all. I do need your help and your support. Look, you've already helped by bringing up the one thing I hadn't considered. I'll phone my German contact straight away.'

His mother was unconvinced, and suggested again that she come over to assist with the move, but he was adamant. 'It's not a form of rejection,' he said when she suggested as much. 'I've made this mess and I need to fix it. We're flying over on Friday,' he continued. 'I'll let you know when we arrive and I'll update you then. Hopefully we'll get down and visit you the first free weekend, though I imagine we'll be busy settling in for the first month.'

He could imagine his mother's distress at the turn of events, but he could not afford to include her in his worries. There would be time enough to sit down and discuss things with her and his father; for now he had to concentrate on the children and the move.

His mother phoned him some five or six times during the course of the next day as she thought of things he ought to do. 'Your father said to remind you about Mer's records and X-rays from the hospital,' she said. 'Just in case...' 'Any winter clothing that still fits the girls from last year...' 'Bring some photographs so that you can put your mark on your new home...' 'Don't forget to cancel the milk...'

The trip to Germany was uneventful.

He had dozed on the flight, Cassie beside him clutching a teddy bear he had not seen her hold since she was about four years old. Its ears were askew and chewed, its fur rubbed away in places. Ali and Mer were across the aisle, Mer reading a book and Ali staring stonily ahead of her. He knew they had phoned some friends and told them about their forthcoming 'year abroad', as they put it. He knew there was pain and loss in those phone calls, but that the girls did not say what had really happened. Like him, they seemed to want to get away, to close the door on the past, to have a clean start. He was unsure if he was deluding himself on that front, but certainly Ali had propelled things along during the week as if she could not wait for the moment of departure. He thought then about shame and how that was currently his overriding emotion. He thought that they might feel that too, along with a sense of bereavement. He realised that it was, in some ways, like a death, but instead of grieving over a body in a coffin they were grieving for a living, sentient human being who had just walked out.

He realised that if he, as an adult with more rationale than they, still could barely get his mind around the fact that his wife, their mother, had left him for someone else, then they must be even more bewildered. He could scarcely bring himself to think about how that someone else was a woman. It made no sense to him. It seemed even worse than the notion of her leaving him for another man.

He had tried to work that through in his mind; surely the betrayal was all that mattered? And yet, he felt that being left for a woman made an even greater mockery of his marriage and all their shared dreams and hopes, when in reality someone of her own sex could give her what she needed and wanted. He could tell himself a thousand times, as he had indeed done this last week, that this was not a reflection on him. He had been honest. His actions and intentions had been honourable, he had not lied to her when he took her to bed; it was her betrayal, but he felt diminished and the only way he could handle this was by pushing the thoughts aside, to avoid the million or more loving memories which now seemed hollow if not meaningless.

He started at one point to think of what had been going on in his own house, under his own roof with his three daughters living within the lies his wife had concocted, but the thoughts were truly agonising and his mind could not contain them. All he could do was to get the girls as far away from that as possible. He thought too of Elsa, the au pair for whom they had done so much, and how she had eaten away at the very core of his family. And after Elsa had shown her true colours, not just as the seductress of his wife but also as a potential blackmailer who had threatened to expose his wife if he did not give her money... even Miriam had been shocked then, or so he had thought. But now he wondered what Miriam had truly felt, and he realised he would probably never know. He had forgiven Miriam for her actions a year earlier. It had hurt at the time, desperately in fact, but he had believed her contrition and her pleas for forgiveness. He had agreed to invite his mother over, knowing that she would encourage him to keep the family together. He had done what his mother had said. 'Forgive utterly. Show compassion. Move on.'

He had been helped by his mother's reaction, although surprised at Miriam wanting her to come over. At the time, Miriam had seemed to be terrified by Elsa's threats. His surprise was due to the fact that Miriam didn't mind his mother knowing what she had been doing. Now he was no longer sure what Miriam had really been thinking. He thought that maybe Miriam was just not ready to leave back then, that Elsa's timing had been wrong, that Miriam was more afraid of public exposure than anything else, that she clearly did love Elsa and clearly forgave her for pushing her in the horrible way she had. But how could she forgive someone for putting a gun to her head like that?

His mother had spoken to him of the mistakes that people make, and while she could barely contain her anger, she was as ever pragmatic in her thinking. She had told him then how she had once forgiven his father for what she described as 'an indiscretion', and that while it hurt deeply at the time, she cared too much for family and she loved him. Of course he had known about all of that, she had told him when he was eighteen and she felt the time seemed right. He had listened then, had nodded, had understood, and had been glad that she had taken back his father, glad of the stability there had been in his childhood, relieved that his parents had managed to overcome their differences.

Now he wished he had not listened to her. He should not have agreed to Miriam's insistence that his mother come over. He had been weak then, stunned by the events in the house and Elsa's attitude. If he had rejected his mother's pragmatism and her experience a year earlier they would be further forward now. The pain would have passed and they would all be in a different place. Even in thinking that, he wondered what he could have done. Thrown Miriam out? He knew he would not have been able to do that.

He wondered at how Elsa had managed to keep in contact with Miriam, and how Miriam must have lied over and over this past year as all the time she was still in love with Elsa. Love? He doubted it. Lust was more likely, he thought. But that burns out, his thoughts continued. He had genuinely believed that the despicable nature of Elsa's behaviour, her turning on the family and attempting to blackmail them, would have turned anyone against her. He was furious with Miriam too, but knew that he had to curtail the anger if he was going to maintain the family unit. He had fought his own emotions, his anger and his disbelief a year earlier. He had struggled to change his ways and to spend more time at home. But no, it was not enough apparently. His once loving wife had found Elsa and her blackmail preferable to the wonderful home they had made, the three beautiful daughters they had created, the comfort and happiness that surrounded them. He felt anger surge in him again, anger and disbelief.

\*\*\*

The plane landed in Frankfurt. Everything went according to his plan, more smoothly than he could have hoped. When the plane finally stopped, he pushed the thoughts aside and worried instead about the little things that he could now actually achieve: the collecting of suitcases from the carousel, the purchasing of tickets, the ushering of the children on and off trains, the journey to a place where he had once been so happy. He could only hope he would find happiness there again and that the girls would find it too.

They took the train to Stuttgart, another train to Tübingen, queues at ticket desks, the bustle of the railway stations, Mer holding Cassie's hand tightly at Karl's request as he feared her slipping away.

They were met at the railway station by his friend from the university, Christian Waldfeld. There were greetings at the station, the shaking of hands, the introduction of the girls. Two taxis were organised to get them and the bags to the house off the market square. They surveyed the outside of the tall, narrow house with its wooden-shuttered windows. The tiny garden at the back boasted a single tree and neatly cut lawn that was just about large enough that the girls could lie out on rugs in the last days of summer. Red and yellow roses studded the garden wall, and the window-boxes of geraniums added to its charm.

The family of his predecessor had emptied the house but left the furniture. Two of the bedrooms were relatively small, and each held a single bed, a wardrobe and a desk. The study was even smaller. In the meantime it had been emptied of its desk and bookshelves and now contained a chest of drawers along with a bed. Cassie chose the study as hers, not realising that Ali had deliberately admired its small dimensions to encourage her little sister to demand it for herself.

The study was on the top floor next to the main bedroom, and Cassie plonked herself down on the bed and said, 'This is mine.'

With a grin, the first he had seen on Ali's face in a week, his eldest daughter begrudgingly said, 'Oh, all right then, you have it,' as she and Mer went to inspect the two bedrooms and bathroom on the middle floor. Downstairs, on the ground floor, there was a decent sized living-room with a small kitchen and dining area off it. A vase of freshly cut flowers and a bottle of wine awaited them on the table. There was a cellar beneath the house where their cases would be stored, and where the washing machine was plumbed. Karl liked the house, loved its proximity to the centre of town, its shuttered windows, its narrow staircase, the short walk to the river, which the girls immediately found on their first foray.

'What do you think?' he asked them as they surveyed their surroundings.

'It's lovely,' Mer said hopefully.

'Our house at Seapoint is better,' Ali said, but then, seeing his face, she added, 'I like it. It's a good place to be.'

There was a tiny balcony off the bedroom she had chosen. He rather wished that Mer had got that room as he knew how she liked to sit staring out of windows, and the balcony would have been an additional benefit for her, but she seemed happy enough with her bedroom, and was the first to unpack and put her clothes in the wardrobe and her albums under the bed. They ate out that first evening in a local pizzeria, and the girls were startled at the size of the pizzas. 'We could have bought one between the three of us,' Mer said, staring at her plate. 'Maybe we can bring the leftovers home,' Ali said. 'Lunch tomorrow...' 'And dinner,' Mer added with a laugh.

***

They settled in, more quickly than he had expected. Routines were created. He made breakfast and ushered the girls out. School started early and they were gone from the house by 7.40 in the morning. They seemed to adapt easily, and if there were arguments among them they were kept to the minimum. Occasionally he would overhear something, like Cassie saying, 'But when are we going home?' and then Mer's gentle voice cajoling her. 'Don't let Dad hear you saying that. This is home for now. Let's make it nice for him.'

'But when's Mummy coming back?' Her voice went babyish when she asked that.

He grimaced as he thought how Miriam had objected to the terms *mum* and *mummy*, and how Cassie had now begun to call her by a forbidden name. He knew that she was still clutching the old teddy bear and that she was sucking her thumb again, but that aside, and the occasional sobbing from her in her sleep, they seemed all right. He did not dismiss her distress, though, and made a point of letting her sit on his knee before bedtime, and reading to her, often carrying her up the stairs while she clutched him and the teddy bear.

For his part, he was sufficiently distracted by his new but old surroundings and the way so much had changed and yet so much was still the same. For the first time in years he looked forward to winter, to the cold and the snow and forest walks, visiting his parents and skiing with his girls. He enjoyed cycling to the building where he taught, although he would walk or take the bus once the snow came. He liked sitting at home in the evening at the dining table going through Cassie's class work, correcting essays or just reading. For some reason there was a simplicity attached to it that made it easier. Perhaps it was to do with not having to balance a wife in his life and the demands she used to make. Occasionally he would think about the immediate past, but he knew it was difficult to decipher what was real and what was the slant he was putting on it because he was still too close to it. Regardless, he knew it was over and would never return. There was no contact from Miriam. It was as if she had dropped off the face of the earth, and while he certainly did think about her, he was glad of that lack of contact even though he had a problem understanding how she could not want to know about the girls, how she had simply packed her bags, written a letter and then departed.

Occasionally he thought about her letter, and a sentence in it that said he had used her just to have children knowing that she had never really wanted more than one. He did not know that; it made no sense to him. It was he who had organised contraception, which was impossible to acquire in Dublin in the sixties. There was an implication that he had forced himself on her, which bore no resemblance to his memory of events. He knew that Mer's illness as a baby had devastated them, as it would any parent, and when she had fallen ill the previous year there was real torment repeated all over again. Was that what Miriam had not been able to endure? Of course, that was the time when

Elsa pulled the blackmail card. But he could find no real explanation, and time and again when the thoughts arose and he considered what had happened, he was forced to dismiss them as there were no answers.

He was proud of the girls, proud of the way they got up in the morning, assisted by a bit of cajoling from Ali, proud of the way they settled into school and made friends. He had the feeling that things were going to be all right. A visit to the clinic with Mer and her file of X-rays and reports meant that she was quickly under medical supervision, although the doctors, as in Ireland, said there was nothing that could be done about the flaw in her veins. They did, however, ask for her to return in four months so they could monitor the lesions inside her mouth, which appeared to be growing again.

'Do you want to ask us any questions, Merope?' they inquired of her.

She shook her head. She seemed to detach completely when she was being examined. 'Is there any pain?' She shook her head again and smiled her sweet smile. 'So brave,' one of them said to Karl, and he was taken aback. He had not seen her as being brave, or indeed being anything other than just Mer.

'You are brave,' he said to her on the way home.

'How do you mean?' she asked. They were walking to the bus stop and she slipped her hand into his.

'You go through all of these examinations and you never complain about them.'

'Would there be any point?' she asked, looking up at him with her serious little face.

'No, probably not.' But he admired her capacity for acceptance.

'Anyway,' she said, 'I don't want to feel brave or to have anyone thinking I am brave because that implies that there is something to be brave about, and if I start thinking that then I might worry and I got the impression that there is nothing that can be done to make me better, to make me like everyone else with ordinary veins, so there doesn't seem any point. In worrying, I mean... or in thinking that I'm brave. I'm not. I'm just me.'

'Yes,' he said. 'You are just you, but that's good.'

'Miriam once said she loved me because I was her little fighter,' Mer continued. 'I didn't want her to love me because I was a little fighter. I wanted her to love me because I was just me. But it turned out that she didn't love me enough anyway...'

'Why do you say that?'

'Because she didn't love any of us enough to stay with us,' Mer said. 'Can we have an ice-cream when we get down the mountain?' The clinic was high up on the hill and it was cold waiting for the bus.

'Isn't it a bit cold?' Karl asked her.

'It's never too cold for an ice-cream, especially one with hot chocolate sauce.'

He laughed, and the moment was gone, the first time that she had mentioned her mother in weeks. He knew he was being foolish to think that the girls were all right, of course they weren't, but he was glad of the way they were coping and the way she had almost casually mentioned her mother. He would have preferred no mention of Miriam at all, but he knew that was unrealistic, that she had to be in all their thoughts, and that to refer to her was probably a healthier approach.

Two days later his sister, Anneke, appeared on the doorstep.

'Anneke,' he said in surprise when he opened the door. It had been quite some time since he had seen his sister. She worked in Bonn in one of the Government's offices. She had never married, but had no shortage of suitors. She surrounded herself with friends. Her dark hair was neatly cut into a bob, her forehead high and clear, sunglasses pushed up onto her hair despite the weather, smartly dressed in a navy blue suit. Her normal large smile, which was the dominant feature of her face, was absent.

'I would have come earlier but I couldn't get away until now,' she said, shaking her umbrella onto the street before turning back to him. It was raining that day, the first real sign of autumn.

'It's good to see you. You're looking well.' Karl thought that it must have been two or three years since they had seen each other. There used to be regular family gatherings at Christmas until Miriam insisted they stayed in Dublin for the festive season, and reluctantly Karl had agreed. Now Anneke was here on the doorstep. They hugged briefly and he took her raincoat and hung it up.

'Come on in,' he said, leading her into the living-room. 'I said to the girls recently that we should see more of you.'

'Where are they?'

'They'll be in from school shortly. This is the one day I finish early. Are you staying? You don't have a bag...?'

'I checked into a hotel farther up the town. Mother said you wouldn't have room here. I should have phoned, but I wanted to surprise you.'

'You have surprised me.' He was puzzled at her sudden appearance, but pleased too.

'It's just a brief visit. I only have two days off, but I wanted you to know that I care.'

They looked at each other. Theirs had been a troubled relationship, vying for everything when they were children. She was only months younger than he, and they had competed at every level, in school, in sports, in trying to outdo the other, even in contending for their parents' attention and love, which had never been in short supply. She had been adopted when he was too young to remember.

'Thank you,' he said. She embraced him.

'We never did that before,' he said.

'Well, we should have.' She seemed less brittle than he remembered her. Even her face seemed gentler. She used to wear her hair tied tightly back; now he noticed the new cut and how it softened her face.

'I'm glad to see you,' he said, at the same time hoping she was not going to ask for details of what had happened.

'You seem changed,' he said.

'I'm sure we've both changed,' she replied, looking around. 'It's nice, Karl. Your home I mean.'

'I think it could do with a dust,' he said with a laugh. 'There never seems to be time to do the small things.'

Coming home from school shortly afterwards, the girls too were surprised but pleased to see her. She fussed over them, taking them out to dinner and to the cinema. Cassie held her hand and several times asked, 'Are you going to stay here, Tante Anneke?' Karl could see that Anneke was pleased.

'I have to go back to work, I'm afraid. They can't run the country without me, but I was thinking if you are planning on a holiday next summer, perhaps we could go together,' she said. 'I was hoping to go to the Adriatic, a lazy two weeks in the sun with lots of swimming and nice Italian food. Or somewhere down on the toe of Italy, but with exactly the same ingredients.'

'Oh please, let's,' Mer said.

Karl nodded in agreement. He was pleased. He had the feeling that positive things were on the way, something for the girls to look forward to, and for him, too. A real holiday with someone there to help him, to relieve the burden on Ali and to make sure that Cassie didn't get lost, which was his biggest fear as she seemed incapable of staying in one place for any length of time.

'It's a great idea,' he said. Her visit uplifted him, and the house was full of excitement that had hitherto been missing.

'Moving around in Germany is a lot easier than when you were living in Ireland. You can be in the mountains in less than an hour, over a border in less than two… you must use this opportunity, Karl, to widen the girls' experience. Did that sound too bossy?' Anneke looked at him. 'I didn't mean to sound like that.'

'No, you're right,' he said. 'When we were living in Ireland, it was all I could do to get the annual air fare to fly us here to visit our parents. From here, we can get anywhere as you said. It's only a few hours to different countries; I have lacked the impetus. No, it's more than that, I even lacked the imagination to think about it. Thank you.'

'You're welcome. I think it's important that you plan trips, even short ones. They will act as a distraction, and will also give the girls a look at other places.'

When she was leaving on the Sunday evening to take the train back to Bonn, they embraced again. 'I can't tell you how much I appreciated this,' he said to her.

'What? My visiting you?'

'Not just that. It was more than that. It was the feeling of comradeship, of support, a holiday to look forward to: something that hadn't occurred to me. This weekend has done me… us… more good than you might imagine.'

'For me, too,' she said. 'Promise we'll keep in better contact.'

'I will. Both of us, we both will. And thank you, Anneke.'

He smiled, realising that her appearance had managed to bring joy into their home.

*\*\**

He was pleased when his mother arrived later in the week. He could see that outside influences were good for them all. It broke the routine in a positive way and gave a greater feeling of normalcy.

'My darling granddaughters,' she said as she came into the house.

Cassie wrapped herself around her grandmother before sitting on her knee and hugging her.

'The house is lovely,' Oma said to the girls. Karl made tea and they sat in the living-room.

'Sit beside me for a little,' Oma said to Cassie. 'That way I can drink my tea and not spill it on you.'

'Yes,' said Cassie. 'You might get burned. My mum once got burned with a hot water bottle and that's why we never had hot water bottles in our real home.'

'And do you have hot water bottles here?' Oma asked.

'No,' Cassie said. 'The house is much warmer, so we don't need them.'

'Well that is a bonus,' Oma said. 'I always look for bonuses. They make things better.'

'What's a bonus?'

'It's something that's good. Now tell me all the bonuses.'

'We can't dance at the sea,' Cassie said.

'I know, darling,' Oma said. 'But tell me the good things, the things you *are* enjoying.'

'There's a girl in Ali's class with a moustache,' Cassie said.

'Hmmm,' said Oma.

'We can walk to the river,' Mer contributed. 'And there's a great pizza restaurant just around the corner. And you can get waffles with apple sauce in the market place.'

When the girls had gone to bed, Karl sat with his mother and opened a bottle of wine. 'And how are things really?' she asked.

'All things considered, we are doing all right. All three are settled into school. Early days I know, but so far all is positive. Ali runs the house, the shopping, the cleaning...'

'Karl, she is still a child. Yes, I know she is sixteen, but she is a child and you have to make sure that she doesn't carry the burden...'

'She's so efficient,' he said. 'She only does half the things herself, and gets the other two to do the rest.'

'I shall get a cleaner for you,' his mother said. 'I will find someone who will come in one or two days a week and do the vacuuming, the laundry, the ironing. It will be my gift to the girls. You don't want Ali to be doing everything. '

'Can you afford that?'

'Of course I can. Your father and I... well... our needs are simple. We have everything we want, and few expenses. Now, how are you?'

'I'm good,' he said. 'I'm enjoying my work, a new approach I suppose, and it's actually nice to be lecturing in German again, through the medium of German I mean.'

'But how are you really?' she asked. 'Emotionally, I mean.'

He shrugged as he poured another glass.

'I think it's a journey,' he said. 'Not just for me but also for the girls. Cassie pines I suppose, but she would pine if she were in Dublin. At least here there are fewer reminders.'

'And are you pining?'

He shook his head and grimaced. 'I'm angry. I suspect there are phases one goes through when this happens. Shock, bewilderment, grief, and now anger.'

'What do you think the last phase is?'

'You probably want me to say forgiveness, but actually I think it's forgetting. Who knows? I certainly don't.'

'Do you regret my intervention last year? I keep thinking about that time.'

'When you came over? No, not really. In some ways I think that if you hadn't come the marriage would probably have ended then; and so the girls and I would be that bit further forward now. But having said that, at least the girls had one more year of their mother. Anyway, I don't blame you in any way if that is what you're asking. It was Miriam who wanted you to come over and I agreed, so you have no reason to be bothered about this.  You did the right thing; you came when we asked you. I know Miriam was afraid; at least I think she was.'

'Afraid?'

'Afraid of exposure, of losing everything... I don't know. It's something I think about a bit too much. But at the time I truly thought she was frightened and regretful. Yes, I got that wrong, but at the time...'

'I agree with you. I picked up those same emotions from her, and I thought that what she wanted was forgiveness and a clean start.'

'Well, she got that in the end,' he said, somewhat bitterly.

'Do you still love her?'

'Love and hate are very close,' he replied. 'I know that I have to find a place where I feel no anger and then, hopefully, I can let it all go.'

'How can I help you?' she asked.

'Practical things,' he said. 'The girls need clothes. I should take them shopping, but it would be great if you did it. I just don't seem to have any time. I could have asked Anneke when she was here last week, but I didn't think of it. The weather seems to have got colder suddenly. Nothing seems to fit them, and because we brought only a certain amount of things with us there is little to be passed down. Mer is so much smaller than Ali anyway that it seems like it will be years, if ever, before Ali's things will fit her.'

'Mer is looking well,' his mother said. 'She's a far cry from the sick little girl of a year ago. I will take them shopping for clothes, shoes and boots too, winter coats. I can stay until the weekend and bring them home with me. We can shop on Saturday in Offenburg or Strasbourg, and I will put them on a train home on Sunday evening. Would you like to come, or could you do with some time for yourself?'

'I'll stay,' he said after a moment. 'You're right. There's no quiet time at the moment except when I am cycling to work. I've let paperwork pile up, and I've essays to mark and seminars to prepare. Thank you.'

'Oh, Karl,' she said. 'If we should talk, if you need to talk, you know I'm here.'

'I know,' he said. 'One of the problems for me is that I feel that no one could possibly understand what I'm feeling. Betrayal... yes, definitely betrayal, but it's more than that.'

'I know about betrayal,' his mother said. 'It's one of the things that I do understand. Perhaps not the level of betrayal that you are experiencing, or not the same betrayal, but I do know how it feels, and I think that more people know about that feeling than you might imagine.'

'Anneke?' he asked.

'Yes.'

'But did that not work out for the best?' Karl asked.

'Yes, it did. But I'm really referring to the difficulties I experienced when your father brought her home. I knew at once that she was his, and to be fair to him he didn't try to hide that.'

'But?'

'Well, there were the issues of forgiveness and that took time. Of course it was a different era, that time between the wars... But I have no regrets about that. It's just that I fear that my experience was more in mind last year than it should have been. I think it would have been better for you if I hadn't come when Miriam called. I've never asked you but I assume she knew that Anneke was your father's child?'

'Yes,' he said. 'I saw no reason to hide that.'

'Of course not. She was your wife. But I think she used that information to save her marriage at that time. She used me. I think she knew that I would encourage you to forgive her. And as a result, here you are again facing the betrayal you experienced a year ago. I did you no favours.'

'Mother, it doesn't matter. Not now. We all did what we thought was right then.'

He had the feeling that she was going to say more on the subject when the door opened and Mer appeared. She did not reply to their greeting or their concern at her sudden appearance. She was wearing blue pyjamas and her feet were bare. She walked past them to the window and moved aside the lace net curtains and looked out at the street. He had forgotten to close the shutters.

'Merope,' Karl said, startled, getting to his feet.

'Be careful. I think she's asleep,' his mother said. 'Don't waken her.'

Mer came back across the room and looked at one of the framed photographs on the shelf, and then she stood there staring at the floor.

Karl came and put his arm around her. 'Let's go back to bed,' he said gently to her, steering her to the door.

# CASSIE'S TALE

Ali shouted at me. I remember her standing in the hall and shouting. She was always bossing me around, but then when we moved she just shouted and shouted when Dad wasn't in the house. She said I was cleverer than the rest of them put together and to do my reading and to shut up, and she bet I couldn't learn Latin. She said I had brains to burn. Mer, gentle Mer, hugged me in bed and told me stories.

Back and forth goes my mind. Is it now or then? I can hear Mer's voice, from then? From now? She tells me the story of Daedalus and the labyrinth he constructed.

'Who is Daedalus?' I asked her.

'He was the father of Icarus,' she said.

'Who is Icarus?' I asked.

'Daedalus made him wings with wax and feathers and told him not to fly too close to the sun.'

'Would the sun melt the wax, Mer?'

'Yes,' she said. 'It would and it did. And he plummeted to his death.'

'What is a labyrinth, Mer?'

'It's a maze,' she tells me.

'Do you get lost in it?'

'Yes, but there is always a way out.'

'Did Icarus live in his father's labyrinth?'

'No. The Minotaur lived there.'

'What is a Minotaur, Mer?'

'He was a monster, a creature with the body of a man and the head and tail of a bull. They fed him human sacrifices.'

'I bet his parents didn't want him to be born.'

I am lost in the labyrinth.

Papa says we control our own destiny.

'What is destiny?' I ask Mer.

'It's our lives,' she says, 'the things that happen to us.'

Little girls have no control over destiny, if they did we would have stayed at the house at the sea, we would have swum in the swirling water among the rocks, we would have worshipped Poseidon and danced among the stars. Mer tells me about Poseidon, god of the sea. She says that Zeus ruled the sky, Hades the Underworld and Poseidon the sea, the endless, breathless sea.

'I bet you can't read all the books in the house.' It's Ali again.

I rise to the bait. I read at night curled up in bed. It's another world where adults live, but our father, always right, is wrong. He seized the strings from the puppeteer and tried to construct a new show. The labyrinth he constructed becomes our playground. We wander in it, fledgling nymphs, not knowing that the Minotaur is lurking around the corner. He drives us to the north coast where the sea is grey. He brings us to Konstanz and we take a trip on the lake. We visit our grandparents and ski. We ski too in the Alps and eat Toblerone and look at cuckoo clocks. We visit the rising of the River Danube and later, another day, another trip, we boat on the river and see the Austrian border from the water.

Mer tells me stories as I go to sleep.

'Do you love me, Mer?'

'Of course I love you,' she curls up on the bed beside me.

'Will you stay with me, Mer?'

'I'll never leave you. I'll never let you go,' she wraps her arms around me, one big, one little and we sleep with the pale moon shining through the tree and casting shadows across the walls. The Minotaur hovers on the edge of imagination.

But now, horrifyingly horrifically now, his day has come.

# CHAPTER EIGHT

It was some time before Mer realised that she was sleepwalking. She had been puzzled sometimes in the mornings by the dust on her feet, recalling that she had had a bath on the previous evening before going to bed. Sometimes she felt uncommonly tired when she woke, and sometimes she had odd memories of peering out a window into the night, looking for someone or something but she could not remember what.

She dreamed once about the nun in the hospital whom they all had said could not have been there when she had the tumours removed from her tongue and inside her lips. She had since found an explanation for that, at least a sort of explanation, one that she could live with. The nun had been alive when she was a baby, and she had been nursed in that hospital when she had had cancer when she was just months old. She reasoned that somewhere in her subconscious memory that nun must have remained. She was sure that the nun had nursed her back then as a baby, and then when she fell ill later the memory must have resurfaced. But now, when she had the feeling she had been looking out of a window with lace curtains, it was that nun she sought in the darkness of the night. A dream, she thought at the time, just a dream.

They went with their grandmother back to her village and the farmhouse for the weekend. She curled up on the sofa with her grandfather and he told her how he would take them skiing once the winter came. 'I'm not allowed to do sports,' she said sadly to him. 'They're afraid I might bang my head, you see.'

'I know you've been ill, but what's wrong with your head?' he asked, looking at her pale, pretty face and her fair hair. 'It looks pretty good to me.'

'Well, it's the veins,' she said. 'I'm supposed to be careful...'

'Can you walk?' he asked her.

'Of course I can, Opa.'

'Can you run?'

'Yes, I can run.'

'Well, how about cross-country skiing?' he said. 'It's just as much fun as downhill skiing.'

'Really?' She remembered the downhill skiing from when she was a little girl visiting her grandparents one Christmas, and it had been the best fun she could imagine, other than swimming of course.

'The others can still go downhill skiing if that's what they want, but you and I will go across the fields on our skis. That's my favourite thing now that I've got older, and I wish I had discovered it as a sport when I was younger. I'll get you your own special skis, and as soon as the snow arrives...'

While Ali, Mer and Cassie went shopping for clothes with Oma, Opa went and bought her a pair of pink skis and presented them to her that evening. 'Our secret,' he said. 'We'll keep them here in the garage, and when your father brings you down here when the snow comes and they head for the mountains, you and I will have our own fun.'

'Opa, thank you,' Mer said. 'They're so lovely, so pretty, I love them.' She had not thought that skis could look pretty, but these did.

'Something for the two of us to look forward to,' he said, patting her head.

'But where will we ski?' she asked.

'Right here, behind the house, in the fields beyond the farm. Come, let's go for a walk and we'll map our route.'

Their grandparents lived down in that no man's land on the banks of the Rhine just east of Alsace at the foothills of the Black Forest. It was a place that, as a little girl, Mer held almost as dear as their old house in Dublin at Seapoint. The winters were cold and the fields were heavy under snow with the picturesque view of the forest behind stretching upwards as though protecting this perfect valley. Her grandfather was a silent man, not given to communicating much, but he and Mer found a common ground on this visit. They walked across the fields and he pointed out the bunker that was once part of the Siegfried Line, long since gone, in the fields beyond the garden. He farmed the fields around the bunker, and that afternoon he helped her climb down into it. She was frightened down there but he held her hand. It was cold and dark. 'It's a little piece of history,' he said to her. 'The fear that once was here is gone now.' She shivered in the semi dark and the cold beneath the earth. 'Did you hide here when you were a child?' she asked.

'No,' he shook his head. 'Your father played here as a child. Later there were soldiers here, other soldiers, not me. I fought my war somewhere else. Now, let's get out of here. I'll lift you up and you climb out and then I'll follow.' He was strong and agile and he pushed her up through the entrance and the autumn sun warmed her skin. 'Opa,' she said, as he followed her. 'Why is it all broken, the bunker I mean?'

'It was blown up after the war.'

'Did people die in there?'

'I think so,' he said. 'Long ago. Not a problem for now, anyway. There are other problems, of course, but not that one.'

She did not ask then what he meant, but later, when he drove them to Strasbourg to look at the clock at the cathedral, they were stopped at the border. There were soldiers there with guns. 'Why are we being stopped, Opa?' she asked.

'Just a border control,' he said reassuringly as a soldier approached the car.

He unwound the window. 'Good afternoon,' he said. The soldier glanced into the car at the three girls in the back and then nodded them onwards.

'Are they looking for Baader and Meinhof?' Ali asked as they drove on.

'They've been captured, but they are still hunting others from the group,' he said.

'Who are Baader and Beinhof?' Cassie asked. She was sucking her thumb again.

'Thumb out, Cassie,' Oma said turning around. 'Baader and Meinhof. They're terrorists,' she explained.

'What is a terrorist?' asked Cassie.

'Lawless anarchists,' Ali said, quoting her father.

'Bad people,' Oma explained. 'They have no plan other than disruption. The one thing we really don't need.'

Cassie, not understanding, looked out the window at the posters of the wanted criminals, which were stuck along the border post. Those already caught had a red cross through their portraits. 'I'd like to have my picture pinned up like that,' she said, taking her thumb out of her mouth.

'Well, I'd prefer if you had your picture pinned up at the border it was for some other reason,' Oma said. 'I really would not like you advertised as a criminal.'

Crossing the border, they drove into Strasbourg, where Opa parked the car and they walked to the cathedral. Outside its doors the statues of the Church and Synagogue stood. 'Who are they?' Mer asked.

'One is Ecclesia and the other Synagoga. They represent the transition from the old law to the new. Synagoga is blindfolded,' Opa said.

'But why?'

'Because she has not understood that things have changed. Now, your grandmother and I each have favourite statues. Let's go inside so I can show you,' Opa said.

They walked up the steps and in the door, and he led them across the floor. 'This is my favourite.' He gestured to a pillar. 'It is called the Pillar of Angels.' The column rose high above them, with the four apostles on the bottom level, and above them on the next level were the four angels blowing their horns, announcing the Last Judgment.

'It doesn't look sturdy enough to hold all of that,' Mer said.

'It's been there for seven hundred years,' Opa said to her. 'It has survived time and wars. It will last.'

'What's your favourite piece, Oma?' Ali asked.

Oma led her to the sculptures of wise and foolish virgins. 'This is mine,' she said.

'Why are they foolish?' Cassie asked.

'The wise virgins brought enough oil for their lamps to the wedding. The foolish did not, and they had to leave to get more, and when they came back the bridegroom had arrived and they were excluded.'

'Couldn't the wise ones have shared?' Cassie asked.

'They were wise enough to know that there would not be enough oil if they shared,' Oma explained.

'I think they were mean,' Cassie said. 'You're supposed to share.'

The girls slept in an attic room in the farmhouse where there was a double bed and a single one. Ali took the single. Mer got into bed where Cassie was already asleep beneath the low-beamed ceiling. She could smell Cassie's teddy bear and pushed it away. She wondered if teddy bears could be washed. Oma would know. She would ask her in the morning.

She lay there thinking about the day, feeling the clean, stretched sheet beneath her body, finding peace and comfort in the attic room.

She had recently asked Ali if she thought much about their mother, and Ali had said, 'I find it easiest if I just live in the present and make plans for the future. I get too sad if I think back...' She had found that reassuring.

Mer found it difficult that their mother was never mentioned. Sometimes she cried quietly at night in her bed; mostly she just did not understand. She had stopped taking her photograph albums out. They made her sad. She wondered what had happened to the camera, and thinking back she realised that it was long gone. Perhaps Elsa had taken it when she had left a year earlier, or maybe her mother had just put it away and then taken it with her when she had departed. There were no photographs from that last year, and she had only just realised it. The past seemed full of sad things, she thought. Opa and his memories of the war; she had seen the sadness in his face when they were in the bunker in the slanted light from outside. Ali seemed to have the best way of dealing with things, just not to think back. She started to think about the sea, and she could suddenly hear the waves in the caverns of her mind, washing over and over onto the beach, throwing up the tiny stones and shells that they used to gather and sort each spring. The shells had looked nice on her windowsill, arranged in rows according to size. The glass pieces needed to be kept in water or they dulled and faded. And then she was asleep.

She dreamed that she was going down to the sea to watch the tide and the night sky, but try as she might she could not find them.

Her grandfather woke at about three in the morning. He lay there puzzled, wondering what had disturbed his sleep, and then he became aware of some small change in the house, perhaps a change of temperature or a different noise level above the hum of the boiler, and he slipped from his bed and put on his slippers and went downstairs. The front door was open. He looked outside but could see nothing. He put on his coat, which was hanging in the hall, and walked down the path to the road. Glancing to the right he could see across the fields lit by the autumn moon, which was exceptionally large and close to the earth. There was a child walking across the frosty fields away from the house. He began to run and was about to call her name when he remembered that his wife had said that Mer had sleepwalked the previous week while she was staying with them. He realised he could not catch her before she got to the bunker, and in despair he called her name. 'Mer!' he called over and over as he ran as fast as he could, his voice echoing across the fields, his fear of her falling into the bunker adding to his speed.

She stopped and seemed to listen, and then she turned around just before he reached her. 'Opa, Opa, why am I here?' she said.

He picked her up and lifted her off the cold ground. 'It's all right, Mer,' he said. 'You went for a walk. It's all right.' He carried her back to the house as she began to shiver in his arms. 'You were sleepwalking,' he said.

'Sleepwalking?' She was surprised and frightened. 'I think I've done this before,' she said, as he brought her into the living-room and wrapped her in a rug. He sat beside her and stroked her head.

'I better get your grandmother,' he said. 'I think you might need to have a bath to warm you up.' He took the fleecy throw from the back of the sofa and added it to the rug around her. 'I'll be back in a moment.' He did not want to leave her but he could not shout for his wife as he did not want to wake his other two granddaughters asleep in the attic.

Oma came running down the stairs, her face covered in thick, white cream, her hair in a strange pink cap. Mer got another fright when she saw her. 'Oma, what happened to you?' she asked. 'Oh this,' her grandmother pointed to her face. 'To prolong my beauty,' she said with a light laugh, but Mer could see the worry in her eyes. 'Now, my little Mer, what have you been doing?'

'I don't know,' Mer said. She was still shivering.

'A bath,' her grandmother said. 'You run it,' she said to Opa who was also shivering. 'We'll get her into it and warm her up, and then I'll make hot drinks. Everything is fine,' she said to Mer. 'You're not the first person to sleepwalk and you won't be the last. Everything will be just fine.'

Later, warm again and wrapped back up in the rugs, Mer drank hot sweet tea and enjoyed them fussing over her. 'What if Opa hadn't found me?' she asked.

'There are no *what-ifs*,' Oma said. 'He did find you.'

'But what if I do that again and I get lost?'

'That won't happen. From now on, we lock the doors and remove the keys and that way you can't get out. It won't happen again. You're safe now,' Oma said. If she was worried, she now hid it well. Mer believed her.

She slept the rest of that night in bed with her grandmother, and her grandfather slept on the sofa in the living-room. She woke in the morning to hear Cassie shouting, 'Mer, Mer, where are you?' before her sister burst into their grandparents' room complete with the smelly teddy bear, blonde, curly hair askew.

'Oh, I want to sleepwalk too,' Cassie said, when everything was explained.

'No, you don't,' Oma said to her. 'You would get very cold feet and maybe a cold and you would be sick and would have to stay in bed for a week.'

'Does Mer have to stay in bed for a week?' Cassie asked.

'No, she doesn't. We warmed her up and she is just fine. Now, who wants a cooked breakfast? I'm thinking pancakes and hot chocolate,' Oma said.

# CASSIE'S TALE

Crisis averted. No matter what Oma said, walking in your sleep sounded fun. Where was Mer going? What was she looking for? Oma said she was trying to find something familiar. Would she just have walked and walked had Opa not realised something was amiss? What if we had never found her? What if she had reached the forest and disappeared among the trees, climbing out of the valley, out of the labyrinth, lost forever? In one of Ali's fairytales the children were brought into a forest and abandoned. They left crumbs to find the way back but the birds ate the crumbs.

I asked Ali what we would have done if Mer had disappeared that night. 'We would search for her,' Ali said. 'We're sisters. We would never let one of us disappear and not search forever.' It was enough to have lost our mother. Would they have made a poster with Mer's picture and a sign saying 'Lost'?

Much later they put my poster up. Ali and Mer and the police all put my poster up. I saw it on a newspaper stand in Rome. I knew the face, I knew the name, but I did not realise it was me. The picture of a girl in her teens, blonde curls, blue eyes, although the photograph was in black and white. I seemed to remember it being taken some time earlier. Perhaps at a party. I knew the girl, I knew her well but I could not stop to look again, to read, to see why she was wanted, what she had done. I had to run. I had to get away.

We ran away when I was eight years old. We took planes and trains and left the sea and the mist over Howth Head; we went to a place with a market and waffles and icing sugar, and when I looked out the window of our tall house it was like looking into one of those glass balls that you shake and the snow fills the glass before falling gently down on the houses and the man with the accordion at the street corner, always playing the same tunes, over and over. Shake the glass and it is all repeated. Winters come and go.

I remember going to school and learning where to put the umlauts on the vowels, and how to multiply in German. The grass in our garden was green, then white, then green again. Time passed. The snow in the glass ball poured out of the sky, and the three little girls grew. A single bird sang a plaintive song, perched on the branch beneath the summer foliage. Tante Anneke came. Grandmother came. We went to our grandparents. Ali and I skied down the mountains with Papa, as we now named him so that we fitted in with everyone else, calling to us to follow him and to stay on the beaten track.

We hid our secret, our lost mother, we conformed, Papa, Oma, Opa, meine Schwestern, we spoke the language, we ate the food, we became little German children, children with a secret. Mum gone to a houseboat with pretty Elsa. I did not tell my sisters. Perhaps I thought they knew. Perhaps I thought that if I told them I would be in trouble. 'Our mother died,' I heard Ali once saying to someone who asked about our home. 'A long time ago,' she added. Mer's face was closed. Like me, she listened. Unlike me, she pushed away the past. I tried, but I failed.

You can't push away the past. Each day leaves a past of its own and it follows you. It eats into everything that you do.

# CHAPTER NINE

Ali knew that Mer followed her example. She saw, as one of her strengths, the fact that she had that power over her. Mer had always been in her thrall, and the bond that connected them was very strong. Cassie was different though. Cassie connected better with Mer, but that was mostly because Ali had not been too keen on an addition to the family, and at eight, when Cassie was born, she was old enough to know that. Cassie delayed her responses and reacted badly to Ali, but eventually did what Mer did, though usually in the most roundabout way.

Ali had thought that her mother had said to her that people lead by example, though she now began to wonder if it was her father who had said that, as it did not make much sense such words coming from her runaway mother's mouth. There was a time when she had truly adored her mother, but that passed when she hit her teens and found herself always curtailed by her parent, who kept leaving her in charge of the younger two. The image she once held of her composed and loving mother had evaporated, and in its place there was a conniving woman who had used them all. She had created a wonderful home with their father and they had, without doubt, been very happy for a long time. But all of that happiness faded, and all Ali could really contain about her mother was the fact that she had lied and cheated and used Ali to fulfil her own needs.

'Our mother died ages ago,' she told enquiring classmates. It brought her sympathy she did not want, but it put an end to any questions. She had settled in quickly, enjoying the novelty of being the new girl in her class, a rival for the other top pupils, with a reserve and poise that attracted attention. It pleased her. Once again she was curtailed by her family life, by the need to get home as soon as school ended, to look after Mer and Cassie even though she felt that Mer was old enough to do her share of caring for Cassie. It was she who organised dinner with a school book propped beside her. She was grateful for Oma's input into their family, and for the cleaning woman who popped in twice a week and left the place spotless and the laundry ironed. She sauntered home from school with her new friends, but always conscious of the time constraints, one eye on the watch on her wrist. She was fearful of returning to Dublin. Unlike her sisters, she did not pine for their home at the sea. She missed it, but did not want to be there.

'Papa,' she said. It was the following year, and like the others she too had changed the way she addressed him. 'Are we going to stay here?'

'Yes,' he replied. 'This is now home. We're going to stay in this house for the next few years. The owners have decided not to sell.'

'I meant are we really staying here in Germany. I thought... we still have the house at Seapoint,' she remarked thoughtfully. 'Does that mean you are thinking of going back there at some point?'

'No,' he said. 'Not for a long time. We have good tenants there. I've been assured they're looking after the place.'

'Why didn't you sell it?' she asked, still looking for reassurance that there would be no return.

'It's not that simple,' he replied. 'I can't just sell the house. It's not in my name.'

'Oh, I see.' She had not thought of that. She wondered how that worked. He was renting out the house and as far as she knew he got the income.

'The tenants love the place, and that's the way things stand for now. Do you want to go back? Is that why you're asking?'

She shook her head. 'No, I want to finish my schooling here. And we all love it here, don't we?' she said to her sisters, possibly with more force in her voice than she intended, but they both nodded.

Later, in her room, standing on the tiny balcony with Mer beside her, she said, 'You do like it here too, don't you Mer?'

Mer nodded. 'I miss some things,' she said, 'but yes, I like it here.'

Ali had joined a drama group in the school, and had talked about reading English and going to acting classes the following year when she finished her final exams. Their father wanted her to study two subjects. 'It will open more opportunities,' he said. 'If you decide to become a teacher, two subjects are better than one.'

'A teacher?' Ali said in disgust. 'Me? I'd never do that. All that noise and disruption, and never getting anywhere with children who have no interest; I couldn't bear it.'

'It's not quite that bad,' he said to her. 'Surely it depends on the quality of the teacher.'

Ali knew that was true. Some of the teachers maintained excellent discipline in class and things would move along smoothly enough. Ali suspected that she would be a good teacher, but it was not what she wanted. She was good at manipulating things in the home so that she got her own way while keeping the peace. This was easy enough to do with Mer, less so with Cassie. Cassie had a determination that Mer did not have, and while Ali shone, both because of her brains and her looks, Cassie sparkled in a different way.

When Ali looked at her two sisters she was sometimes startled at how different they were from each other. She was tall and dark, with Oma's posture, and clear, beautiful skin. Her beauty was classical, and on some level she was starting to know this, although she still felt awkward. She remembered that she once had felt more confident, in her looks and in herself, remembered walking in a polka dot bikini into the sea hoping that she looked attractive, more than that, maybe even knowing that day that she looked good. But those feelings had evaporated. Mer was thin and pale and rather wistful. She seemed to live inside herself. Ali wished she would stand up for herself more, though not, of course, in dealings with her. Cassie, on the other hand, was curvier and more bubbly. She was also very noisy. Banisters were made for sliding down, according to her doctrine. Trees were for climbing, baths were for splashing in, regardless of how many suds ended up on the bathroom floor. Floors were for dancing on. So were streets. 'Can't you walk in a civilised fashion?' Ali remembered their mother saying a dozen times a day when Cassie was little. But no, Cassie could not walk in a civilised fashion. She could twirl and twist, jump and tap-dance, but walking was not in her repertoire. Her school reports referred to a lack of focus, and twice their father had been called in because of her disruptive behaviour, most recently because she had brought two mice into school and released them in the school canteen.

'Imagine if I became a teacher and had children like Cassie in my class,' Ali said to Mer that evening on the balcony. Side by side they rested their arms on the iron railing.

'I don't think there is anyone else quite like her,' Mer pointed out.

They were looking down on the garden with its single tree where Cassie was hanging upside down by her knees on the strongest branch. 'She's like a bat,' Mer said.

'No,' grimaced Ali. 'Bats only come out at night and they steer clear of humans.'

'I read that some bats come out during the day,' Mer said.

'Yes, all right; then Cassie the Bat is a good name for her.'

The similarity began and ended just with Cassie hanging upside down, but she did remind them both of a bat that evening. She was dressed in black jeans and a dark jacket and she just hung there in the garden in the slowly fading light.

'Do you ever want to be like Cassie?' Mer asked.

'How do you mean? Always in trouble? Always being a total pain? A walking irritant? No, I don't.'

'I didn't mean that. She's very clever, very articulate, stoic I suppose. She seems to bounce along. Anyway, I didn't mean that. I just wondered what the world would be like hanging upside down,' Mer said.

'Go out and hang there with her and you'll soon find out.' Ali suddenly stopped and looked at Mer. 'I'm sorry. That was silly of me.' She was too aware of the voices of Mer's doctors, and knew that Mer must be even more conscious of her own limitations, of the things she must not do, of blood flowing through her veins and not flowing out again, of the pockets in her head. 'You are much better, aren't you?' she said.

Mer nodded. 'You know I am. I probably get as much exercise as you do; swimming in the pool, cross-country skiing with Opa. And I feel better and stronger. I...'

She stopped. Ali looked at her. 'Go on, what were you going to say?'

'I hate the operations,' Mer said. 'I like the anaesthetic, and the drifting off to sleep, and I want to hold on to that. I just hate the whole recovery thing, the knowing that I can't eat, and the diet of soup...' She had recently had more of the lesions removed from her mouth and her lips were swollen and cracked again, and Ali knew her sister was still in pain as she was only taking soup and water. She knew she was just trying to reassure herself that Mer was getting better.

It was the first time Mer had spoken about it. Ali put her arm around her. 'They'll find a cure,' she said.

'How? How can there be a cure for weak veins? I read about it in the library. Women with varicose veins have the veins removed or stripped or something. You can't do that with the veins in your head. I'd end up with no lips and...' she paused and touched the side of her face where the inoperable tumour sometimes swelled and caused her pain.

Ali looked at Mer's mouth. 'You know, once the stitches heal each time, you can't see anything wrong.'

'I feel that when I smile there are gaps,' Mer said.

'Well there aren't. It may feel like that, but you have a great smile.'

'Do I?'

A wave of anger swelled up in Ali's chest. Anger at Miriam for leaving Mer. She needed a mother, someone to tell her nice things about herself, to give her some self-esteem. Didn't Mer have enough problems in her life with her short arm and her little hand and the swelling in her jaw?

'You're very pretty, Mer,' she said, still railing against her absent parent. 'And you're loving and kind. Anyone who can be consistently kind to Cassie the bat has a nice nature. Nicer than mine anyway.'

She knew that her father did his best with them, and he was good with them, but maybe the younger two did not get enough individual time; maybe that was why Cassie was always in trouble in school, and Mer was so withdrawn. She did not want to think about these things. She wanted them not to be her problem. She felt frustrated with everything to do with her home, and she wanted to get away and leave it all behind.

'I've applied to the University of Strasbourg,' Ali said, changing the subject, as down below Cassie swung upwards like a professional acrobat.

'Strasbourg? Why there?' Mer asked in surprise. It had not occurred to her that Ali was planning on leaving. Living in a university town, she had just assumed Ali would continue her studies right there.

'I'll be eighteen when I finish next year. I don't want to stay here. We need to find our own way,' Ali said. 'Anyway, I'm going. They've accepted me and I'm going to study English and German.'

'In French?' Mer said bewildered.

'Yes, in French.' Ali's modern language skills had always been excellent and, unlike Mer, she had steered clear of her father's obsession with the Classics. She found the idea of studying through French more interesting than any of the universities that her father had suggested.

'I'll miss you,' Mer said. Her voice sounded wistful.

Ali felt sorry for her again. As much as she loved her, she was aware of the enormity of the four year age gap at that time. Mer seemed such a little girl, almost like someone from a different species with her skinny arms and legs, and her big eyes in her tiny face. 'It's not for ages yet,' Ali said. 'But it's good for us to talk about these things so that they don't come as a surprise. We've had enough surprises I think.'

'You mean you won't do a runner like Miriam did.'

Ali ignored the comment. She had the feeling that Mer was trying to make a joke, but it was all too bitter, with a sense of something too raw to confront.

'I worry about you,' Ali said. 'You need to stand up for yourself more. You too need to make plans for the future. Don't find yourself trapped here.'

'Of course I won't,' Mer said. 'And I don't feel trapped. I like it here. I'm going to study too I suppose. But I have ages to go before I need to think about that.'

'I know,' Ali said. 'But you should be thinking about what you want to do, what interests you most. In four years you'll be finished and the world will be yours.'

She was protective of Mer, in her own way, and while her father talked with her about the future, she was unsure if he talked to Mer in the same way.

Night had fallen and it was getting cold. Their father had called Cassie in from the dark a few minutes earlier. The streetlights lit up the road, and the tree in the garden shimmered slightly in the rising splinter of moonlight. 'Friends come and go,' Ali said suddenly, 'but sisters are forever.'

Mer held her hand. 'I know,' she said.

They both had missed their friends from Dublin, but both had acquired new ones.

Ali said, 'It's odd how friends change. I really pined for some of my friends when we came here, and I wrote the odd time, but then I let them go. I couldn't explain what had happened and why we left. Not the truth I mean. Now I will lose my new friends as they are going to universities all over Germany, and I suppose the same thing will happen, letters for a while and then no more...'

'But it's not quite the same,' Mer said. 'Your friends all come from here now and when you come home during the holidays they will be here.'

'I don't think it'll be like that,' Ali said. 'I think when you say goodbye it's goodbye.'

'Strasbourg is really very close,' Mer said, wondering if her sister feared homesickness or loneliness. She had no idea what Ali was thinking.

'And you have Opa and Oma. They're just across the border. And I'll be down every weekend that I can; at least once a month. And there are letters, and the phone... well, maybe not the phone,' Mer added.

Their father hated them using the phone. They all dreaded the arrival of the phone bill; it was the one time he ranted and raged, calling it a complete waste of money and his working time. 'I don't work so that you girls can chat to someone you see every day at school or on the street,' he said every month when the phone bill came in. 'If next month's bill isn't down I'm cancelling the phone.' It was the only time he showed annoyance.

Ali laughed. 'Yes, maybe not the phone.'

'But you are excited about going... about your plans?' Mer asked, and Ali could hear in her voice that Mer wanted reassurance. It was, of all the changes in their lives, the most significant one to date. Well, perhaps not *the* most significant one, she thought, but she wanted to see it as such.

'Yes,' she nodded. 'Of course I am,' she added looking at her sister's face. 'Growing up is exciting. It might not always seem that way, especially at thirteen. But it is. Change is good.'

She needed out and away. She was tired of looking after the younger two, tired of her father's constant checking on them all, tired of the effort of pretending everything was just fine. She remembered a moment of almost-freedom, swimming in the sea and two boys swimming with her. She felt that freedom sometimes when she was skiing, weaving her way down the mountainside, and once on the river, rowing in a boat with some of her classmates with the sun beating down on them... that was freedom; away from the constraints of home, of Cassie's noisiness, and Mer's pale, hopeful face always looking to her for guidance. Sometimes she hated herself because she loved Mer and did not want to hurt her, but sometimes her tongue got the better of her and she would snap out some cruel words just to be left alone. And Mer never said anything. She would retreat into herself, and then the self-loathing would begin. What she did not tell Mer was that she would have liked to have gone farther away to study, but she had chosen Strasbourg so that she would be close enough if Mer needed her. It was her compromise, and her secret, because she did not want Mer to know how she really worried about her.

Now in these moments of honesty with her sister, she said, 'Mer, if I say something unkind to you, and I know I sometimes do, you should say something back. People shouldn't walk all over you. You have to fight for yourself.'

'You're not unkind,' Mer said. 'Sometimes you snap at me, but that's all right. I know you don't mean it.'

'You're too nice,' Ali said. 'Too forgiving.'

'There's nothing to forgive,' Mer said, no irony in her voice.

Ali felt that her sister just did not understand. She saw goodness in everyone even when they were mean and horrible. She seemed to look past the obvious and ignore unkindness and cruelty.

'We had better go in,' she said. 'It's getting cold. I'm glad summer is coming...' Buds were forming on the tree and the grass needed cutting.

Mer nodded. 'Do you remember the Dance of the Waves?' she asked.

They both laughed then.

'I wonder if Cassie remembers.' Mer said.

'It's probably why she hates me so much,' Ali said.

'She doesn't hate you,' Mer said with a smile. 'Cassie loved the Dance of the Waves. Remember her squeals of laughter? Just because she doesn't do what you tell her to doesn't mean she doesn't like you.'

'She does the opposite of what I tell her,' Ali said as they stepped back into the room and she closed the wooden-framed glass doors and pulled the curtains.

'Yes, but you're great at getting her to do what you want,' Mer said with another laugh. 'You tell her to do the exact opposite of what you actually want and so she does whatever it is. She's working her way through every book in the house and is even reading the books I borrow from the library. I even saw her with one of my Latin textbooks, and that was because you told her that you bet she couldn't learn Latin.'

'I don't think I've any parenting skills, but even I can see this mightn't be the best way to raise a child,' Ali's voice was scathing. 'Anyway, she does what *you* want, which will be a bonus when I am gone.'

Ali settled down to an hour's study before going to bed. She decided never to have children because of the constraints brought about by their very existence. She wondered if that was selfish, but she felt it was a lot less egotistical than having children and then discovering she did not want to care for them. She was determined not to repeat the patterns of her mother's family, taking off when it suited them and leaving those behind to survive as best they could. She had wondered during that first year as each birthday came and went if their mother would send even a card. She was aware of a conflict of feelings. On the one hand, she would have liked a card, an acknowledgment of her birth, of her very existence, but on the other she knew she would tear it up in anger. She wondered if Miriam even knew that they had moved. Maybe there were birthday cards lying in the house in Dublin on the hall table. It made her think of that letter her mother had left and she wished she had opened it and seen its contents. She wondered if Miriam thought of them at all, or was she so content within her new life that she had closed them out, just as she, Ali now closed the shutters and shut out the night. She forced her thoughts back to her school work and settled down to read.

She had the feeling that there were good times coming. She was going to get her driving licence soon, and during the summer she was planning on waitressing with the sole intention of saving enough money to buy a car for when she was in Strasbourg. Her father and their aunt, Anneke, were planning a holiday but she would stay at home, though she had not told them yet. When she left, Mer would have to look after the cooking, so she could take over that role while she, Ali, waitressed. It would be good practice for her sister. She sighed. None of this was what she wanted, really wanted, deep in her bones, but it seemed to be the best that she could do at the moment. She had thought of asking in the local pizzeria for work, and she was reasonably sure that they would give it to her, so well known were she and her sisters. But there was a hotel in town that she thought might be easier work, and probably better tips, and she would not have to deal with Cassie and her friends, who often had a pizza on a Friday evening, accompanied by one of their unfortunate parents. She would go into the hotel on Saturday and ask. She looked at the clock beside her bed. It was already ten thirty and she knew she ought to go to sleep, but she was restless. She went downstairs to get a hot drink to bring back with her to bed. Her father was reading in the living-room, a single light from the standard lamp shining down on him and his book.

He looked up when she came into the room. His face looked anxious for a moment.

'I was afraid you were Mer walking in her sleep again,' he said.

'She's stopped, hasn't she?' Ali asked, looking at him and wondering for a moment about his problems and his worries. He never seemed to go out or to socialise. His life revolved around the home and the girls and she felt sorry for him. After their mother had gone and they had first moved to Germany and she had time to think, there had been a period when she had felt anger towards him as well as towards her mother. She felt that he, as an intelligent man, should have known better than to marry someone as incapable of bearing responsibility as their mother.

'Dad... Papa...' she corrected herself. They all had moved, almost seamlessly, into German speech and thought, but occasionally words and phrases emerged from the past. She remembered the first night that she had dreamed in German, and knew that a transition had taken place, and both her sisters had experienced the same thing.

'Papa, I think you should get out more.'

'Out where?' he said, looking puzzled.

'I don't know. Maybe going out with friends from work, or even... dating,' she suggested.

He smiled at her. 'I'm not ready for any of that yet,' he said.

For some reason this gave her reassurance. It meant that he knew where he was in the healing process, and it also meant that he knew, or at least had implied, that there would be a time when it felt right again for him to go and do normal things.

'Are you lonely?' she asked.

He shook his head. 'There's not much time for loneliness around here. Between work and home I am fully occupied, and in many ways I'm enjoying that. This time of evening, when the house is quiet, I sit and read or make plans for tomorrow. For some reason, that seems just right for now.'

'Will you be all right when I leave?' she asked.

'Of course I will. I'll miss you, but that's part of being a parent. And you won't be gone for another year, so I'll have plenty of time to get used to the idea. It's odd though, because when children are little you just can't imagine such a time coming: the time when they want to spread their wings... I'm proud of you, you know.'

He had never spoken to her like this before. She didn't know. It wasn't something she had considered. She had just done what had to be done. 'You're intelligent,' he continued.

'Not as intelligent as Cassie,' Ali said.

'There are different kinds of intelligence,' Karl said. 'Anyway, I didn't mean that I was just proud of your intelligence or indeed because you are a good looking girl. I meant because of how you use your attributes. You use your intelligence. You fulfil your potential. As a parent I think that is the most we can ask.'

She wondered if these were things he had discussed at some point with Miriam. She wondered if they had worried over their three girls and what would become of them. Of course they would have worried over Mer constantly. She supposed they must have been afraid, just as she was afraid each time Mer had to have an operation. Mer's stoicism was definitely one of her attributes, undemanding, always finding a smile; that was Mer.

'Do you worry about Mer and Cassie?' she asked.

'I worry about Cassie, I suppose,' he replied thoughtfully. 'She's so bright but doesn't seem very interested in any kind of academic achievement. Or, indeed, any achievement. Articulate beyond her years, that's what the principal said when I was last called in for a 'discussion', which felt more like a reprimand.'

'But Mer,' Ali said. 'Do you worry about her?'

'Only with regards to the sleepwalking,' he said. 'But as you said, that seems to have stopped. That episode when you went to stay the first time with your grandparents seems to have been the last, although I am careful to lock the door and remove the key at night.'

'I meant about her health, and how she's doing in school,' Ali said.

'Of course I'm concerned about her health. I hate her having these endless operations, but she bounces back out of them. They hope each time the lesions won't return, and this time they were more hopeful... but she is so pragmatic about it all that it rubs off on me. And her school work, well, she's doing fine. She has to work harder than you, and she does. She'll be fine. She'll find her way.'

'Is it difficult having no one to talk to about these things?' Ali asked. She was sitting on the sofa now and she pulled a rug over her legs. It was becoming chilly in the room. The nights were very cold and, even though the boiler was left on overnight, its timer reduced the temperature when they went to bed. She shivered.

He smiled at her. 'I'm talking to you,' he said. 'That's sharing my thoughts, clarifying them, I suppose. And I do talk to colleagues at work. I'm not the only one who is a single parent. It's one of the advantages of being here as opposed to Dublin. Here you can acknowledge separation and divorce. It will be a long time until divorce arrives in Ireland.'

'Are you divorced?' she asked in surprise, wondering if she had misunderstood him.

'Yes. I petitioned for it earlier in the year and I attended the court and I'm divorced.'

'You never said. How did you do that? Was... was she there?'

'No. She never turned up.'

'But did you ask her to... I mean... how... did you contact her?'

'No, I didn't. I got a lawyer to deal with all of that.'

'Oh.' Ali was stunned. She thought she had her finger on the pulse of everything that was going on in the home, but had no idea of what her father had endured. 'I wish I'd known,' she said. 'I would have gone with you, supported you.'

'Thank you,' he said. 'There seemed no reason to involve any of you. I waited until she was gone six months and then I filed for divorce. It was all very straightforward, the more so as we had married here in Germany.'

'What grounds... is that the term... what reason did you give?' she asked.

'Desertion,' he said.

'I suppose that is the perfect word,' Ali said. 'For what happened, I mean.'

Later, in bed when she turned out the light, she realised that he must have an address for her mother in order for his lawyer to contact her. She wondered briefly where her mother was, and then decided that she did not care, that knowing would add nothing and that she was just as well being left in the dark.

# CASSIE'S TALE

Like a knife that slices through a loaf of bread, they were divorced. The stairs didn't creak in our German home, our gingerbread house. I can listen at the silent doors.

When Oma comes to visit she bakes bread and cake and biscuits and the house smells of cinnamon and icing sugar. The warm yeast rises in water. It froths and bubbles. Mer helps her, she writes down the recipes and little by little she learns how to cook like Oma. We come home from school and Mer opens the bag of flour and takes the butter she has left out that morning so that it is soft. She opens the yeast, she measures and sifts and she makes Hefekuchen. The sweet cake rises under a warm towel near the stove and goes into the oven.

The house is warm and smells of nearly happiness.

I did my reading sitting by the stove. The smell is in my clothes and in my hair. These are things I will remember later when I am trying to remember my name and why I am running on the streets. I will remember looking into the eyes of the Minotaur and know that I must find my way out of the labyrinth. I will try to find that gingerbread home in its glass globe with the falling snow, but it is muddled. I think it is by the sea. They had given me back my passport on the last flight. I remember the plane. I remember the smell. It was the smell of fear. I looked at my passport and then at the man who gave it to me and he said, 'When we get to Rome...'

And I thought, what makes you think we will get to Rome? We had seen the desert sands in Africa; we had seen landing-strip after landing-strip. We had seen the Acropolis when we took off from Athens. Yes, I could remember some things. But not the sequence. There were things I did not want to remember. I closed my eyes. I don't know what else he said to me. Something about a doctor maybe. Something about shock. He gave me a drink. There was silence again on the plane. I knew I must not think. I feared the gun at my head. I feared looking out the plane and seeing the ground and knowing that when the trigger was pulled I would fall from the plane on to the hard surface and that I would die there and be forgotten in the dust of ages, eaten by vultures...

No God's acre for Cassie Peters.

The memories are coming in too fast. They jump from glass globes with falling snow, the old man and his accordion, the cobbled streets of our German town, to the maze and the Minotaur. I can't get rid of the Minotaur but I don't remember how he found me. In the myth, he eats the boys and girls. They are fodder for him. I painted it once. I remember the sketch, and the winding pathways in the labyrinth. I painted them trapped, frightened, ready to be devoured; there was no rescue for his victims. Even if they had escaped, I wondered what would happen to them. Would they know how to readjust to a world that had abandoned them? What hope would there be for them to find their homes, to be reunited with those who had once loved them? Or had they been forgotten? Lost in the maze, adrenalin pumping, fighting against the inevitable.

# CHAPTER TEN

Mer sometimes wondered where time went. She felt that it made no sense. The growing up years in Dublin, and now the German years, were often marked by anaesthesia and the feeling that what she encountered in that morphine-riddled world had more meaning than so-called reality.

She told no one that the nun from her childhood memories often visited her in her dreams. She sometimes saw this dream as a guideline, and more and more she took refuge in mythology, finding succour in other worlds. As a child, before her first real memory of the world behind anaesthesia, she had loved her father's stories of ancient Greece and Rome. She liked thinking about the links between the stories from different worlds, and in the meantime knew that every culture seemed to have created similar stories to explain the world, the seas and the skies. She grew both physically and emotionally the year before Ali left. She saw herself as a link between her sisters, and was close to both of them but in different ways. She had mothered Cassie while Ali had just bossed her around, and that was the way it had been long before their mother had evaporated.

Sometimes she thought her happiest times were curled up in bed with Cassie, telling her stories from ancient times. Cassie, who longed for attention, lay quietly beside her. Sometimes Mer read to her, novels borrowed from the library, books taken from the shelves downstairs, but she always returned to the myths. Cassie did not appear to mind what Mer read or told her, as long as she had that comfort time with her before going to sleep.

'Once upon a time...' Mer told her myths and legends in a particular way, and if she paused for any reason, Cassie took her thumb from her mouth and would say, 'go on...'

'Once upon a time, a very long time ago in an ancient world of gods and goddesses, of nymphs and fauns, of babbling brooks and star-filled heavens, there was a beautiful girl named Persephone. Her father was Zeus, god of the skies, and her mother was Demeter, goddess of the harvest. Everyone loved Persephone, everyone including Hades, god of the Underworld, who wanted her for himself. One day, while Persephone was out collecting flowers, Hades split open the earth and reached up from the Underworld and seized Persephone from the flowering fields and took her with him back to his home in the land of the dead. Only Zeus and the sun, which was called Helios, had seen what had happened. Poor Demeter, her mother, searched everywhere for her, broken hearted, wandering from place to place in her efforts to find her missing daughter. Eventually, Helios took pity on her and told her what had happened to Persephone. Demeter was so angry and so upset that she stopped looking after the earth and it ceased to be fertile. Nothing grew. Zeus, who had been busy with other things, sent Hermes, the winged messenger of the gods, to visit Hades and to tell him to release Persephone. You see, Hermes, being the messenger of the gods, used to guide the souls of the dead down to the Underworld, so he knew the way. Hades did not want to let her go because he loved her and wanted to keep her to himself, but he agreed. It was not a good idea to have Zeus as an enemy. Before he let Persephone go back to the world of the living, he gave her a pomegranate to eat, and because she ate its seeds and had now fed in the Underworld it meant that she would always have to return there, every year for a part of the year. The rest of the time she stayed with Demeter, her mother. Every year when Persephone returned to Hades in the Underworld, Demeter stopped caring for the earth and it became infertile again, and that season of the year became known as winter.'

'But Mer, why did Zeus not tell Demeter where Persephone was?'

'I don't know. For some things there are no answers.'

'But didn't he love his daughter?'

'I'm sure he did.' Mer wasn't all that sure, but it seemed wise to give Cassie the answers she wanted. 'Sometimes parents don't know what's best for their children; sometimes they are busy, distracted by other things.'

'I feel sorry for Demeter, looking for her daughter all that time,' Cassie said, turning on her side. 'I wonder why the sun told her.'

'I think that he might have wanted to shine light into the darkness.'

'That's nice,' Cassie said. 'Hopeful.'

\*\*\*

The summer Ali waitressed in the local hotel, Mer took over the kitchen completely. Her interest in food had developed during recent operations when she found herself drinking soup from cans, heated slowly in a saucepan. She remembered too clearly the aroma of the things she could not eat during those periods, and now she took it upon herself to learn how to cook like her grandmother. She enjoyed pottering in the kitchen, marinating meat, preparing vegetables, making sauces and baking. She bought little pots of herbs and watched them grow. The smell of crushed garlic on her fingers pleased her, the zing of a lemon cascaded in the air and she smiled even as she cut onions and placed the knife under cold water to stop the burning in her eyes. She cut and peeled and chopped, absorbed in the activity. Cassie, who had hitherto just eaten whatever was put in front of her, now commented on the dinners that Mer so lovingly served up. 'Can we have this again tomorrow?' Cassie would say after a chicken roasted with lemon and garlic was enthusiastically devoured. 'Did you really make this ice cream?' 'Why does Sauerkraut taste nice when you make it?'

Ali came home from work, sometimes early, sometimes late, depending on her shift in the hotel. 'Where's my dinner?' she would ask at ten thirty at night, and Mer, looking up from a book or away from the television said, 'Sorry, Ali, I thought you were eating in the hotel,' and she got to her feet to go and prepare something for her sister.

'I did eat in the hotel,' Ali said. 'I was just teasing. There's just a nice smell when you come in the door...'

'I can fix you leftovers,' Mer said.

'I was joking,' Ali said.

Mer was no longer sure when she was joking. Ali had detached herself in some way during those summer months, and while Mer grew into her new role in the house, Ali seemed to grow away from them.

Tante Anneke had reappeared as promised, and they had gone on holiday, not to the south of Italy as originally suggested, but to Crete. Ali had convinced her father that she should stay at home and work to save for a car. He had wanted her to join them.

'Come with us, Ali. You need a holiday as much as the rest of us.'

'But Dad, it will be a holiday for me. It'll be just as much of a break. I really want to save for a car, and I've found work for the whole summer. They won't just take me for a month. And I can look after myself; it'll be good preparation for when I go to university. Please, Dad.' He knew she was probably right, and so he agreed.

Their holiday was both uneventful and a success. On alternate days they lazed at the beach and swam. The other days they went to see sights, with Tante Anneke insisting on doing the driving. In the back of the car, Mer and Cassie alternately held each other by the hand or clung on to their respective doors. Anneke had no fear of hairpin bends on the mountains and no problem at honking at wayward goats.

'I'd forgotten you failed your driving test the first time round,' Karl said to his sister.

'I remember you were thrilled,' she said with a laugh.

'Only because it meant I didn't have to share a car with you.'

'Oh, I always assumed you were just glad I had failed.'

'Was I that mean? I hope not.'

'Actually, you weren't a bad brother,' Anneke said.

The thin walls of the apartment in which they were staying did nothing to protect the privacy of conversation. There were evenings after Mer and Cassie went to bed, tired but finding the heat difficult to bear at night, leaving them restless, and Karl and Anneke sat in the tiny living-room. Anneke had the other bedroom in the apartment, and Karl slept on the fold-out sofa bed in the living-room. They sat with the windows open and talked quietly, unaware that much, though not all, of what they said drifted into the next room.

'I probably was a bad brother,' Karl said, referring to the conversation in the car earlier.

'I was probably a bad sister. So needy. So busy trying to be a Peters, not knowing I really was one until I was eighteen. And we were very close in age. It must have been difficult for you.'

'I don't remember you not being there,' Karl said.

'Neither do I. There are no prior memories. It must have been difficult for Mother though, my being landed on her doorstep, I mean.'

'I sometimes thinks she thrives on difficult situations. She rises to them. And she certainly loved you as her own. Were you angry when they told you when you were eighteen?'

'Yes. Probably. I don't remember that particularly. I think I was just more bewildered. For ages afterwards I thought maybe my real mother was still alive. Maybe I even hoped it. But she's not. I went to the village where I was born, and she really did die in childbirth. And for some reason that helped. I hadn't been stolen or abandoned. She had died of natural causes, and considering the history of our country from that period, that was a relief. And our father took me to your home because he loved me, wanted me, and in so doing he protected me. He saved my life, and later Mother did too. Not telling me my past was a form of protection.'

'You mean that your mother was Jewish?' Karl asked.

'Yes. We didn't have to hide that, you and I, I mean, because we didn't know.'

'I wonder would it have been easier for us as so-called adopted siblings, growing up knowing all of that.'

'Maybe. Maybe not. It's difficult to tell. I think now that it was easier not knowing that I was Jewish. Can you imagine having to hide that through those years? It was awful enough as it was. I think we would still have enjoyed sibling rivalry,' Anneke concluded with a laugh.

'Enjoyed?'

'Well, it had its benefits. We both achieved. Do you see rivalry in your girls?'

'It's different,' Karl said. 'They are linked in such a different way. Ali and Mer have always been close. Ali was so jealous when Mer was born, and I remember once thinking that Mer's illness as a baby had its own benefits. I didn't think it at the time, but later... Ali cared so much for Mer. Though I have to admit the age gap seems wider at the moment.'

'That will pass,' Anneke said.

'No doubt. Actually I think they lack rivalry, and again that could be because of the age difference. Ali has always achieved; she's good at maths and modern languages. Mer on the other hand is following my path, Classics. Cassie is still finding her way. So intelligent, so articulate, brilliant in fact, but of the three of them I suppose I worry about her the most. I'm never quite sure what she will do next. She has a fearless streak. When we first moved to Germany I had this fear that she would get lost. Silly I suppose, but very real at the time. She could never stay in the same place for more than a minute. Now I'm less concerned about that. It's still early days for her, though I could do without being called into her school to discuss her lack of progress. They said she has linguistic skills beyond her years; that she is probably the best read child in the school, let alone her class, but she is always in trouble. I'm not good at handling that. I want her to be like the other two; to put her head down and to work, but her physical energy never seems to deplete. She climbed up the fire escape in school onto the roof to sunbathe. Topless. She hit some other girl with her tennis racquet during a school match, which the principal implied was bullying. I never see any of these traits at home. I think she might be bored or frustrated.'

'What did she say when you spoke to her about these things?'

'She said she didn't want to sunbathe topless in the playground. She said the girl she was partnering in the tennis match was useless at serving and shouldn't have been on the team. She never seems to see the wider context of her actions.'

'Did you punish her?'

'I spoke to her very firmly.'

'Karl, you need to take away her pocket money, or not let her out at the weekend or something like that, something that might make her think twice about her activities. Is there anything she really likes doing?'

'Art.'

'Well, at least she's putting an effort into something,' Anneke said. 'I was going to suggest curtailing something she enjoys, but I think that is something to be supported. Have you thought of getting her extra art classes? If that is her main interest maybe it would help if she saw you encouraging her.'

'I hadn't thought of that. Maybe I could ask in the school. I find the whole school thing so difficult. Miriam used to deal with all of that.' He sighed.

'Would you like coffee or a glass of wine? I need something.'

'Let's go with the wine this evening,' Karl said. 'We had such a busy day, and it's the best way to unwind. For me anyway.'

'Mother said Miriam left you a letter...' Anneke said as she fetched a bottle of wine from the fridge. She handed it to him with the corkscrew. 'She only told me recently, in case you wonder why I didn't ask before.'

'Yes.'

'Do you want to tell me about it?'

'I don't know that it throws any real light on anything. She said some very cruel things. By the way, do you think I'm vain?'

'Did she say that?'

'Yes. That and things to do with selfishness. That I forced her to have three children when she only wanted one...'

'My God,' Anneke said. 'Did you? It doesn't sound like you.'

'Of course I didn't.'

'Karl, tell me you destroyed that letter,' Anneke said suddenly. 'The girls must never see it.'

'I did. I kept it for a long time, and then one day I thought I don't need to read this again; it felt etched into my soul. And I burned it. The odd thing is that I can't remember it properly. I just seem to remember the cruelty in it. But maybe that's all there was anyway.'

'I'm glad you got rid of it. It can't do anyone any good to be re-reading something like that. And for the record, I don't think you're vain. I think you're careful with your appearance and there's nothing wrong with that. I think you're a great father. You've made a success of your life and you're doing well by your children.'

'Thanks, Anneke. I appreciate that. The thing is, it doesn't feel like a success. There is so much I just don't understand. Way back when I first met Miriam, you probably remember, I had thought of a career in the diplomatic service. Now I think that that was very important to her. She was angry when I changed direction. I go over and over these things. It was as if she had mapped out a course and I had diverted from it.'

'I don't think she was a very nice person,' Anneke said.

'Really? Did you always think that?'

'It isn't important, but yes. She never really had enough time for me; or not the amount that I wanted anyway. Mother felt the same.'

'Did she? I had no idea.'

'Well, you can't really say those things to someone who's in love. They have to live their own life.'

'Maybe I would have been better off if someone had pointed a few things out to me about Miriam and her nature.'

'And you would have listened?' Anneke said with a snort.

He laughed then. 'You're right. Of course I wouldn't have.'

'It bothered me that she had dropped out of university without completing her studies. It struck me that she was placing all her trust in you. Not that she shouldn't have trusted you; that's not what I meant. But she could have got her degree. It struck me that she didn't know how to complete things.'

Lying in bed, Mer heard some of this. She wondered if Cassie was awake and really hoped she wasn't. Cassie's breathing seemed even, but she was not tossing and turning as she had done on previous nights. Mer did not want to hear their conversation. She put her hands over her ears and thought about the trip they had made that day to Knossos.

Tante Anneke had bought her a camera and she and Cassie had taken it in turns to use it. Mer had concentrated on people and scenery, and it was Cassie who took photos of the sights. She remembered Cassie photographing an urn, and on it was a painting of two women.

'They're Thyke and Nemesis,' their father had explained.

'Who were they?' Cassie asked.

'Thyke was the goddess of Chance, and at one point Nemesis was viewed like that too; the distributor of both good and bad fortune. But later her name took on another meaning, and now it means to give what is due and she's seen as a goddess of retribution or vengeance.'

'They have their arms wrapped around each other,' Cassie said.

'That will be a nice photo,' Mer said, pleased at Cassie's curiosity about the things that interested her, too.

She fell asleep thinking about that.

The next day when they were on the beach, she said to Anneke, 'The walls in the apartment are very thin.'

Anneke, who was lying beside her on a towel, propped herself up on her elbow and looked at her. Karl and Cassie were in the sea.

'Voices travel?' Anneke asked or said. Mer was not sure which.

'Yes,' she said.

'If you heard something you didn't understand, you must ask me or your father,' Anneke said after a moment's pause. 'We were chatting and I suppose we thought you were asleep. Certainly we had no idea that our voices were that loud.'

'I wasn't listening,' Mer said. 'But just in case, I thought I should say it. Cassie, you know...'

'I'm glad you mentioned it,' Anneke said. 'But, Merope, I meant what I said. You can ask me anything. I probably don't have the answers though...'

'I know,' Mer replied. 'I was just thinking of Cassie. I don't have any questions. Not any more.'

'What do you mean, not any more?'

'We made a new life. I don't want to think back. Ali said it is better we live in the present.'

'And do you?'

Mer smiled. 'I've found other ways to handle things. And we're happier now. I am anyway. I used to sleepwalk. I don't do that now. That means I've moved on. Cassie used to suck her thumb. She's stopped. We don't need to think back. Not like that, anyway.'

Anneke touched her lightly on the shoulder. 'Growing up is difficult enough. I sometimes think it doesn't matter what happens to you as a child... I mean, of course it matters, but a time comes when you get to make your own choices. You get to choose perspective and how you want things to be. Your father and I, we fought as children. We were particular people, with our own personalities and our own needs. We were very lucky. I'm not sure that I saw that then. I was always vying with him, always wanting more. But a time came when we were both able to make choices and to decide what we wanted to do. It's important to make those choices wisely.'

'Do you think Papa did not make wise choices? Is that what you're saying?'

'No, it's not what I'm saying. He made choices and they seemed wise at the time. The one thing I do know is that he wouldn't change the past. And do you know why?'

'No,' Mer said.

'Because if he did change the past, then he wouldn't have you, Ali and Cassie. And I know that you three are the most precious things in his life.'

'Do you really truly believe that?' Mer asked.

'I do. I have absolutely no doubt about it. I know of his love for you, his concern, and his belief in the three of you. I also know that he's proud of you. He probably doesn't say that; he's not the kind of person to say it to you anyway. But he has said it to me.'

Mer thought about that for a bit.

'Do you think he's happy?' she asked.

'I think he is as happy as he can be at the moment. He's still dealing with the past. Maybe he carries guilt, feels it was entirely his fault.'

'That what was his fault?'

'That he got his marriage wrong, and that you girls got hurt because of that.'

'We're all right,' Mer said. 'I only brought up the sound thing because of Cassie.'

Anneke looked at her and nodded. 'I understand.'

There were no more overheard conversations in the apartment, but both Mer and Anneke noticed that Cassie was sucking her thumb again.

# CASSIE'S TALE

**W**ords from that letter came back like snakes into my head.
One child wanted, two children not.

I had forgotten. Much better to forget.

I need to forget, not remember.

So much mythology in that holiday in Crete. With winged sandals I ran across the hot sand and threw myself into the sea. The water washes away the snakes but they return on the beach. Poseidon cannot save me on that golden sand.

King Minos ruled. All civilisations come to an end. They think they have it all, and then there is betrayal or war, or just evil, pure evil. Evil destroys. As does lust and even love. Once there were oak and cypress trees around King Minos's palace, now there are vines and olive groves. All things change and the changes influence the changes.

Once we had a house by the sea. It turned into a house with warm yeast rising and falling snow, the pavements hard packed, the accordion player on the corner playing his tunes. Apple sauce in the market place. The taste of icing sugar on my fingers.

All who looked into Medusa's face turned to stone. Her hair of snakes writhing and hissing. Perseus killed Medusa by never looking into her face, through a glass darkly he cut off her head. Her spilled blood made the Red Sea red, the drops of her blood turned into snakes and slithered across my mind into the desert. *'The lone and level sands stretch far away.'*

It was Theseus who killed the Minotaur. He told his father he would put up a white sail on his boat when he was journeying home. The white sail would tell his father he was still alive. If he was killed, the sail would be black. He forgot to put up the white sail, and his father thought he was dead.

I sought an image for that mother of mine. I was yet to find it. She is yet to tell me the story while we sit, sipping tea, in that houseboat floating on the water on Camden Lock. There was no sail at all on that boat. She is yet to tell me that it is better that she left, that she had nothing more to give us, and that she did as her father had done, and had opened the door, and walked down the gravelled pathway.

'Was it because of me?' I will say. She will shake her head.

'Your father and I wanted different things. I was tired of conforming to the pattern of his life.'

'But what about Ali, Mer and me?'

'I couldn't take you with me. I knew you would be better off with Karl. He seemed to have parenting skills that I lacked.'

She did not seem to see that Ali, Mer and I did not care about parenting skills, we just wanted the parent. How could I say that to this woman who had a photo of me on her wall, but did not understand that I wanted real contact, not a framed image of me in her life?

The Minotaur looks into my face but he will not see what I once was, what he once was, a child formed from love or lust. Innocence where did you go? Why did I seek to lose you? Why did you abandon me?

When the Minotaur unleashes his weapon and pulls the trigger, he will not see that he has destroyed dreams.

Soon he will not see at all.

# CHAPTER ELEVEN

After Ali's late shifts waitressing in the hotel, she either did not come home until after midnight, or else she came in, flounced about for a little and then went to bed.

'I should have passed you the role of chief cook and bottle-washer a lot earlier,' she said. Mer felt that she was trying to pick a row with her.

'I wouldn't have learned how to cook if it hadn't been for you,' Mer said.

'Yes,' Cassie said to Ali. 'She only learned to cook because you are such a rotten one.'

'That's not what I meant,' Mer said.

'You can never take a joke, can you?' Ali said to her. 'And Cassie, shouldn't you be in bed?'

'You're not in charge now,' Cassie said.

Mer knew she wasn't good at being teased. No matter how often the others finished their sentences by saying 'it's a joke, Mer,' she fell for it every time. Now Cassie was clearly trying to annoy Ali and Mer was tired. For the first time in her life she stood up to the two of them. 'Shut up, both of you,' she said. 'I'm doing my best. Can't you two do the same without bickering over everything?'

There was a stunned silence, and then Ali began to laugh. Cassie joined her in an unusual moment of conciliation between the pair of them.

'At last,' Ali said. 'At long, long last. And on that note I'm going to bed.'

That year passed and their father once again spoke to them about staying on in the rented house. The landlords were asking for a new contract that would last for five years. There were no objections, just queries about their home in Dublin, although they now understood that a return there was not an option because of his work.

'Is it still the same, do you think?' Cassie asked.

'Well, there is a shower now in the bathroom,' Karl said. 'The tenants asked if they could install one and I said yes.'

'Brilliant,' said Ali. 'I hated that ridiculous hose that was attached to the bath taps and that always came off when I was washing my hair.'

'And they've put more gravel on the driveway,' Karl said.

'Really settling in, huh?' Ali said.

'All good improvements,' Karl said.

'Do you have to do anything here? I mean, are we expected to make improvements?'

'No, though any improvements we want or need to make will be all right with the landlords,' he said. 'They are talking about decorating this room sometime soon, though.'

'And the kitchen?' Mer suggested hopefully.

'All right, all of downstairs then,' Karl agreed. 'I can ask them to do it all. Or maybe we just do it ourselves. I need to check the contract and talk to the owners.'

'Wait until I'm gone then,' Ali said. 'I couldn't bear the disruption.'

Karl suddenly realised that, while he dreaded her leaving, he also was looking forward to it. Filled with mixed emotions, he watched as she seemed to withdraw from them. It was like their nest had suddenly become too small for her. He could feel her frustration; it seemed aimed at them all and even at the tenants in Ireland. He knew she was working hard for her exams, but wished she wouldn't be so irritable. These last few months he had taken to going back to the university in the evening just to escape from the bickering.

He had a feeling that what was going on at home was normal, certainly his colleagues spoke of such things but he found it difficult to bear as the squabbling seemed relentless. It took more energy than he had, to constantly diffuse the arguments between Ali and Cassie, and he felt that he was letting them all down by not being able to cope.

To the outside eye his life was probably nothing more than work, be it his work in the university or his work as a parent. He, however, felt that he had got more out of being a father than most. These last years had brought with them a paternal fulfilment that he had never expected. Arranging skiing weekends, or hopping in the car to drive away for a long weekend with the girls was fun, and brought with it a sense of achievement. He was glad that Ali did not socialise adequately, and if he thought about that at all it was with a sense of relief as, so far, he had managed to avoid the arguments with her that he knew took place with other teenage girls and their parents. He did not see that she was just looking to escape.

*** 

Ali was gone soon enough. She passed her driving test and bought a second-hand pale blue Volkswagen. She brought them out to see it parked on the street, and could not help the note of pride in her voice. 'It's lovely,' Mer said. 'Just perfect. It suits you.'

It was the first real thing that Ali had ever bought, and she kept going to check on it. Then the day came and she packed her bags and her books and then she was gone. Mer waved from the end of the street before wandering slowly back home.

That year she visited Ali twice. The first time she stayed over for the weekend, but felt in the way. Ali was busy with university and friends and had little time for her. They talked a little but did not seem to connect.

'I came first in my class in Greek,' Mer said.

'That's good,' Ali replied, and Mer had the feeling that Ali had not really heard her.

'Cassie has started Latin. She's really good at it.'

'Great,' Ali said as she brushed her hair.

The second time she saw Ali, she and Cassie had gone to stay with their grandparents and Opa drove them to Strasbourg and they took Ali out for lunch. Sitting outside a restaurant overlooking one of the canals, safe with her grandparents and Cassie, Mer felt more comfortable, less like the first visit where she had felt young and awkward and in the way. Some students passing by their restaurant table greeted Ali, and unlike on the previous visit, Ali introduced them to her family. 'My grandparents, my little sisters,' and Mer felt or realised that Ali had moved on in some way; that the gap between them had widened. Mer decided not to visit her again unless she was invited.

As it happened, Ali phoned her some months later on a Sunday evening. 'Hello, Mer,' she said.

'Hi, Ali.' Mer was thrilled to hear her sister's voice. Ali had only phoned twice during that first year away. At Christmas they had all met up in their grandparents' house, and Ali had not visited home since her departure the previous September.

'I was hoping you would answer the phone,' Ali said. 'I was wondering if you would be free to come to Strasbourg this Tuesday, for the day, but you could stay over if you wanted.'

'Oh, I would love to,' Mer said. She was uplifted that Ali wanted her to visit. 'But I can't,' she continued. 'I've an essay to hand in on Tuesday, and school of course, and I can't afford to miss it... I miss so much every time I have to have an operation. But Cassie and I are going to stay with Opa and Oma next weekend. Maybe I could come over and see you then...?'

'That's a pity,' Ali said. 'I'm not sure I'll be around next weekend. Never mind. We'll do it another time. '

'Is everything all right?' Mer asked. Her sister sounded buoyant for someone who had just been let down.

'Everything's fine,' Ali said. 'Really fine. Couldn't be better.'

The following Friday after school, Mer and Cassie took the train down to visit their grandparents, whom they had not seen since Easter. 'You're always writing when we're on the train,' Cassie said once. 'What are you writing?'

Mer looked up from the blue copybook on the table in front of her.

'Things,' she said vaguely. 'There are always things to write.' She did not want to share it with Cassie. She had always been interested in myths and legends, and borrowed from the library, books on ancient Greece and Rome, stories from different countries in Europe and from around the world. Now she was writing them, putting those stories into her own words. She was working on the story of Persephone, taken by Hades to live with him in the Underworld while her mother, Demeter, goddess of the Earth, searched for her.

'But what?' Cassie asked.

'Oh, just stories, things I like. I'm writing one now...' her voice drifted into silence.

'But tell me what?' Cassie persisted.

'Another time,' Mer said, picking up her pen again and turning the page.

Opa and Oma were waiting for them at the station; Oma looked sad, Opa pragmatic. 'My darlings,' said Oma hugging them both.

'We got a letter from Ali this morning,' Opa said as they walked from the station to the car. 'She has written to your father as well. She got married earlier in the week.' He handed the letter to Mer and she and Cassie read it side by side standing by the car.

*Dearest Opa, Dearest Oma,*

    *I have been seeing a man called Maurice Callier. He is doing his doctorate in politics and economics and we decided to get married. Neither of us is into pomp and circumstance so we married quietly on Tuesday and then went back to class. We are going away this weekend for a two-day honeymoon, and will be back on Monday for lectures. I have written to Papa to tell him; please will you tell my sisters? I know they will be with you for the weekend. I can't wait for you to meet Maurice.*

*Love to you both,*

*Ali Callier.*

Mer was shocked. She read the letter several times with Cassie peering over her shoulder, and then looked at her grandparents. 'Is this real?' she asked, as though they were pulling some joke on her.

'What is pomp and circumstance?' Cassie asked.

'It means celebration and fuss,' Oma said.

'It appears to be real,' Opa said, opening the boot and putting in their two small weekend bags.

'Does she mean us?' Cassie asked.

'What do you mean?' Mer said.

'Pomp and circumstance. Is that how she sees us? Well you can call me Pomp,' Cassie said, handing the letter back to Mer. 'And you can be Circumstance,' she said to her sister.

There was silence in the car as they drove back to their grandparents' house.

'Do you cut the grass with a pair of scissors?' Cassie asked her grandfather as they pulled into the driveway. 'It's always so tidy, never a blade out of place.'

Opa laughed. Mer thought how safe their home looked, with the grass, as Cassie had pointed out, so perfectly neat, and the flower boxes on the window-sills with their tumbling red geraniums, and the blossoms forming on the walnut trees.

'Papa is going to go mad when he gets this letter,' Cassie said.

'Papa is going to be devastated,' Mer said.

'They're gone for the weekend, Ali says in the letter,' Oma said, 'otherwise we would be over there today to see what is going on. As it is we will have to leave it until next week. Your grandfather and I will go over on Monday or Tuesday and see what is happening.'

'It's rather obvious what is happening,' Opa said. 'She has met someone and has got married, and that is that.'

'She's not going to exclude us...' Oma said.

'She already has,' he said.

'I mean she is not going to exclude us from this point on,' Oma said. 'You can't cut off your family just like that.'

'Mum did,' Cassie said. 'I think I read in a book something about that. Like mother like daughter, it said. I didn't know what it meant until now.'

# CASSIE'S TALE

I read Mer's stories in her neat notebooks while she was asleep. I liked Cerberus, the three-headed dog guarding the way to the Underworld, and Charon the ferryman who ferried the dead down the river Styx. I liked Demeter searching for her lost daughter, Persephone. Oh Persephone, taken to the Underworld. Only a mother could find her. Only a mother could save her.

I waited then, waited until I was nearly eighteen and then I went to search for Demeter. My mother. Bits of it are coming back. Camden Lock and the river Styx became as one. Elsa, once an au pair, now merged into the fanged faces of Cerberus, or Cerberus turned into Elsa.

She guarded the gates. No way in. No way out. She guarded my mother.

Demeter, mother of the lost Persephone with her once smiling face and her clear, tanned skin etched in my memory, changed slowly but systematically into something from Mer's Underworld, a cross between Hades, a dark shadow, and something indefinable. Metamorphosis hovers and the multi-headed dog that guards the doors to knowledge becomes Medusa, the vipers on her head replace her hair and hiss in my direction.

If my mother had seen her life with my father as some form of entrapment, did she not see that she had replaced it with another? Of course I did not know this when Ali went to study in Strasbourg, sailing away in her little blue car, full of optimism and the opening of new doors.

Ali met a man-boy, or so he looked, but he was a boy-man, handsome face, dark eyes, good looking. No one had taught him how to behave. At first he held the doors open for her, and later he closed them in her face, her beautiful bruised face. Not a bruise that you could see, but something inside her.

Mer asked her 'Is it nice to be married?'

'Nice?' Ali said. 'It's wonderful.'

Mer believed her, but I saw something else. Something had changed in Ali. She tried to appear nonchalant; a permanent smile on her face when we were looking at her, but it was gone when we were not.

What has happened to you? I wondered.

The cold, dark eyes of Maurice Callier casually glanced at me, stared at Mer's small hand, and took my eldest sister for his own and married her on a spring morning quietly in Strasbourg excluding us from this tribal ritual as he would try to exclude us from everything to do with my nymph sister.

# CHAPTER TWELVE

Their lives continued despite this new development. In due course they met Maurice when Ali brought him to Tübingen. They made a handsome couple. Maurice was all charm, the shaking of hands, the greetings to his new father-in-law and his two new sisters-in-law.

'We married suddenly,' Ali said.

'But you had to post the bans,' Karl said. 'That takes time.'

'Well, yes,' Ali said. 'But we wanted to do it all quietly and quickly. No fuss.'

'We wish you well,' Karl said. His voice was slightly stilted, his reserve apparent.

'Who were your witnesses?' Cassie asked.

'One of my brothers and a friend,' Maurice said.

'I see you've had the rooms painted,' Ali said as she looked around. 'Nice colour.'

'It must be six months since we had that done,' Karl said.

'If you'd visited us you would have known,' Cassie said.

'I've been busy,' Ali said. 'Study, you know.'

Karl and Mer caught each other's eyes. They had discussed Ali's prolonged absence, her sudden wedding, and their feelings of hurt and even of betrayal. Mer had come home from her grandparents that awful weekend and had thrown herself into his arms.

'How could she?' she sobbed. 'She phoned, you know, last weekend. She asked me if I could come down for the day on Tuesday. I thought it was just for a visit, and I said no. I'd have skipped school had I known...'

'Now, you listen to me,' Karl said. 'There's no way that you're going to bear any guilt connected to this. She didn't tell you what she was going to do, and that's not your fault.'

Neither said anything now. Karl had pointed out to Mer that expressing their feelings of confusion and sadness, and even of anger, might make the situation worse, and the one thing he did not want to do was to have Ali feel that and to cut her links with them, although right at that moment he had the impression that she had already cut her links. He felt wounded to the quick when he received her letter stating that she had married, and now felt even more so on finding that Maurice's brother had been at the wedding. He wondered if Maurice's parents had been there too.

He found it difficult to get Ali on her own, as Maurice was like a shadow, appearing in doorways seconds after his new wife.

'Can you get him out to the garden or bring him to the market?' Karl said quietly to Mer and Cassie. 'I need to have some time with Ali.'

Cassie took Maurice by the arm and dragged him out onto the street. 'I have to show you the river,' she said.

'Isn't Ali coming too?' he asked.

'Oh, I think Papa wants some time with her,' Cassie said firmly.

Mer admired her sister's determination and bluntness. After all, Cassie was right. Why should their father not have some quiet time with his eldest daughter whom he hardly saw any more?

'Stay, Ali,' he said as she prepared to follow the others. 'I want to talk to you.'

'I'm a married woman,' she said gaily. 'There's nothing you can't say in front of my husband.'

'Yes, there is,' he said. 'I can hardly ask you in front of him why you married him so suddenly, which is what I am asking you.'

'We love each other,' she said. 'And I'm not pregnant if that's what you are thinking.'

'It never occurred to me that you might be,' he said carefully. It had occurred to him of course, but knowing her it seemed unlikely. He was pleased to see her looking so well and so happy, but the hurt she had inflicted on them all would not disappear lightly.

'I just don't understand why you would marry so suddenly. You can hardly know him. We saw you at Christmas and you never mentioned him. You didn't invite us to your wedding? What are you hiding?'

'I'm not hiding anything,' she said, pushing her hair back off her face. 'We met and fell in love and it is the best thing that ever happened to me.'

'Don't push me away,' Karl said. 'I've loved you all your life and I'm not going to stop loving you now, but I just don't understand.'

'What don't you understand?' Ali said.

'Don't be obtuse,' he said. 'You're too intelligent for this. Why would you marry him so suddenly and so secretively?'

She turned her head away then, and for a moment he thought he saw a look of sadness on her face. 'Because he asked me,' she said simply.

Karl put his arm around her.

'I love you,' he said. 'That won't change. I need you to understand that. It's just that I don't understand how you could exclude us like this. It is hurtful.' To say the least, he thought.

'I didn't mean to hurt you,' she said. 'It was just that Maurice wanted us to marry quickly and quietly. I didn't know he was going to ask his parents. He never said. And I did try to ask Mer...'

So the parents were there, Karl thought and while that intensified his hurt, it did not surprise him now.

'He didn't tell you his parents would be there? Were they not surprised to be suddenly invited to his wedding? What did they say?'

'I had met them before,' Ali said. 'A couple of times. They like me. I thought he meant it when he said no one would be there except us.'

'Wasn't that a bit deceitful of him?' Karl asked.

'Well, I was deceitful too, if that is the word you want to use,' Ali said as she went and sat on the sofa. 'I asked Mer... and that wasn't in the plan.'

Karl shook his head. 'But why would you agree to marry him so suddenly? You could have lived together for a while. It might still be frowned upon in Ireland to live with someone, but here it is perfectly normal, and I would have understood. It's part of growing up. I just don't understand the urgency in tying the knot.'

'Didn't you marry Miriam quickly and quietly?' Ali asked.

'No We'd been together for a while, we were older than you... too young, I might now say, but still several years older than you are. We were together for several years before we married. We didn't exclude family...'

'But none of our mother's family was there at your wedding,' Ali objected. 'She told us that once.'

'That was because she didn't have any family. It's not the same thing at all.'

'I love him, Papa,' Ali said. 'I don't have to do anything other than look after him...'

'But you've done so much caring for others over the past couple of years. Surely you need time for yourself?'

'I have time for myself,' Ali said.

Karl was troubled. How could he of all people offer his daughter any advice? She was not asking for it anyway. The secrecy and the speed of her decision and actions horrified him. It occurred to him that maybe this was the teenage rebellion that other parents spoke about, and in her case it had just come a bit later.

He tried to see what it was that had drawn Ali to Maurice, and some of it he could indeed see. Maurice was older and he carried himself with confidence. He put his arm around Ali and they looked at each other with clear affection. At times he was charming but there was an edge to him that disconcerted Karl. While Maurice's German was good, it was not fluent, and so it was difficult to work out if the warmth that he would have expected was actually missing or was being blurred by a different language.

Later that day, just as they had arrived so suddenly at the house in Tübingen, so did they leave. There were hugs and kisses, a promise of another visit soon, although that promise was by Ali and was not echoed by Maurice.

'May I come and visit you soon?' Mer asked.

'Yes,' said Ali.

'But not for a while,' said Maurice. 'We have exams looming and we don't need any distractions...'

'During the holidays then,' Mer said.

'We're visiting my parents in a few weeks time,' Karl said firmly. 'I'll be over then to see you, Ali, and hopefully I'll get to know my son-in-law a bit better.'

'So lovely to meet you all,' Maurice said. 'I'd heard so much about you. It's good to be able to put names to faces.'

There was something about the way he said that which made Karl even more uncomfortable. They weren't just names and faces; they were Ali's family.

'At least you had names,' Cassie said.

'We came as soon as we had the time,' Maurice said.

Karl did not like the way he dismissed Cassie; he had only met her a few hours earlier.

'Cassie is right,' Karl said to him. 'And when something is important, then we make time.'

Maurice looked him in the eye and Karl had the feeling, for just a moment, that he was being challenged. 'I meant no offence,' Maurice said with a smile. 'And you're right. We should have come earlier. But with exams on the horizon there seemed no time.'

But time enough to get married, Karl thought. He was irritated now, peeved with this young, handsome, arrogant boy who was treating them a little too casually. Was Ali not worth more than that?

'Well, we need to make up for that lost time,' Karl said. 'We'll be down, as I said, very shortly. We'll go out for dinner. I'd like to meet your parents, of course.'

'They're away at the moment,' Maurice said. 'Do phone before you come down so that we will be there.'

And it was there again, that challenge, that feeling that Maurice and Ali were a unit, as they indeed now were, but attached to it the sense that if Ali's family was going to be allowed to meet up with Ali, then it would be on Maurice's terms. Karl's parents had already been over to Strasbourg twice and had knocked at Ali's new home and there had been no answer; Karl knew his parents had felt that there was someone there. The first time they had phoned and asked if they could come by, and Maurice said that he thought they were going out. They said they would be over within the hour if Ali would just stay until they arrived. They wanted to see her and to meet him. There was no answer to the doorbell. The second time they phoned when they had arrived in Strasbourg using a call-box on the street just down the road from Ali and Maurice's apartment. Again Maurice answered the phone and Karl's mother hung up without saying anything, having ascertained that someone was there. But, once again, there was no answer when they rang the doorbell.

When his mother had told him this, Karl had hoped that she was just mistaken. 'Don't waste your time coming down. You need to get Ali to visit you,' his mother had said. Now he was convinced she was right, and that they were being deliberately excluded. He could not see why Maurice wanted Ali cut off from her family. He had the feeling that Maurice saw her as some kind of prize that was his alone.

He glanced at Ali's face as they walked down the street to where Maurice had parked but he could read nothing through her poise. Maurice took out his keys at a flashy new Maserati parked beyond the Market Place. Karl was startled by the car knowing that it was extremely expensive, but it was more than that; he was surprised that Ali would be attracted by someone who would drive something so showy.

'That is quite a car,' Karl said. 'And how is your little blue Volkswagen doing?' he asked Ali.

'Oh, we don't have it any more,' Maurice said. 'My parents gave us this as a wedding present and we sold the Beetle.'

'We only need one car,' Ali said. 'Isn't this beautiful, Papa?'

Karl nodded. He wondered if that had caused Ali any grief. He knew how hard she had worked and how she had saved to buy that car, and he remembered her pride when she had brought it home and shown it to him and her sisters. It was hard to believe that she was happy to let it go and to have it replaced with something like this.

'I hope you did something nice with the money you got for it,' Karl said.

'We traded both our cars in to get this,' she said. 'Maurice chose it,' she added.

That was some trade-in, Karl thought, wondering if Ali had any idea how much such a vehicle must cost.

And then they were gone, with a roar from the car and a slight skidding on the cobbled stones of the street.

'What is she doing?' Cassie asked that evening.

'Who?' Mer asked.

'Our big sister,' Cassie said.

'You're old beyond your years, Cassie,' Karl said.

'I don't like Maurice,' Cassie said.

'He's very good looking,' Mer said.

'Is that a reason to marry someone?' Cassie asked.

Mer shook her head. 'No. I was just looking for a reason to explain why Ali went and got married so quickly.'

'I think she thought it was a grown-up thing to do,' Karl said. 'She's very young, but she is mature in some ways.' He was unsure about talking to his other two daughters about the situation. On the one hand, if he gave the impression of just accepting it, they might go the same route, but on the other, he did not want to say anything that might get back to Ali and that might alienate her.

He had long since realised that he was not good at making decisions. Anything to do with his work was fine and under his control, provided he had sufficient time; but with his girls he was becoming less and less sure. He had felt that he had made a lot of good decisions and that they were reasonably healthy and happy, he had brought them through from the bad time several years earlier to a place where the house hummed with their laughter and their activities, but clearly he had got something very wrong if Ali thought it was a good idea to go off and marry the first man she met.

'She married because she fell in love,' he said. He wanted to say because she *thought* she had fallen in love, but then who was he to say that it was not love? He would have gone with her decision had she but shared it; yes, he would have asked her to take her time, pointing out that if indeed it was love, it was not going to just disappear by not marrying immediately. 'I feel, as her parent, that she has rushed into this and it is important that she knows we are here for her. Blatant criticism is probably going to have the opposite effect to the one desired.'

'He's very domineering,' Mer said suddenly.

'Well, she's clearly met her match there,' Karl said.

'I think she is very busy being a Callier and not a Peters,' Cassie said.

'How do you mean?' Mer asked.

'Well, she let him sell her car, and she wrote her name as Ali Callier on that letter she sent, and there was no need for that, she could just have written Ali... and she sort of looks to Maurice each time she says something, almost as if she's checking it's all right.'

He has her in thrall all right, Karl thought.

'And he said we had to phone before visiting them...'

'I think that's normal enough,' Karl said.

'But it was the way he said it. If Ali had said it... she would have said something like, 'phone before you come to make sure we are home...' but he said it and made it sound like he was going to make sure they were *not* home.'

# CASSIE'S TALE

We mulled over our Ali's choice. To close no doors, Papa said. I thought Maurice was horrible. Ali had pictures of film stars up on the walls of her room, her old room in our market house. All handsome boys, dark hair, dark eyes, lean jaws, beautiful mouths. I looked at those men that night. They still papered her walls.

Was I eleven years old then? I had thought that when I grew up I would marry a man like one of those. In my eyes, back then, one or two looked more handsome than the others. I had thought that was what you did, grow up and marry a handsome man. But not that night. Good looks were suddenly not enough. I took down those posters from Ali's walls and put them in the bin. What need did she have of them now? And I no longer wanted to look at them.

Dad was handsome. And good. And kind. And that was not enough either. Not enough for our mother. Enough for us girls, but not enough to secure happiness. I wanted Ali to be happy. She was the one who told me fairy tales when I was little. The fairy tales are happy-ever-after tales when the pauper turns into a prince and finds his princess, when the frog is kissed, when the glass slipper fits, and the wedding bells ring out. Ali had created her own fairy tale, and had slipped into the pages of it thinking that her prince was really a prince and not a toad in disguise. She will turn many pages of that book before she realises that beauty is skin deep. Not her beauty. It is real. It is deep like she is. Deep and dark and full of sad things. But hopeful too. Ali still had optimism in the early days of her marriage.

Long ago, Hades cleft the land and reached up to steal Persephone. Her mother found her, but not in time. The damage was done because Persephone had eaten the pomegranate seeds in the Underworld and would therefore always have to return to the dark, no matter how often she re-emerged. Persephone never made it to the heavens to be among the stars.

Demeter, her mother, never stopped searching for her. When she is found, and found she will be as there is no place too deep to hide, the seasons will return. The roles reversed. I, as Persephone, searched for Demeter.

The dark places are always there in our minds. Good memories clouded by the bad. The stealing of the human soul. I once had a soul. I once was a girl named Cassie. I once danced in the waves and swung in the trees and watched the stars falling into the sea. Once I reached for the stars to find a constellation that would be mine. But the stars receded beyond my grasp. I could not see a place for me beyond the Milky Way.

My memories are becoming clearer.

# CHAPTER THIRTEEN

Ali had been swept off her feet by the first man she had met. Her
father was right about that. She felt that when things had been
normal, when her mother had been there, she was growing up like
other girls. When they had moved to Germany there seemed to be so
much to do, both at home and in school, that she had pushed certain
things aside. Her pictures of film and pop stars, cut from the magazines
that the girls shared in school and carefully pinned on her bedroom
walls, were typical of a girl in her teens. She had not felt like
entanglements of any sort with the boys in her class. She felt the need
to protect herself from hurt or betrayal, which were emotions that
some of the girls in her class seemed to endure on a daily basis. So she
put the pictures on her walls and admired them from a safe distance.
Avoiding all intimate contact, she worked hard and, while she did
socialise to some small extent, she concentrated on the things that
seemed important to her at that time.

It was different once she arrived in Strasbourg. She felt like it was a
clean start, cleaner than the last one anyway, and that she was on an
equal footing with her peers, not the girl with a secret that hurt, and
not trying to catch up. Here they were all new, starting out afresh. There
were no little sisters or a father to worry about.

She had received permission to sit in on various different seminars
in order to improve certain aspects of her French. One such turned
out to be politics, and Maurice Callier was giving the class. She sat
quietly at the back and took notes, and at the end of the class he asked
her if it had been helpful.

'Very helpful, thank you,' he said.

He smiled at her. 'I'm impressed,' he said.

'Oh? Why?'

'First of all because you are taking an extra class. Not every student does that. But also, when I got a note asking if I had room for you to sit in on my seminar, it said that French was not your first language. So I'm impressed that you are studying through a second language.'

'It's my third language,' Ali said, 'I speak both German and English.' As she said it, she wondered which she now saw as her first language. She had really no idea.

'Well, now I'm even more impressed. A third language, and so fluent.  I'm giving another seminar on Friday at eleven,' he continued. 'If you want to attend, you are welcome.'

'Thank you,' Ali said. 'It clashes with a lecture so I can't.'

'Well, not to worry, I'm sure we'll meet again,' Maurice said as he started to put together his papers.

She met him again a few weeks later when the snow was melting and spring was in the air. She and two of her friends were sitting in a cafe drinking coffee one afternoon when in he walked.

Their eyes met when he came through the doorway. Recognising her, he came over, introduced himself and asked if he could join them. They all moved up and he brought a chair over and slipped off his coat and put it on the back. He sat across the table from Ali. She thought he looked delightful and she felt pleased at how he seemed to fit in. He wooed her with his eyes during that extended coffee break from the library. When they left, he went with them, walking beside her, picking up a book that she dropped on the slushy pavement and wiping it with a perfectly folded white handkerchief that boasted his initials. Ali, who was usually unimpressed by affectation of any sort, was impressed by the fact that he didn't seem to care that his handkerchief was now filthy.

By then she had been on a few dates with two different boys, but they had left her untouched. They had seemed so young and uncertain. This time it was different. This time she had met someone who appeared to her to be no mere boy, but a man, confident in himself, in control, and comfortable in his surroundings wherever he was. This time she wanted someone's attention, his attention, his eyes on her and her alone.

At the steps to the library he took her arm. 'Seeing as you can't come to any more of my classes,' he said, 'would you like to have dinner with me?'

She spent time getting ready for their dates. She went with him back to his apartment that first evening, sipping red wine from slim-stemmed balloon glasses as they sat looking out the window with its view of a park and trees that were slowly beginning to bud before unfurling their leaves. She fell in love with his charm and his courtesy. She got her hair cut, and he told her he preferred it long, and she promised to let it grow and not cut it again without his agreement. She felt she was the focus of his very being, and she was in love. It was immediate. It was accompanied by her heart beating faster when he looked at her, when he spoke to her, when they met up after parting, when he walked into a room. When they were apart she thought about him all the time. She had never felt such things before.

He took her to meet his parents. She was enthralled by both, but by his mother in particular. She loved their reserve, their wealth, the way dinner was served. She felt they were assessing her and hoped she was being accepted. During the drive back to Strasbourg he told her how they were charmed by her, how perfect they thought she was, how she indeed was perfect – perfect for him. He was six years older, and he seemed so wise, so manly, so very sure.

For someone who had been so practical in all her dealings with boys hitherto, Ali was suddenly and completely swept away. She was in love with being in love, and so, knowing deep in her heart that there was no reason for things to move at such a pace, she married Maurice less than two months later. She may have wondered slightly why his parents did not object to the speed of it all, but she did not look beneath the surface. She was indeed slightly surprised at their acceptance, knowing in her heart that her father would not approve. Her life, she felt, would continue the way it was, with the added bonus of not just a boyfriend, but a husband, not just a shoddy room in a large and noisy building, but an apartment that was quiet and peaceful, and no constraints on money as Maurice seemed to have an unlimited supply.

At first it was fine, even though she occasionally felt that he gave her no time to herself, but she supposed that was what marriage was and that you lost yourself and your individuality within the unit. She felt that the unit was everything and she was going to make sure it worked. She found that she no longer had time for a coffee or a drink with the friends she had made since arriving in Strasbourg, and when she pushed for that time, as she occasionally did, Maurice always came too. She was so in love that she loved the fact that he could not seem to let her out of his sight. She loved that she, who had tried to control everything for the previous four years, suddenly had to control nothing. He even chose her clothes, advised her on the colour of lipstick, which she had never worn before, selected clips for her hair and negligées for bed.

She had felt ashamed when they visited her family home in Tübingen; ashamed that she had managed to hurt her father, dismayed that they were clearly let down by the suddenness and secret nature of her marriage. She and Maurice had known each other for three months at the time of that meeting, and it was the first time that she felt he did not acquit himself well. She had thought he was perfect, but that day she felt he was insensitive to her father and too casual with her sisters, as though they did not really count for anything.

It puzzled her too that she had not conidered that they would be hurt by her sudden marriage. For some reason she had thought they would be impressed, but now she was not quite sure why she had imagined that. She had seen something sophisticated in her actions, delighted not just to be a girl with a man, but to be this particular girl in love with this particular man, and he so in love with her that he wanted to marry her. To be wanted for herself seemed so important to her and she had thought that being married would give her status in the eyes of others.

She brought it up in the car on the journey back to Strasbourg. 'I don't think they're too happy,' she said.

'What do you mean?'

'Well, they feel left out from the wedding...'

'I'm sorry about that.'

'Maybe we should have stayed longer, maybe stayed overnight, to give them time to get to know you properly...'

'Ali, we couldn't have stayed there. Where would we have slept? Your single bed in that tiny room? If we'd gone to a hotel, they would have been annoyed about that...'

She wasn't sure if he was belittling her, but she felt put down. It was her home he was talking about, and there was nothing wrong with it. They all had grown to love living there. It might not be as wonderful as their old home by the sea in Dublin, but it was their home, with their possessions in it, and she had always loved her bedroom with its tiny balcony overlooking the garden. She would have liked it if he could see something nice about it.

'I don't think they would have been annoyed if we had gone to stay in a hotel. I think they just would have liked more time. I wish I'd invited them to the wedding.'

'But we agreed to do it low key...'

'But your parents came. You never said that you were inviting them.'

'Of course I was always inviting my parents. We agreed just to have the minimum amount of people there.'

'But I thought you meant witnesses...'

'We need my parents. I couldn't afford to offend them.'

'But I offended my family,' Ali said, struggling to understand how he could not comprehend what she meant.

He had always seemed to know what it was that she needed, and often seemed ahead of her in her own thoughts.

When there was no response, she tried again, 'Maurice, what do you mean that you can't afford to offend your parents?'

'The trust fund set up for me by my grandparents hasn't kicked in yet, so I still need money from my parents,' he said.

'I'd like you to slow down a bit,' Ali said as he took the hairpin bends too fast on the mountain road.

'You're annoying me by going on and on about your family. You're a Callier now, part of my family.'

It was the first time they had argued, and it struck her that to continue it on the mountain road would not be wise, so she retreated into silence. She did not like the way he had spoken about her family. In his eyes they counted for nothing, and that it was only his family that had any bearing in his life; and she was not even sure of that. He treated them more like a personal private bank. She felt like a whole part of her was being rejected, and hurt and anger bubbled inside her. She also felt that in some unclear way he was using his own parents. She wondered why these thoughts had not surfaced before now. She felt uneasy.

They drove for the next hour in silence, broken only when they crossed the border from Germany into France, when she made an effort to move on from the previous conversation. 'It's funny how, when we first moved to Germany in 1972, many of the terrorists were being hunted,' Ali said, looking at the posters of the Baader Meinhof gang that adorned the border post, 'and now, nearly all are behind bars, with pre-trial hearings underway.'

'What's funny about that?' Maurice asked.

'Well, not funny, just... interesting I suppose. It will be good to have an end to this particular era in German history.'

'It can't be seen as history until sufficient time has passed. Anyway, don't you support them?' Maurice asked.

'First of all, I wasn't using the word 'history' in the sense of something passed. We are living in history as it will be viewed some time in the future. And no, of course I don't support a campaign of terror. How could I? Lawless terrorists who have nothing to contribute...'

That was when their second argument began. Ali had no idea if he really did support the anarchists or if he was just itching to continue arguing with her, but something had changed in their relationship and she found herself pulling back and looking at him with surprise. She was seeing a very different side to him.

'I'm the one who's studying politics,' he said. 'I know more about these matters than you do.'

'But even if you can find something justifiable in their aims,' Ali said, still confident in her beliefs, 'how can you justify their actions? How can you have a society that is terrorised on a daily basis? And they have nothing with which to replace that society even if they did achieve their aims.'

'You shouldn't talk about things you don't understand,' Maurice said.

'Well explain it to me so that I can understand,' she said.

'Stop arguing with me. I'm trying to drive.'

She wanted to say that if discussing something rationally meant that he couldn't drive at the same time, then there was something wrong. She wanted to ask why he was bullying her, but the words stuck in her throat. She just wanted to get home now and somehow make this ridiculous day right, but it would not get right. She did not see that then, but she started to see it soon after.

Ali was proud, though she did not acknowledge that. Her pride was in her abilities and her academic achievements, in how she tenaciously stuck to a task, how she systematically hid the fact that her mother had abandoned her, how she needed to make everything that she did a success story. She did not give up because she had no idea how. She was married and that was going to work.

Those first arguments were not the last, though Ali learned to steer clear of anything that might be controversial. She was used to being able to discuss things as they did in her family; her father always made time to listen and to comment, and dinners were a time when they each aired their views and, while they argued, it was not like it was with Maurice. His opinion had become the only one that mattered in her new home. He had changed from those first weeks when all he seemed to want was to listen to her. She now wondered if indeed that had been true; perhaps it was she who had wanted to listen to him.

She had thought that they were equals, if different, and that each was bringing something to their marriage. Now she saw that there was no equality whatsoever. She loved him, and she forgave him, time and again. His anger escalated into verbal abuse and she found she was withdrawing into herself in shock. She had had no idea such things could happen, and each time she assumed that it was her fault. It was a superficial assumption, because deep inside her she knew that this was all wrong. Her problem was that she did not know how to rectify it.

She was ashamed as well; too ashamed to tell anyone or to ask for advice and for help. For the first time she had the feeling that she was too young. Being the eldest daughter, her role had appeared clear cut, even in difficult times, but now she was handling something she had never heard about before. She had no idea there could be such violent words in a loving relationship, and she did not doubt that their relationship was loving. After all, she had fallen in love and so had Maurice, so she looked for ways to keep his anger at bay, or to steer it once it had erupted. For his part, he became more controlling.

There were occasional dinners with his parents, his mother talking kindly to her, his father organising the wine and food, ordering for them all if they were in a restaurant, or pontificating about politics in a way that Ali now found objectionable. Once, when she was helping her mother-in-law clean the dishes in the kitchen, she tried, tentatively, to bring up the subject.

'Maurice and his father have very strong views,' her mother-in-law said, 'but deep down they are very sensitive.'

'But don't you ever want to have your say?' Ali asked, as lightly as she could, accompanying the question with a smile.

'Oh, I leave politics to the men. It makes for a happier marriage,' her mother-in-law said.

Ali retreated then. Who was she to tell her mother-in-law that her opinions might count for something, when her mother-in-law seemed happy with her lot? But she felt uncomfortable, seeing things a little clearer than she had previously. She tried to see it from the other woman's viewpoint, but the word 'sensitive' did not sit well with her. Sensitive surely meant taking the other person's views into account, letting them have their say, even encouraging them.

She thought of her father and Mer and Cassie sitting around the dinner table, and for the first time she felt a pang of homesickness and the smallest twinge of regret.

# CASSIE'S TALE

I begin to remember sequences now, not just marked by the turning of the leaves on the trees, or the mosquitoes from the river in summer, the heavy snows of winter and the blanket of white that covered the world overnight. The buds formed on the trees and burst out into leaves. A single bird, that dear little bird, sang his plaintive tune. I remember my pens and pencils, my painting box that I was given on my fourteenth birthday by Mer, the drawing paper I stole from the cupboard in the art room in school.

The house was emptier when Ali moved out. Two female role models had come and gone, now just Mer to show me how to grow up and be an adult. Mer... in and out of hospital for years and years, and now suddenly not so ill. She grew, and while she would never be tall, she now looked almost her age. She always wore loose, long-sleeved t-shirts, even on the hottest days, so her scars were covered. I remember the sands on a Cretan beach, and Tante Anneke said, 'Take off your t-shirt, Mer. The sun will do your arm good.' Tante Anneke rubbed cream so gently into Mer's arm.

Mer told me once that she didn't care about the scars, but that it was easier not to have to explain. We all hate having to explain. Do I mean hate or hated?

It is so much easier to take things at face value, but perhaps not so wise.

But I remember good times then.

Mer and I, side by side. She cooked and baked and wrote her stories. I drew and painted. The kitchen smelled warm and aromatic. The rooms had been repainted and the light from outside came through the many-paned windows and lit up those rooms. There were books everywhere, papers stacked on a side table, my schoolbag on the floor in the hall. There was love in that house. Mer encompassed love.

Papa... I remember I once called him Dad – he looked in the mirror in the hall and I caught his eye. Or was that another story when Perseus sought to kill Medusa? The stories blur.

Something terrible happened. Something beyond words. I can't remember. I must not remember.

It was not Papa whose eyes I saw.

I saw the Minotaur's eyes. His eyes saw mine.

Something... someone died.

# CHAPTER FOURTEEN

Mer was more upset by her father's distress at Ali's sudden marriage than by the marriage itself. She had been very conscious of her sister pulling away, and finding herself growing into someone new when she moved to Strasbourg to study.

She trusted Ali implicitly and always had, and because of her unquestioning love for her she did not think as the others did that Ali had done something less than sensible. It was true that she had seen Maurice's arrogance and she had not liked it, but she was impressed by the way he looked at Ali, how he had put his arm around her and she had thought that he had seen her sister as a goddess who would enhance his life. Engrossed in her Greek and Roman myths, and her school work, she somehow thought that true love was what it was all about, and that that was what Ali had sought and had found.

Unlike her sister, who concentrated on modern European languages, Mer's fortes were Latin and Greek. She found that immersing herself in ancient times offered a good balance to just living in the present as Ali had once recommended. She thought Maurice was very handsome and she could see what had drawn Ali to him. He had the imposing presence of their father, possibly even looked a little like a young version of him, and he was comfortable in himself in a way which she envied.

Ali had become like that in the last year or so, as if she did not doubt herself, while Mer doubted herself all the time. She had no confidence in her looks or her abilities. She worked hard to fulfil assignments, and buried herself in books of ancient lore, which opened up other worlds for her.

One evening, while she was preparing dinner and Cassie was sitting at the table drawing instead of reading, she came around the table with the cutlery and saw Cassie's sketch of a large dog, three headed with a swirling tail and a vicious look in each of his six eyes. She stopped in amazement. 'What is that?' she asked.

'Oh, nothing,' Cassie said, pushing it aside.

'It's Cerberus,' Mer said. 'You've painted Cerberus. It's very good...'

'Thank you,' Cassie said, trying to sound casual. Mer, recognising something in her sister's voice, looked at her face and Cassie shuffled uneasily.

'You've been reading my stories, haven't you?' Mer asked.

'They're very good,' Cassie said.

'You had no right...'

'I know, but I had to read them. And they're really very good. I've painted pictures to go with all of them, some are just line drawings...'

Mer was torn between anxiety at someone taking her stories and reading them without her permission, annoyance at Cassie for invading her privacy, and curiosity at what Cassie had made of them.

Cassie showed her. Line drawings, paintings, a picture of the River Styx winding down into darkness with the gnarled roots of trees along the banks, Hades reaching through the earth to seize Persephone... Mer sat down at the table and slowly leafed through the pages, shaking her head.

'They are wonderful,' she said. 'Better than my stories.'

'No, not better than your stories. They only have meaning because of your stories,' Cassie said.

'Are there more?'

Cassie nodded. 'Yes, they're in a folder in my room.'

'May I look at them after dinner?' Mer asked.

Cassie giggled. 'If you were me, you wouldn't ask, you'd wait until I was asleep and then you'd go and get them.'

'Yes,' Mer said. 'But fortunately I'm not you. You need to learn a bit of respect for other people's things,' she added.

'Are you angry?'

Mer shook her head. 'I love what you've done. How can I be cross? I really want to see the rest though.'

Before Cassie went to bed that night she brought down another folder and left it for Mer, who was writing at the dining table.

'Good night, Papa, good night, Mer,' Cassie said as she put various things into her schoolbag before going back upstairs to have a bath and then to bed.

'Don't show them, sure you won't?' she whispered to Mer before going to kiss her father goodnight.

Mer put a finger to her lips and smiled. Unlike her younger sister she understood discretion. She opened the folder and looked at the contents one by one. They were all wonderful and she knew it. She had always known that Cassie's artistic abilities exceeded both hers and Ali's, but these were beyond anything she had imagined. They were so skilled and so insightful. She could immediately see which belonged to which story, and where in the story each should be inserted.

Turning the pages, she came to a poem or possibly a song, she was not sure.

*'I don't want to say goodbye, not now, not now, I don't want to leave, not now, not now, Give me back the sea and you, Bring me back, yes take me back, give me back to you.'*

She felt tears forming in her eyes, and she brushed them away with the back of her hand. She had no doubt what the poem was about.

She slipped it back in with the drawings and paintings.

The following day she spoke to Cassie about the folder. 'I love your work,' she said. 'Your drawings are so good.'

'You can have them,' Cassie said.

'I wondered if I could ask you a couple of favours,' Mer said. 'Well, one is a favour.'

'Ask and you might or might not receive,' Cassie said with a cheery laugh.

'Well, I have almost finished my Greek myths and I sent three of them a while back to a publisher who wants to see the rest of them. May I send your artwork too? They sort of belong together...'

'Really?' Cassie was amazed. She didn't know what to say. 'Really?' she said again.

Mer nodded. 'That's not to say that they will publish them, but they're interested, and they're written for children so they may well want illustrations, and yours are so perfect.'

'Of course you can,' Cassie said. She was thrilled. She danced around the room. 'I can't believe it.'

'Can't believe what?'

'Well, that you sent your stories off, and that they are interested and that you want to put my pictures in with them... it's the most exciting thing.'

Mer smiled at her. 'Well, let's see what happens,' she said cautiously. 'There are no guarantees.'

'You said there were two things,' Cassie said.

'Yes. There was a poem in among your paintings which I think you might want back,' Mer said, rooting through the folder to find it.

'Oh, that...' Cassie said. 'It was just a first effort. I've finished it in the meantime, and a boy in my class has put it to music. He plays the guitar. It was for a school project.'

'It's lovely,' Mer said. 'Will I get to hear it?'

*\*\**

She did get to hear it, a few years later, at her own graduation when various pupils in the school performed. Cassie's song moved her again as it had done when she had read that first draft. The melodic strumming of the guitar, Cassie's voice so plaintive, the chorus of three of her friends, repeating the words *'Bring me back, yes take me back, give me back to you.'*

When they came home from the graduation there was a package awaiting them, and in it were six copies of Mer's first book. She had signed the contracts almost a year earlier and knew that the publication was in motion, but had no idea when that might be. Cassie was over-joyed at her pictures in it, and at the front cover which showed the shadowy figure of Hades lurking in the dark far down the River Styx.

Their father was staggered. 'I had no idea,' he said. 'I am proud beyond words. Of both of you. What an amazing achievement, and you worked together. No parent could feel like I do at this moment. This is wonderful.' He read the book that evening, while Mer pretended not to be aware of his activity as she busied herself with tidying up before going out with her friends.

Karl sat and read, turning the pages slowly, sometimes just admiring the artwork, sometimes so engrossed in Mer's writing that he had to turn back to take in the accompanying picture. It occurred to him that he really had no idea when the girls had done all this work. He had thought that he knew what was going on in their lives and now, like with Ali, he realised that he had little idea of their activities.

He put the book down when Mer was ready to leave. 'I'm so impressed,' he said. 'Why did you never say?'

'I think I didn't really believe it would ever happen,' Mer said.

'And do you really have another one on the go?'

'Yes,' she said. 'Plus a deadline. My Latin Myths are to be ready in six months time for publication next year.'

'And then?'

'Well, Cassie is already drawing and painting for them. I'm still on the final draft. Cassie has already done most of them. And then... well, I'm thinking of moving on to European myths, although the publishers have suggested a complete book of short stories on the nymphs of Ancient Greece. I have time to decide.'

'But what about university?' Karl said. 'You haven't given up on that?'

'No,' she said. 'I'm deferring for this year so that I can give all I can to the writing, and then I will go as planned.'

Cassie, coming into the room at the end of this, asked, 'Can I defer school for a year?'

Karl laughed. 'No, you jolly well can't, but that's not to say that I'm not inordinately proud of you.'

'There are a lot of negatives in that sentence,' Cassie said.

'I love the inscription in the book,' their father said, opening the title pages.

*'For those who love us, with our love.'*

# CASSIE'S TALE

A parent's praise is a wonderful thing, especially when I could only remember being told to calm down, or to settle down, or to walk like a human being, and not to climb everything I could see.

I basked in Papa's joy that day. I basked in Mer's. I basked in my own.

I had always had more confidence than Mer, but I was needier than she. She was shy but content within herself. She enjoyed her own company whereas I needed friends. I needed activity in a way that she did not. Now, for the first time, I took pleasure in my own abilities, in settling down to paint or draw, in doing things that I enjoyed, and in working to get them right. It rubbed off on my school work too. '*A massive improvement*' my report said, and for the first time I cared. For the first time I saw potential – my potential, even though I was still not clear what my potential could be. I remember that, that moment of achievement, of success, of prowess. I remember too the pleasure of working to a deadline, I who had never handed in a school essay on time.

Ali in her ivory tower, constructed too high, so inaccessible, so difficult to climb over the balustrades and to find the earth again, the terra firma that was none too firm regardless of whether one was in an ivory tower or not. Her Underworld was created on the pinnacle of her confidence. Mer was the stay-at-home child, with her new spectacles and her books and her blue stockings. I was getting ready to fly. Call me Icarus.

My wings of burning steel, or is that burnished? Were they just feathers moulded to my back with wax? I thought they were stronger. I thought I was stronger. I thought my father Daedalus had created a winged child. I thought I could fly.

Instead of a train I took a chariot. Instead of a plane I took Pegasus. I saw the top of Mount Olympus. I reached for the sky, for Zeus, for

Demeter. The stars twinkle in the heavens, and when I touch them they recede. I was never meant to be in the Pleiades; my constellation was a different one. But I could not find Andromeda and Perseus as I seek to be among the stars. I look down. I am looking down. Pegasus gallops across the sky, and I am airborne time and again. The sun burns down on the silver wings. His galloping hooves turn into wheels for each landing. Then they rise again. Again, again, I fly and fly.

Then I will fall, and fall, and fall...

# CHAPTER FIFTEEN

Things moved apace in their ever-dwindling household. They seldom saw Ali as she never seemed to be at home when they visited, and she never had much time to talk on the phone. She turned up late one Christmas day for dinner in their grandparents' house, but could only stay for an hour. She had rushed in shortly after they sat down to dinner. 'Sorry I'm late,' she said, hugging them all and exchanging Christmas greetings.

'Where's Maurice?' her father asked.

'He's still at his parents'. They had dinner in the middle of the day and he didn't feel like coming out again.'

'You've already had dinner?' Cassie asked.

'Just a little,' Ali said. She did not put much food on her plate, and what was there she pushed around with her fork. She seemed stressed and did not say much. She kept glancing at her watch and, just over an hour later, said that she would have to leave.

'All that way for just an hour?' Cassie commented.

'I know. It just isn't long enough, is it?' Ali said, getting up and kissing them all. 'But I really must go.'

'You can talk to me for a few minutes,' Karl said, following her into the hallway.

She shuffled uneasily, and he was struck at how chic she looked, with her dark hair pinned up and her smart, black dress. She was pulling on her coat, and he assisted her by holding it as she slipped in her arms. 'That looks like a very expensive garment,' he remarked.

'Maurice gave it to me as a present,' she said.

'Excellent taste,' he said. 'Very stylish.'

'I have to go,' she said again.

'I have come twice to Strasbourg to see you and you haven't been there. I had written beforehand saying I was coming...'

'I never got any letters from you,' she said, surprised.

'Have you ever received any letters from me?' he asked.

'No,' she said.

'How does your post arrive?'

'Maurice looks after the post,' she said after a moment's pause. 'We have a letterbox outside with a lock on it. He keeps the key.'

'Ali, is everything all right? '

'It's fine,' she said hurriedly, glancing again at her watch. 'Maybe you don't have the right address,' she suggested.

He looked at her thoughtfully. 'I have the right address,' he said. 'I've long since checked that. Ali, please talk to me. We haven't seen you in I don't know how long. You arrive here in a hurry, you leave in an even bigger hurry...'

'Papa, I'm fine,' she said. 'I want my marriage to work. Maurice doesn't socialise much. He likes it to be just the two of us...'

'But you've just come from his parents' home, haven't you?'

'Yes, but...'

'But what? Couldn't we alternate Christmas dinners so that you come to us every other year so that we can have some real time with you?'

'I don't know,' she said awkwardly.

'Are you happy?' he asked her.

'Of course I am.  I will come up and visit as soon as I can.'

'And when will that be?'

'The weather is so bad, and Maurice doesn't like me taking the car in the snow.'

'But you took it today,' her father said looking out at the snow, which was beginning to fall again.

'I must go,' she said again.

'Promise me you will phone,' he said. 'You never seem to be home when I call.'

'I promise,' she said, pulling keys from her pocket and reaching up to kiss him.

He put his arms around her and stroked her hair.

'We miss you,' he said.

Thereafter she rang occasionally, but the calls were hurried.

***

Mer had one book published for each of the next three years while she took her degree. Cassie illustrated each of them with care. She started coming straight home from school, and staying in so that she could concentrate on her art.

Mer stayed at home in Tübingen and studied in her father's department in the university. She met a boy in one of the seminars she was taking and they started going out together, long walks through the town and along the river banks, holding hands and smiling at each other. He was as shy as she.

'Are we going to meet him?' her father asked one Saturday night when she came in late.

'Soon,' she said. 'There's no rush. We're just enjoying each other's company. He's like me,' she added.

'In what way?'

She hesitated. She wanted to keep him secret, her secret, but she would not hurt her father as Ali had done.

'He was ill as a baby, but his cancer came back. He's well now, but we understand each other.'

She knew the word *understand* did not explain their relationship at all. It was too small a word. They communicated well, but also knew what the other was thinking.

'Does he make you laugh?' Cassie asked.

'Yes,' Mer smiled. 'He does.'

'What's his name?'

'Bernd.'

'Don't...' Karl hesitated.

'Don't what, Papa?' Mer asked.

'Don't get pregnant or run away and get married,' Cassie said. 'That's what he wanted to say, isn't it Papa?'

Karl laughed wryly. 'These are things parents worry about,' he said. 'But I don't think I have to say them to Mer. But do bring him home. Do let us meet him. We won't make a big deal out of it, but I would just feel more comfortable...'

'I know, Papa. I promise I will bring him home. You don't need to worry. You know his mother, anyway...'

'Do I?'

Mer smiled. 'Yes, Papa. His mother is a lecturer in your department.'

'Really? Who?'

'Frau Meyer. Bernd says she knows you well.'

'Goodness. Leonora Meyer. Yes of course. I do know her. I have a great deal of respect for her. Sometimes we have coffee together.' He seemed pleased when he said that.

Mer smiled. She knew from Bernd that her father and his mother were friends, and she instinctively knew that her father was going to like Bernd. She was in no rush to bring him home.

It all seemed safe but exciting. Mer was happy, and that was clear to them all. She kissed Bernd in the old town at night in the shadows. They sat together outside the library and talked and talked. They shared truths and secrets; they exposed their lies. He touched her arms and kissed her scars. She ran her hand through his brown hair. She kissed his eyelids. He sought her smaller hand and brought it to his lips. She told him of her dream world. He told her of his.

As their confidence grew with each other, their eyes would meet across their desks among the bookshelves. He let his eyes linger on hers and then slowly brought them down to her breasts. She smiled, her eyes now half-closed.

She brought her Bernd to meet her family. He had a gentle, kind face, light brown hair, a cheery smile for them all. He came to Cassie's eighteenth birthday party, which was held months before her birthday to tie in with her school graduation. It started with a picnic at the river, followed by a small gathering in the hotel where Ali once worked to save money for her little blue car. It was an evening with music and dancing.

Mer and Bernd were joined at the hip as they danced to 'Eye of the Tiger' and 'Physical'. Cassie had asked the band to play her favourite songs early in the evening. They came off the dance floor after 'Every Little Thing She Does Is Magic', and sipping their beer they sat down with others from the party. They were playing German songs now. 'Ein Bisschen Frieden' filled the small dance area. Karl was smiling at Mer. 'You dance well together,' he said, and she knew that he was giving her a seal of approval. She had always felt shy and awkward, and in some ways exposed, when she was dancing, but with Bernd it was different. He moved well on the floor and she responded to it and the embarrassment disappeared.

'I've a surprise for you all,' Cassie said as she suddenly appeared at their table and plonked herself down. Mer thought how well she looked, and how alive, her eyes sparkling, her blonde curls bouncing. Her grandparents had been unable to attend because of a storm that had damaged the crops, but her aunt Anneke was there.

'What are you up to now?' Anneke asked. She reached across the table, and taking Mer's camera she took a picture of Cassie and Mer sitting with their arms around each other's shoulders.

Mer said, 'Tante Anneke, take a picture of Cassie by herself.'

Cassie stood up, tossing her curls and smiling at the camera. Click, and the picture was taken.

'I've bought a rail ticket with some of my early birthday money,' Cassie said, pulling out a chair and sitting down. 'And tomorrow I'm off.'

'Off where? How exciting,' Mer said. If she was concerned she didn't show it, knowing that her father would worry, and knowing Cassie, she would go anyway.

'I'm going to get on a train and see where it goes,' Cassie said. 'And then get another train and see where it goes.'

'Wait a moment,' Karl said. 'When are you doing this and with whom are you going?'

'Karl,' Anneke said. 'Isn't this exciting? So grown up and ready to fly.'

'I'm going with a girl from my class and we're going tomorrow. I packed my rucksack this morning.'

'Who is this girl, I want to meet her.'

'You did meet her,' Cassie said. 'It's Anna. She was here earlier.'

'I wonder why she never said anything?' Karl said. He knew Anna from various visits to the house. 'How long are you going for?'

'I'm taking the train at two tomorrow,' Cassie said.

'I? Not we?'

'Oh, I mean, well I'm taking the train from here at two and meeting Anna in Frankfurt. She has to go up first thing in the morning. We'll meet in the station there and then... onwards... we're going for the summer, six weeks maybe, back in September in time for university.'

'This is all very vague,' Karl said. 'And sudden.'

'Promise you'll send postcards along the way,' Mer said. 'It sounds like a wonderful trip.' She no longer saw Cassie as her baby sister. Cassie had grown in stature and in maturity and was full of adventure. She felt proud of her.

'I wish you had discussed this earlier,' Karl said. 'I would have preferred if you had waited until you were eighteen.'

'That's why I didn't discuss it earlier,' Cassie said with a laugh. 'It's a growing up thing, Papa. Everyone is doing it. I've finished school. I'm old enough to go to university. I'll be eighteen in a few weeks time. I'm old enough to have a job and pay taxes.'

'You'll always be my little girl,' Karl said. 'Now come and dance with me.' He got up and took her hand, and Mer, watching them with Bernd by her side, smiled at them dancing on the floor in front of the band, an image that became etched into her memory as one of the last clear pictures of her younger sister.

Anneke whispered to her, 'I like Bernd.'

Mer smiled and blushed slightly. 'Do you? Really?'

'I do. But would it matter if I didn't?'

Mer laughed then. No, it would not matter, but approval was good. She wanted Bernd to be liked.

It was she who went with Cassie to the railway station the following day, staggered at the size of Cassie's rucksack and how she could carry it on her back, when she, Mer, could hardly lift it off the ground.

'I wish Ali had come to the party last night,' Mer said.

Cassie shrugged. 'I've just about given up on her,' she said.

'Don't say that,' Mer said. 'We must never give up, not on each other or on anything. You don't really mean that, do you?'

'No, I don't,' Cassie said. 'I just feel frustrated as she had promised to come, swore it in fact. Anyway, on the way back from my trip I intend to come via Strasbourg and I will camp in the parking lot outside her apartment block until I see her. I promise not to come home without having seen her. It seems ages. And for the record, I don't believe one word she says about being a happily married woman.'

'What do you mean?' Mer said in astonishment.

'None of it makes sense. Neither you nor I would cut off our family as she has done. She has no time for us, and yet she makes these hurried phone calls.'

'What are you saying?'

'What do you think?'

'But... I really don't know what you mean.'

'If she wanted to have nothing to do with us, then she wouldn't phone. I don't think Maurice wants her to contact us, and I wouldn't be surprised to find that she doesn't tell him. I think she is very isolated.'

Cassie stood up and kissed her sister on the cheek. 'I've got to go. My train is here. Take care of yourself and Papa. And Bernd. Don't do anything I wouldn't do... lots of leeway there, mind you.' And with a wave and a laugh, Cassie strode down the platform leaving Mer standing, waving, and worrying.

She started going in the direction of home, then she stopped and sat outside a cafe and had an iced coffee while she thought about what Cassie had said. She couldn't take it in for a while, but the more she thought about it, the more she wondered if Cassie was right. It was not impossible, but if Cassie really believed that, then why had she not said something before? And then she remembered Cassie pushing Ali at some point, pushing her about having no time for them, and Ali had said something about being so busy and not really having any choice. The more she thought about it, the more uneasy she felt. Ali was so confident and determined, so sure of herself and what she did. She wondered for a moment if Ali could not admit to her family that she was in trouble. Was Maurice was so controlling that Ali really did not have a choice? The more she thought about it, the more concerned she became, wondering why she had not seen it earlier.

She had nothing much to do herself. The summer stretched ahead of her. Bernd was working on his thesis, and she had just started a book of stories for children based on tales from the war. It was a change of subject matter for her, but she wanted to try something slightly different, and she had often thought over the years about the bunker in her grandparents' field and what might have happened there. She was still sitting sipping the end of her iced coffee when Bernd appeared on a bicycle.

'Hello,' he said, coming to a halt. 'I was just going over to your house. I wondered if Cassie was gone and if you were feeling lonely.'

'Come and join me,' she said with a smile. 'I was just sitting here thinking about things.'

Bernd signalled to the waitress. 'What will you have?' he asked Mer. 'I've given up on work for the day,' he said. 'It's too hot. I'm thinking of a glass of cold white wine and then going to sit at the river with my feet in the water.'

'Sounds excellent,' Mer said. 'Same for me.'

He ordered the wine and then said, 'Everything all right? You didn't look happy when I arrived. Did Cassie go off all right?'

'Yes, she's gone, with a bag almost the same size as her. When she walked off down the platform it looked like a rucksack with two legs. She was fine.'

'So, what's up?'

'She said something before she went.'

The waitress brought their wine, and they sat for a little in silence with the sun beating down on them. Bernd moved the parasol over the table so Mer's face was in the shade.

'Well?' he said gently.

'You haven't met Ali yet...' Mer began.

'The elusive perfect older sister,' he smiled.

'Cassie said she thinks...' Mer hesitated.

'Thinks what?'

'That Maurice is keeping her from us, that he is controlling her. That's what she implied.'

'Are you being serious?' Bernd looked surprised. 'Do you think it's possible? You once said to me that she was the one who organised you all and made sure the house ran smoothly.'

'The more I think about it, the more I realise there is nothing I understand about what she's doing, or why she's so elusive. She was to come to the party last night, and then she never appeared, no explanation... She married almost four years ago, and I can count the amount of times I have seen her since on the fingers of one hand...'

'So what are you going to do?'

'My first thought was to tell Papa, but if I'm wrong I will have upset him unnecessarily, and I really don't want to do that. He doesn't need that.'

'Well, you don't need it either, being upset, I mean, if it isn't true, so you need to find out if it is or not. But, wouldn't he have noticed, even if you didn't?'

'Cassie and I have only seen her a few times, and Papa even less, despite his efforts. He cares for us all, but he doesn't always notice things. I know he is concerned about her, but he said that she said she was happy.'

'Do you get the impression she is happy?'

'I don't know. I want to think she is, but every time we see her she's in a terrible rush. She never says very much...'

'What do you want to do?'

'I need to make a plan,' Mer said. 'Step one, I will go down to Strasbourg and find her...'

'Shall I come with you?'

'Can you?'

'Yes. I can drive you and maybe we can visit your grandparents? You're always talking about them. I'd so like to meet them.'

'Yes.' Mer looked at her watch. 'It's half past three,' she said. 'We could go now...'

Bernd put down his wine glass. 'Give me twenty minutes; I'll go home and pick up some things for the night. I'll phone my mother and tell her I'm taking the car. I'll meet you back at your house.' He called the waitress, taking his wallet from his pocket.

At home, Mer packed an overnight bag, and was about to leave her father a note when she decided to call him instead. 'Papa,' she said when he answered the phone.

'I'm in the middle of a meeting with a student,' he said. 'Is everything all right?'

'Yes, Cassie went off safely. I won't keep you. Bernd and I are going to drive down to visit Opa and Oma for the night. We'll probably be back tomorrow.'

'Have fun,' he said. 'Give them my love and drive safely.'

The drive was uneventful. They had the windows open to let in what little air there was on that scorching summer's day. In Strasbourg, they did not find Ali. There was no answer from the apartment bell. Maurice's car was not parked outside, and Mer did not know where else to look.

'We can come back tomorrow,' Bernd said. 'Let's leave your sister a note to say we were here and that we're going to your grandparents', and ask her to phone you there. What do you think?'

'Okay,' Mer said reluctantly. 'I hate leaving here not knowing... but you're right. We'll leave a note. I hope she's all right. I now feel worried.'

'We'll come back in the morning anyway. A day more or less,' Bernd said. 'It will make no difference.'

# CASSIE'S TALE

The wheels on the train went round and round, northwards ever north-wards. North, north west. I changed trains twice that day. No Anna in Frankfurt. We were never going to meet. Not in my plan. This was a solo journey. A journey of discovery. To lay some things to rest, to stir up others. To change the course of history. To find answers where there were none. To seek a lock and break it open. To find Prometheus, the Titan who played with fire.

Frankfurt, Brussels, Calais, Dover. There I rested in a Bed and Break-fast, a sleazy place near the port, the sheets not quite clean, the floor dusty; I couldn't find the hostel.

Call me any name:

Homer; my Odyssey had begun.

Hercules; my trials were beginning.

Sisyphus; but he never gave up. He pushed the rocks eternally up a hill.

Persephone; unable to resist the pomegranate seeds, those tiny red jewels that she placed in her mouth. Temptation by Hades, stolen into the Underworld, and lost.

I broke my journey to visit Brighton, to walk on the beach and to stand at the sea watching the waves. Then a train to London and the Under-ground to Camden. None of the journey so clear now. The market in Camden Town was busy, my rucksack heavy. I walked and found the Lock and then I had no idea where to look. Along the pathways I saw the house-boats, long and narrower than I had imagined. I put my rucksack down and sat on a bench.

The dog star Sirius had risen with the sun and the sultry heat of the day was intense. Sirius, hound of the hunter Orion, helping to heat the sky and scorch the earth.

I saw her then, walking along the towpath. I made to get up but my knees were weak. The temperature. Lack of water. Tiredness. Disbelief. I started to slip and then she was beside me. 'Are you all right?' she asked as she looked at my face. Her mouth went into an O as she stared at me and I at her and our stares became one stare.

*If you stare into the abyss for long enough, the abyss stares back at you.*

Almost ten years since I had seen her. Different now, but the same. Hair cut short, lines on her face that I did not remember. Smile lines. Perhaps not. Perspiration on her forehead and neck. The day was so hot. Smartly but inexpensively dressed. Bare-legged. Open-toed sandals. Black skirt. Pale blue blouse, two buttons open. A whiff of perfume that I recognised when she helped me up and brought me to her watery home.

How did she recognise me? Mystery soon solved when I sat on the hard seat in her narrow houseboat and saw a photo of me, and one of Ali and one of Mer, framed and hung on the wall. Not old photos from childhood, but ones Papa had taken a few years later, perhaps around the time Ali finished school. She made us tea and I sat there still staring. I would stare for a very long time. No sign of Medusa. We would talk, but not yet. For now we drank tea and looked at each other.

'I always knew you would come,' she said.

'Me? Not Ali or Mer?'

She waved her hand into the air. I did not know what the gesture meant.

'You only just caught me,' she said.

I had caught nothing. Tykhe, goddess of Chance had helped us meet. Tykhe is often depicted on Greek vase paintings with Nemesis. Perhaps I should have remembered that. I searched. Both Tykhe and Nemesis had found us at a bench on the side of a canal.

'I'm flying to Athens in two days' time. Elsa went a week ago. I couldn't get more than a couple of weeks off,' she said.

'I work in a bucket shop,' she said. A bucket shop? What did they sell? Buckets? 'It's a sort of travel agency,' she explained. 'We sell last-minute flights. I have one for Athens.'

'You can come too,' she said. 'I can get you a ticket tomorrow. We'll all go to Athens.'

That was the day she told me that her life with us did not fulfil her, that Papa's dreams and hers did not coincide. I must not think.

The Acropolis stands against a blue sky, the Aegean below; Elsa, now Medusa, dressed in shorts and a cut-away t-shirt. Medusa puts honey on her food. Medusa smiles and nods. Demeter is torn. She wants to talk to

Medusa. She needs to talk to me. She needs to talk to Medusa. She wants to talk to me. I want her to want to talk to me. I stand back and watch. My first Herculean task is not to throw myself off the cliffs behind the Parthenon. The second is to look into Pandora's Box and gaze at all the things that are unleashed.

I can't see into the bottom of the box. Out flies betrayal, abandonment, cruelty, the intertwinement of Demeter's and Medusa's fingers, a swirl of colour and light before darkness. They hug and embrace, and I don't want to know what else they do. I had opened that box and I looked in and I understood nothing.

They took a ship to the islands. I slept on the deck under a lifeboat that looked like it was welded into the ship. There was a storm and I huddled beneath it in the rain. They were in their cabin. I wished I had not found her. I wished my father had not found her on the towpath all those years ago where they created their Pandora's Box. Demeter became Pandora and still I did not understand. The Gorgons came, the sisters of Medusa, created in her likeness, and they danced and drank.

They swam in blue sea under a blue sky with white painted villages nearby. I swam too. They ate in taverns in the evening. I ate too. Medusa was staying for six weeks, moving on with the Gorgons when my mother left. 'We will have more time to talk,' my mother said to me, 'when we get back to London.'

I wondered. There did not seem much to say. There were too many questions and I was unable to ask them. I had a feeling she was unable to answer them. She promised me time. I think she was buying time using the drachmas in her pocket. I think she had nothing to say to me.

Tick tock. Tick tock. The clock was ticking. The clock was tocking.

Back in Athens, I bought a postcard and sat outside a cafe with my battered sun-hat on my head. I sent Mer that postcard. I wrote her name and address on it. I looked at the blank space where words could be written. I could not think what to say. '*Hello,*' I wrote. '*From Athens, With Love.*'

I packed my rucksack. I met my mother in the airport and I hovered while she said farewell to Medusa. She could not know it was the last goodbye.

# CHAPTER SIXTEEN

On the day when Cassie left on her travels, and Mer and Bernd went to find Ali, Ali had waited until Maurice had taken the car to go to the shops, leaving her lying in bed. She was in a state of shock.

The level of control that he had exerted over her over the previous years had increased inexorably. There were nights when she had got up, made herself a cup of tea and had sat on the sofa looking out the window at the trees and thought of times past and wondered how she had ever arrived at the situation in which she now found herself. Having finished her degree she had talked to Maurice about what she should do next, a Masters or a diploma in teaching or to look for a job. The Masters seemed to her to be the next logical step, but Maurice wanted her to stay at home and to look after the apartment and to be there when he returned in the evening. He was now lecturing in political science in the university, and had long since inherited the money that had been in trust for him.

'I can't just stay at home and do nothing,' she said to him.

'It's not doing nothing,' he had reassured her comfortably. 'It's an important role. Look at my own parents and how it works for them. My mother's care of the home and of my father ensured success for my father, removed excess stress from his life, and they live well. We have plenty of money. I look after you well. I want you to be at home. I like the idea of it.'

'But the roles you describe seem more from a bygone day,' Ali said. 'Your mother was brought up to see herself in that position, whereas I am not yet ready to settle for that.'

'Settle for? What does that mean?'

'I don't mean it in a diminishing way,' Ali said. 'I mean that I still have things I want to do, things to achieve, my own aspirations.'

'But what are these aspirations? You don't even know whether you want to go on studying or to get a job. There is no clear aspiration at all. You are deluding yourself.'

'No,' Ali said. 'I would like to go on studying but I'm aware that I'm not contributing anything to the household and that is why I was talking about getting a job.'

'I have plenty of money,' he said. 'And you would be contributing to the household by actually caring for it.'

'But I hate not having any money,' she said.

'I said I've got plenty of money,' he repeated. 'I can keep you in a very pleasant lifestyle. We will have such a good time, just you and me.'

'But I want more than that,' she tried again. Somewhere, somehow, over the years, she seemed to have forgotten how to exert herself, as if it was easier just to agree in order to keep the peace. She seemed to have learned to accept his control over her, hating when he shouted at her, when he belittled her, when he undermined her confidence so that she no longer knew what it was she wanted to say. From time to time she found the energy to fight against it, but the energy never lasted.

'But you have it all,' he said. 'You're just not grateful enough for all that I give you.'

'Maurice, of course I am grateful. You're misunderstanding me. I need to do something with my life.'

'And being my wife is not doing something?'

They were in a restaurant during that conversation, and she was glad because she knew that if they had been at home he would have shouted at her before getting up and leaving the room.

'Now, choose a dessert,' he continued. 'Enjoy the sweet things in life.'

Reluctantly, she had lifted the dessert menu and hidden herself behind it as she tried to think of how to pursue the matter.

'What will you have?' he asked.

'I don't feel like dessert,' she said.

'Then I will choose for you,' he said, calling the waiter to the table.

'Crème caramel for my wife,' he said. 'Coffee for me.'

Ali sat there with memories of his father choosing from the menu for them all, and wondering if her mother-in-law had once wanted to have a say in matters, even things as simple as whether or not to indulge in something sweet.

'Doesn't that look nice?' Maurice said as the pudding came to the table with a flourish. He smiled at her. 'I said,' he repeated after a moment, 'doesn't that look nice?' This time there was a hard edge to his tone.

'Yes, lovely,' she said. She wanted to say, I don't want your carefully chosen dessert. I want to go back to university and to go on studying. But she was afraid.

'My wife will have cream to go with her crème caramel,' he said to the hovering waiter.

For a long time after that she could not sleep properly. She sat on the sofa and asked herself what it was she feared. His raised voice? The hard edge to it? The sense of a threat behind it? She wondered how these things came so easily to him and why she had no idea how to handle him when he was like that, other than to comply. Her mistake had been in ever complying. Had she stood her ground the first time he had behaved like that, she thought she might have set a different pattern, rather than having evolved into the role of someone who always acquiesced.

She also noticed how he seemed to thrive on the aftermath of such arguments, if such they could be called. His anger and his need to enforce his will on her always made him want to take her to bed, and his lovemaking was more passionate, more intense on these occasions. Initially she had responded to this in an effort to pacify him and to restore equilibrium between them. But as time went on, she grew to dread not just the arguments, which she seemed to lack the will to win, but also lying in bed allowing him to resolve his anger on her. She resented it.

Time and again as she sat with her two-in-the-morning cup of tea, she thought of how to stand up to him, how to say to him, 'No, Maurice. I want to do this or that. I want to do something else with my life other than to change the sheets, do the laundry and cook you dinner.'

But when those moments arrived, she did not know how to handle him. She had become afraid of him but she was afraid of leaving too. Failure was her worst fear.

She agreed to take a year off, to see how it would be just staying at home and fulfilling his every need. Frustrated and isolated, she struggled to fill her days. He never left her much money, and he went through the shopping, accounting for every last item. She scrimped in order to have enough cash to phone her family, which she did from a call-box as he also kept a close eye on the phone bill. The more she acquiesced, the worse it got, and the less she was able to stand up for herself.

She could not tell her father or sisters that her phone calls were so short as she was watching the coins dropping through the machine, knowing she would be just cut off if she did not wind up the call in time. She could not tell them that he seemed to despise them and wanted her to have nothing to do with them. She could not tell them that the Christmas day she had taken the car and driven in the snow to spend that short hour with them had cost her dearly. He was so angry that he removed her name from the insurance, saying that she could not be trusted, and therefore she could not use the car.

Her frustration had risen then. 'I just wanted to spend a little time with them,' she had said. 'And if you hadn't sold my car I wouldn't have taken this one. I would have had my own.'

'You just don't understand, do you?' he had said.

'No, you don't understand. It's Christmas and I wanted to see my grandparents and my father and sisters. One hour. That was all I wanted. That's why I went.'

'You stole out of the house,' he said. 'You took my car without asking. You won't be doing that again.'

Little by little, he undermined her every move, curtailing her and controlling her every action. And she, once so strong and forthright, no longer knew how to handle him. She could not let herself down by telling her father. She felt shame and disbelief, and when she spoke to her family, she hid it. She sometimes felt that they must have given up on her, although they always seemed pleased to hear her voice, always asking if she would come and visit, always understanding when she said how busy she was. She could not tell them of the issues she faced, and instead she stayed home and read the books she would have read had her husband permitted her to continue her studies.

Every so often she tried to bring up the subject of returning to university, and his anger and frustration outmatched her on every level. She feared his raised voice, the hand that he once lifted and dropped before he struck her. 'See what you almost made me do,' he shouted.

She thought, if you ever hit me that will be my excuse and I will go. She could not see that she already had a thousand excuses to leave, and so time passed.

But an evening came, an evening when his irritation over dinner had been such that, after she had cleared away the dishes, washed and dried them and put them away, she slipped out of the apartment to get some air, to walk down the street to the corner and back, just to soothe the distress in her head, and then she returned. She hoped he would not have noticed her absence as he was dozing in front of the television when she left, but he had, and he was irate.

She had no idea afterwards how the ensuing row escalated, but one moment he was shouting at her and calling her ungrateful, and the next he had her arm twisted behind her back and she was screaming in pain. The pain did not diminish. Instead it came in waves, and she dragged herself to the bed where she sobbed in anguish. For once, he left her alone.

She drifted in and out of sleep until morning. She waited until she heard him leave and silence settled in the apartment. Through the open window she heard the car door slam. She managed to get off the bed, and she slipped her feet into a pair of sandals and picked up her shoulder-bag and let herself out of the apartment. She was still wearing the clothes from the previous day: a summer skirt and a blouse. She fought the pain as she walked across the car park. Out on the street, she turned left even though it was the wrong way to the bus stop and meant that she had to walk almost a kilometre, but she knew that when he returned it would be from the other direction. She took the bus, struggling to get the coins from her pocket. She sat with her eyes closed, head leaning against the window.

She had intended to get herself to a hospital, but she passed the stop and did not realise it until she was in the centre of Strasbourg.

Getting off the bus, she looked around in despair. She did not know what to do now. She felt like she was going to throw up, but she had eaten nothing and knew that if she could just keep breathing above the pain she could get away. She saw a bus that was going to the other side of the border, a town near her grandparents' home. She got onto it. A man sitting beside her asked her if she was feeling all right. She nodded and tried to lean back but was unable to get comfortable. She took her identity card from her bag and stuffed it down the side of the seat. She dozed again as the throbbing came in waves.

When the bus stopped in Offenburg, the driver came to waken her. Her face was white and her hand clammy when he took it in an effort to rouse her. She gave a small moan and he raced back up the bus calling for an ambulance.

'What's your name?' she was asked by one of the medics as he felt her pulse. 'Ali Peters,' she said, and she managed to give her grandparents' address.

'What happened?' he asked.

'My shoulder,' she whispered. 'Something is wrong with it.'

'If I try to lift you, it is going to hurt even more. If we can get you to your feet we can try to walk you to the ambulance. '

He helped her stand, but then she slipped and fell against him as her knees gave way. He lifted her up and carried her up the aisle and down the steps.

'Dislocated shoulder I think,' he said to his colleague. 'She's blacked out.' One held her as the other pulled the trolley from the ambulance, and together they laid her gently on it. One sat with her as the siren heralded their way to the hospital.

Ali had disappeared into a haze of white pain. She was beyond caring whether Maurice found her or not. Nothing, she felt, could be worse than how she now felt. She was aware of people talking to her, of worried faces asking her questions, of shock in those faces as she was undressed, and the relief of the painkiller shot into her arm. 'My God,' said a voice. 'What happened to you?' And then she was asleep.

When she woke, Oma was sitting by her bed wiping her forehead with a cool, damp cloth. Ali looked into her eyes and then away. 'I fell,' she whispered to her grandmother.

'Did you?' Oma said. Her grandmother knew, or at least suspected. She could see it in her eyes. There was no more hiding, she realised. 'You're safe now,' Oma said. 'And you will stay safe. I promise.'

'He mustn't find me, Oma,' she whispered. 'He will never forgive me.'

'Forgive you for what?' Oma asked. 'Did you do something to deserve this?' Her teeth were clenched. The doctors had explained the extent of her granddaughter's injuries, a dislocated shoulder and a cracked rib and bruising on the ribcage. 'Sleep now,' she said, having given Ali a drink. She did not say that the police had been called and that when Ali next woke she would, hopefully, be able to give a statement.

'Maurice,' Ali whispered. 'Please don't let him know that I'm here.'

'He won't get in,' Oma said. 'I promise you. He won't find you.'

He didn't find her. They took it in shifts for three days until Ali was released. Mer and Bernd had arrived at the farmhouse that night to find Oma pacing the floor and Opa on night shift in the hospital.

'Oma,' Mer said, 'what's happened?'

'It's Ali,' Oma said. 'I don't know how to put this into words.'

'Is she all right?'

'She will be. She's in hospital and your grandfather is with her now. She's got a cracked rib, a dislocated shoulder...'

'Maurice?' asked Mer.

'What? Yes, how did you know...?'

'I didn't know. I guessed.'

Mer told her then how Cassie had suggested something was amiss as she was about to depart on her train trip.

'But why did she not say something earlier?' Oma asked.

'I don't think she really believed it,' Mer said. 'I think she thought it, or suspected it, I think she may even have asked Ali but got the brush off. She certainly didn't think Maurice was violent, more that he was controlling Ali, keeping her away from us. She was vague about it, concerned but not concerned... I just don't think she believed it, but after she suggested it, things started to fall into place...'

'It never occurred to me,' Oma said. 'I feel it should have, but it didn't. We've tried to visit Ali over the last few years. Once we succeeded and we met and had a drink and she was in good form. She seemed to have allied herself with her new family, or that is what we thought. We're both shocked. Your grandfather and I, I mean.'

'How bad is it?' Bernd asked.

'She's going to be all right,' Oma said, 'but really only because she ran this morning. Somehow she got herself together sufficiently to see that she had to leave. As far as we can make out, Maurice left her in bed this morning and went out, and she had spent the night with a dislocated shoulder. I don't think he had physically abused her before yesterday, which has to be something. She is so badly hurt I could cry, but I can't even find the tears. I just feel so shaken.'

'Perhaps a drink,' Bernd suggested to Mer. 'We should make sure your grandmother is all right and then if we go to the hospital we can stay the night and your grandfather can come back to be with her.'

He was practical, pragmatic, organised, and he took control in a way that surprised and pleased Mer. It also impressed her grandmother when she thought about it later.

Ali came home from hospital to her grandparents' house a few days later, quiet and withdrawn, pale and shaken. Their father had arrived in the meantime, and had done all he could to encourage her to press charges. 'I don't want to, Papa,' she said. 'I would have to face him in court and I don't want that. I just don't know what to do.'

'What do you think you want?' her father asked her.

'I just want to be happily married to him, for things to be the way they were in the first weeks and months of our relationship.'

Horrified, Karl withdrew. He spoke to his parents and Mer. 'She's talking about going back to him. I think she's endured this for so long that she can't see clearly. She seems to think she can make it right...'

'I'll talk to her,' his mother said. 'Don't worry. There is no going back. We won't let her.'

***

Oma sat by Ali on the living-room sofa. She held her hand. 'Ali,' she said. 'There are times when we have to close doors, to move on, to start afresh.'

'But I loved him... love him... I don't know. I married him for life. I don't want to give up...'

'This time you ended up in hospital. Next time... and Ali, remember that you said to us that he must not find you.'

'I meant until I was well again. I just need to get well and then I will make this all better.'

'And how many times have you thought just that over the last few years? How many bruises and broken bones will it take until you see him for what he is? He is a wife beater. Once someone starts doing that... He is cruel, sadistic... apart from what he did to you, and God knows I can't even comprehend how a man could do that to you, or to anyone, but apart from that, he left you overnight in agony with a dislocated shoulder. You wouldn't leave an animal like that, would you?'

Ali shook her head.

'Ali, my darling granddaughter. There are things we try to fix, and they are the things that are worth fixing. This one isn't.'

'I want to make it right. I don't want to be like my mother who just ran...'

'First of all, there is no comparison. None whatsoever. And secondly, your mother and father did try to work things out between them. Good things are worth saving. Please, please listen to me. Things happen in marriages, in relationships, and people have to work out what is worthwhile. Things have happened in my marriage, and I worked to fix them because the marriage was worth saving. This is different.'

'What kind of things, Oma?' Ali asked.

'Every family has secrets. Things that you don't talk about. You must know that by now. I doubt that your father talks about what your mother did. Your grandfather and I have our own secrets. There are things we worked through. In the thirties, when I had just given birth to your father, one day your grandfather brought home a baby. It was a difficult time for many reasons and there I was, just a young mother with a baby, and suddenly a second one arrived on the scene. What would you do if your husband brought home his baby that he had had with some other woman?'

Ali shook her head. 'I don't know.'

'I took him back and took the baby in and we raised her as our daughter. I struggled to handle this development, but I loved my husband, your grandfather, and I had no doubt that he loved me. Things happen in war or in times of potential war, and his daughter was one of those things. But she was a human being with no one now to care for her but us. And so I did.'

'Are you talking about Tante Anneke?' Ali was puzzled.

'Yes. I am.'

'But you love Tante Anneke?'

'Yes, I do. I had no trouble in loving her. But that's not the point.'

'But you forgave him, Oma,' Ali said.

'Yes, I did. That is the point. Our marriage was worth saving. That is precisely my point. Yes, he had hurt me, and I have not asked for the details of what happened or why, all I know is that the woman died. Whatever relationship they had may have given him some comfort at a terrible time in our lives. I can find rational excuses and I can live with them. There is no rational excuse for what has happened to you.'

'I feel like a failure, Oma,' Ali said.

'You're a failure because someone beat you? I don't think that makes *you* a failure.'

'But what would I do if I didn't go back?'

'If you had not married Maurice, what would you have done?'

'Gone on studying I suppose. I would have tried to find a career.'

'And are those things inaccessible now? You're only twenty-five. It probably feels old to you, that you're on the shelf and that life and opportunity have passed you by. But listen to me, Ali, twenty-five is young. Your whole life is ahead of you. Do you want to live it in fear? Do you want to be beaten again? Because he won't stop, believe me. And the next time he might kill you.'

Ali closed her eyes. She remembered wishing that she were dead, that he would just obliterate her completely.

'I'm afraid,' she whispered to her grandmother.

Oma put her arms around her and said, 'Let this be the last time you are afraid.'

There was safety there in her grandmother's arms. The others came in and Mer sat beside her holding her hand. Her father and her grandfather sat near her. They had already made plans. 'You won't have to see him again,' Karl said. 'If that is what you cannot bear, we will go to his parents and tell them what has happened. We have pictures of your injuries and a report from the hospital. We will get you a quick divorce and settlement.'

'He'll never agree,' Ali said.

'I think he will. We'll do this through his parents. From what little you've told me, his family will never tolerate the police case that will ensue. We've already reported what happened. There are hospital records. All it takes is a statement from you.'

\*\*\*

'I want to kill him,' Karl said to his father.

'I know. But you won't. You will ease Ali out of this situation so that she can move forwards. You don't want her to look back.' He put his hand on his son's shoulder. 'It's almost over,' he said. 'And this is best for Ali.'

'I know,' Karl said, slowly unclenching his fists. 'But to let him get away with that?'

'We do what is best for our children. She wants no further contact, not to have to deal with him.'

# CASSIE'S TALE

My hijacker let me sit beside my mother as the plane flew south into the sun, then away from the sun, then east as the earth turned and the sun sank somewhere behind us. Night came suddenly, and I tried to sleep with my head on my mum's shoulder. She held my hand. I was her baby again, if only for a little while.

'I love you,' I whispered. 'I need you to know that.' There was still time to ask more about why she left, but I didn't want to know. I wanted these few precious moments when all that was there was she and me.

I moved my head. It was too hot and my hair was stuck to my scalp. She took her perfume from her pocket and sprayed it onto my wrists. For a moment it was all I could smell, and the sweat and the fear shifted. 'Keep it,' she said.

I put it in the pocket of my jeans.

I wanted to say to her that I was afraid, but the words were pointless. No one on Pegasus was not afraid.

Our pilot, Charon, had come from the cockpit with a gun at his head. I knew that feeling. His eyes met mine. We were on the same boat, ferried by outside forces. His eyes gazed into mine. I knew what he was thinking. He knew what I was thinking. He was the ferryman and I his passenger. He was supposed to bring me down the river. He could not row against the tide. I tried to smile at him. It was a grimace, there was no smile inside me. I wanted him to know that it was all right. I needed him to know that he could ferry and we would sit tight. This was one boat we would not rock.

In that moment when our eyes were locked he too made a grimace, but I think it was the best smile he could muster. His grimace mine; my grimace his.

We were coming in to land again when night fell. Or was it dawn? Had the world reversed? I could no longer differentiate between the red and yellow lines of dawn and sunset. If we were in the Underworld, then day and night could be reversed. No. There would be just night. It was the Underworld. It was so dark. I did not know that there could be such fear. I wanted my sisters and I wondered where they were, and if Ali was safe, and if Mer and Bernd were out walking in the night air, and I knew that Armageddon was coming.

The drone of the plane shifted. I could hear the wheels being released and lowered. The fear rose in contrast to the falling wheels. We sat tight, so tight. I clutched my mother's hand. She clutched mine. Our hands merged into two arms entangled by our grasping fingers. Our sweat mingled. The perfume on our wrists wafted together. We tethered that long-since-cut umbilical cord, we tied it together in fear.

The plane landed, bumping down the runway. 'Oh Charon,' I thought, 'keep your hands steady on the tiller.' I thought of Ali and Mer singing in the school choir when I was still too young to understand the words, but yet I found those words now. We were in the school chapel and I was about seven years old. I was with the little ones at the front. Ali with the older girls at the back. Mer somewhere in the middle, the middle child of three. God as a shepherd. I felt like a sheep in a flock of many on a plane. They were herding us to the slaughterhouse. I shall not want. Oh, but I did want. I wanted green pastures and the crashing of waves on the beach. I wanted my dolls' house and my dolls, and my little blue tricycle that I had inherited from my sisters when I was four or five. I wanted to swing in a tree and grin at them upside down.

I wanted to be me, and not this caged, impotent animal.

# CHAPTER SEVENTEEN

Ali and Mer Peters were back in Tübingen. It was the summer of 1982, and Ali was looking through brochures searching for another degree. She was twenty-six years old, and all she wanted was to stay at home and do nothing, but Karl had said that he needed her to find a course and something to occupy herself during this coming year. He was insistent. 'You've done nothing for too long,' he said. 'You're too clever for this. You must look through those brochures. I will give you a week to decide, but we can discuss what you're thinking at any time.'

'I'd like to stay here,' Ali said. 'Study here if I can.' Study if I must, she thought. She just wanted to sit and look at the tree in the little back garden, wipe the table and run the washing machine, but neither her father nor Mer seemed to think this was an option.

'Yes, of course you can stay here. A fresh start.' He put his hand on her shoulder. 'Ali, did I let you down by not doing something earlier?'

She shook her head. 'What could you do? I was so sure I was right, even after I was knew I was wrong, I still thought I could make it right.'

'You're home now,' he said.

Ali and Mer walked by the river together, sometimes talking, mostly not; mostly just listening to the river flowing downstream. They sat on the river bank. Ali stared into the water, and Mer reached out a hand and held her sister's. Sometimes Ali shuddered. Sometimes she sat still. They both had their hair tied back because of the heat. Mer's was light brown; Ali's dark.

'Mer...' she said, one afternoon in August. It was just a few weeks since she had left her husband Maurice.

'Yes?' Mer replied. There had been so many beginnings to a conversation that began just like this, but never proceeded anywhere. 'Tell me,' Mer said gently.

'I pushed him,' Ali said.

'Pushed him?'

'Maurice... I could see no way out', Ali said. 'I had told myself over and over that if he ever actually hit me, then I would leave. That would be the catalyst...'

'I see,' Mer said.

'What are you thinking?' Ali asked.

'Oddly, I thought then that I'm glad that he hit you, but I don't really mean that. I mean that I'm glad that the catalyst, as you put it, actually happened. I can't bear the thought of what you have been through...'

'The strange thing is that what he did to me is not the worst of it,' Ali said. 'Obviously physically it is the worst, but it isn't really the worst.'

Mer tightened her grasp of her sister's hand.

'Do you want to tell me?' she asked.

'There isn't really anything to say,' she said. 'If I repeat a catalogue of events, they don't add up to very much. They really just say that I wasn't strong enough to stand up to him; but it all happened so slowly. I look back and I... I don't know how to describe this really. It's as if I was someone else. I was young and I thought I was invincible. I thought I could do what I wanted. And I fell in love.'

'Who hasn't made a mistake?' Mer said.

'One that big? One that stupid? One that went on that long? It's three weeks since I left him,' Ali said, 'and it seems much longer and yet it seems like yesterday. And I did push him, I know that. I am almost sure I did it deliberately, and yet I remember saying to Oma that I wanted to go back to him, to make everything right.'

'Fortunately our grandmother is wiser than you,' Mer said with a slow smile. 'You know, if she had not talked you into staying with us, I was next on the list to persuade you. We were not going to let you go back to Maurice; that is the one sure thing.'

'I'm glad,' Ali said. 'I look back and I think I must have been insane.'

'You had just had your shoulder dislocated, and a rib cracked.' Mer shuddered. 'You were in shock.'

'I loved him you know.'

'Yes, I do know.'

'But now I don't know why I loved him. I just can't remember anything other than feeling needed and liking that feeling .'

They walked along the river bank, they looked in the market together and they did the shopping. Sometimes Ali sat and cried and Mer stayed beside her and waited for the tears to abate. 'It will be all right,' Mer said. 'It will take time.'

'You seem so wise,' Ali said.

'No, not wise at all. It never occurred to me what was happening. It was Cassie who suggested it.'

'What did she suggest?'

'I think that somehow she saw that he was bullying you into some kind of submission.'

'I wonder where she is and if she is enjoying her train travel,' Ali said.

It was a long, hot summer, one more day in which Ali felt she was putting in time and learning how to live again; a sweltering day and now late afternoon, and she and Mer were at home. 'Cassie's birthday is today,' Mer said. 'It's the first time she's been away from us. I made a cake just in case she comes home today.'

The sun shone low into the rooms and Mer was in the kitchen, bread rising on the stove, the windows open to allow what air there was into the room. The back door was open too, and a single bird was sitting on the tree. She stood for a moment watching the bird under the canopy of leaves, and then she called in to her sister, 'Put on the news, Ali. I'm making a cup of tea. Want one?'

Ali reached for the button on the television and called back, 'Yes, please.'

'Bernd is coming over later,' Mer said. 'I think we might go out for a while. But Papa will be home...'

'I'll be fine,' Ali said. She knew that they made a point of not leaving her alone.

The television warmed up. The clock struck the hour and the news began. '*A hijacked plane flying from Athens to London has landed in Addis Ababa... the demands of the hijackers... the pilot has said...*'

Mer brought in their cups of tea and plonked herself down beside Ali on the sofa. 'Here,' she said, passing a cup to her sister. Ali's eyes did not move from the screen.

'Ali,' Mer said. 'Your tea.'

'Look,' Ali whispered. 'Look.'

Mer turned her eyes to the television and momentarily saw a girl standing in the open doorway of a plane with an arm around her waist and a gun at her head. 'What...?' she said.

'That's not... it's not... it can't be...'

'Oh, my God, it's Cassie,' Mer almost dropped the cups. She put them down on the coffee table as the camera changed and swept over the armoured cars, the soldiers crouched behind them, the shimmering heat washing over the plane, the tanks refilling the fuel and then back to the newsroom.

'*We will have more on the hijacking later in the news.*'

'It can't be...'

But they both knew it was. Ali looked at Mer. 'What do we do? For God's sake, what do we do?'

'Papa,' Mer said. 'He should be home shortly...'

'Phone him,' Ali said. 'Call him...'

There was no answer from his office.

'Change channels,' Mer said. 'Maybe we can find more on a different one.'

'No, we know there will be more on this one in a few minutes. Let's stick with this.'

Karl came in a few minutes later and both girls got up to go to him. 'Papa,' Ali said. 'Papa, Cassie...'

He could make no sense of what she was saying. 'Look,' she pointed at the television as the scene reverted to Addis Ababa and the picture of Cassie in the doorway with a gun at her head and an arm around her holding her to the masked face of her captor, an image that would be on the front pages of all the newspapers on the following day.

'*A flight from Athens to London, hijacked earlier today...*' the newsreader reported.

'It looks like Cassie,' Karl said when he could speak. 'But it may not be. Do we have any reason to think she was in Athens?'

'I got a postcard from her this morning,' Mer said. Her heart was pounding. 'From Athens.'

'No,' he said. 'No, no, no... this can't be happening...'

But it was happening. They watched in continued horror, heard how the plane had just taken off, destination unknown. He made phone calls and information slowly trickled back in. Yes, there was one German on the plane, identity as yet unknown. 'It's my daughter,' he said, 'it's my youngest daughter. Her name is Cassie Peters. She's the girl in the doorway of the plane on the news.'

'My name is Georg Brunner. I will be your contact. I need to take your number.'

Karl gave him their number. He was told to sit tight, that everything possible was being done and would be done, to stay at home and to keep the line clear; there were promises of information as soon as there was any to give.

Oma and Opa phoned. 'We're coming up,' Oma said. 'We'll be there in two hours. We'll stay with you. It's going to be all right, I know it is.'

Bernd arrived at the door, and took in Mer's shocked face. She explained. He sat her down. He made tea for them all as they flicked from channel to channel trying to find more news, a newer update of any sort.

The phone never stopped ringing as school friends of Cassie called to ask if they had seen the news. 'We have to keep the line clear,' Bernd said. 'Yes, we know it is Cassie, thank you for calling.' Karl had stopped answering the phone after the first five calls. He sat on the sofa with his head in his hands. Ali and Mer took it in turns comforting him and then each other. 'It will be all right, it has to be,' Ali said.

At midnight they learned that the plane had landed on a narrow strip in southern Tunisia, but only for refuelling. There was an impasse. Their contact from the German Ministry phoned. 'We have no good news as yet,' Herr Brunner said. 'But equally there is no bad news. I will call again in the morning. You need to try to get some sleep.'

'It's going to be a long night,' Opa said.

'Let's make sandwiches; everyone needs to eat something,' Bernd said to Mer. 'Come and help me.'

She took her eyes off the television and followed him out to the kitchen where she leaned against him. 'I don't know what I would do without you,' she said.

He held her close and stroked her hair. 'You don't have to do without me,' he said.

'You know the way Opa said it's going to be a long night... I keep thinking of how long a night it is for Cassie.' Her voice broke.

'Don't cry,' Bernd said. 'Please don't cry. I'll stay here with you. Cassie may well be asleep. What she is enduring is probably exhausting. But you need to sleep too. Tomorrow is another day. We need to be strong for tomorrow.'

Going back into the living-room he tentatively suggested that bed might be an option after the sandwiches, that he would stay by the phone, that Mer should rest, that they all should. Oma endorsed this. She got to her feet. 'Bernd is right. Whatever happens won't happen in the next few hours. They will be looking for another place to land.'

Karl nodded. 'You take my bed,' he said to his parents, 'and you take Cassie's,' to Bernd. 'I'm going to stay here,' he said, turning back to the television.

Bernd brought Mer upstairs. He kissed her and whispered, 'I promise I'll call you if the phone rings. Now go to sleep. I'm going back downstairs as soon as you are in bed. I'll stay with your father.'

Her head on the pillow, her eyes reddened around the rims, one hand clutching the sheet, she fell asleep. She was vaguely aware of him kissing her on the forehead and then the door opening and closing. She wanted to call to him to leave it open, but sleep sucked her in. She had terrifying dreams that she could not shake. Sometimes she was able to redirect her dreams, this time not. It was like she was enveloped in fear. Like her sister on the plane, her sleep was troubled, distorted by nightmares, frantically trying to escape, but caught in a web or maze. When she woke it was daylight. Glancing at her watch she saw that it was six, and for a moment she did not know if it was morning or evening, then realised that it was morning and that she could hear the phone ringing.

She met Ali on the landing and, both barefoot, they ran down the stairs. Opa was already up and was in the living-room with Bernd and their father was on the phone. Their aunt, Karl's sister, Anneke, had arrived some time during the night, and she was pacing the floor.

'The plane landed, was refuelled again and is back in the air,' Karl said to them. 'We are to sit tight. It's going to be another long day.'

The television was on but it was muted and they glanced at it from time to time as Ali made coffee and opened the back door to let in the sun. They kept the radio on in the kitchen. The day dragged and they ate food that Bernd went and fetched from the market. He returned with his mother. 'You know my mother from the university,' he said to Karl. 'She has come to...' he didn't finish the sentence. He probably was going to say 'to help', but there was no real helping that anyone could actually do.

'I'm Leonora Meyer,' she introduced herself to the room in general. If she felt awkward she hid it well. 'Karl, hello. I am so sorry.'

Karl came over to her. 'Leonora, thank you for coming.'

She touched his arm and nodded. She was dressed in a light skirt and a dark green short-sleeved summer blouse. Her blonde hair was pinned up. He couldn't remember if he had seen her during the previous day at the university. It was, of course, the holiday period, but he went in every day to do some writing and to prepare for the coming academic year. He realised that he did not know what took Leonora into the department most days; the same as what took him in, he supposed, paperwork, preparation, their own work on articles and books. She smiled at him, a tentative but kind smile, as she went with Anneke to the kitchen to help prepare some food. Neighbours came by to see how they were doing. The newspapers were full of the events of the previous day.

'What if no country will let them land?' Mer asked.

'Someone will,' Oma said to her. But her voice was not as strong as usual, not as confident, not as certain. Mer, looking at her grandmother, realised for the first time in her life that her grandmother did not have all the answers.

Towards nightfall, Mer heard Opa saying that something would happen that night. She didn't want anything to happen. As long as the pilot was flying the plane, as long as there was no actual action, she felt that Cassie was safe. She knew that there had to be an end to this, but she wanted to hold on to the moments they had, those moments in which they knew Cassie was alive and where there was still hope.

At the same moment as it was announced on the television that the plane was heading for Mogadishu, the phone rang and Herr Brunner from the Ministry told them the same thing. They talked for some time on the phone.

'Another night,' Karl said when the call finally ended. His hands were shaking. His father poured him a Schnapps. 'Drink this,' he said. 'You need it. Does anyone else want one?' He poured a glass for himself as the others shook their heads, and they sat and watched the pictures unfold on the television.

'Mogadishu,' Ali said. 'Why Mogadishu?'

'I presume pressure was put to bear on the government of Somalia to let the plane land. It had to land somewhere, and Mogadishu took in a plane before.'

Mer and Ali looked at each other. They had hardly talked during the day other than to ask who wanted coffee and if they could do anything for anyone. Ali had vomited twice, and Bernd's mother had sat beside her on the bathroom floor and wiped her forehead and her face. Mer had sat close to Bernd with his arm around her. Once he asked her if she would like to go out for a short walk. She had shaken her head, 'No, sorry.' 'I understand,' he said.

She and Ali both remembered the hijacking of a German plane some years earlier that had ended up in Mogadishu with the killing of the hijackers and the rescue of the passengers. Could history repeat itself? Both were afraid to say anything aloud, as if words might break the spell.

'I think you should have a brandy,' Leonora Meyer said to Ali. she went and got a glass, found the brandy and poured it.

'Come and sit down,' she said to Ali.

'Thank you, Frau Meyer,' Ali said. Her father kept putting his hand to his head and then taking it away again as if he did not know what he was doing. She remembered him taking control ten years earlier on the night when their mother had left; and then the memory changed and she recalled that he had got drunk later that night. She took the brandy and drank it.

They repeated the pattern of the previous evening with Karl and Bernd planning on staying in the living-room by the phone. Anneke would take Cassie's bed. Leonora went home. 'I'll be back in the morning if that's all right? Are you sure I'm not in the way?'

Karl embraced her in the hallway. 'Thank you for coming,' he said. 'We need our family, our friends at a time like this.'

'Call me during the night if you need to,' Leonora said. 'If you hear anything, or if you just need to talk, I have a phone by my bed. Otherwise I will be over in the morning.'

'Thank you. I can't thank you enough. Or Bernd. It's very difficult to think clearly, but I know that the support we are getting is comforting.'

When she left, he stood in the open doorway for a few moments watching her walk up the street. She turned at the corner and raised her hand. He went out the door and called her back. She came running. 'What is it, Karl?'

'Advice. I need advice.'

'Tell me.' Her concern was manifest.

'I don't know how much you know of our past...'

'Bernd has told me a little. I know that their mother left...'

'You know that?'

'Yes. Bernd told me. He has always talked to me. His father left when he was about five; Bernd was ill at the time. We talk a lot. I am sure there are a thousand things that I don't know about Merope, or indeed about Bernd, but he has told me what he thinks I should know, or what he felt like sharing.'

'I was just surprised because I know Ali told people that her mother had died, and I was never sure what the others said by way of explanation. I didn't know if I should tell Ali to be more honest, or if I should leave her to handle things in her own way.'

'Bernd told me that; he told me about Ali's way of handling it. Merope had told him how Ali had always said that her mother had died. I gather that Bernd was the first person to whom Merope had told the truth.'

'I see. Well, at least that means I don't have to start by telling you that Miriam, my ex-wife, is still alive.'

'Karl, do you want to go somewhere and sit down so we can talk?'

'I can't. I need to get back inside. May I tell you something, and then ask your advice as a parent?'

'Of course,' Leonora said.

'That last phone call… they said that there was a Miriam Peters on the plane; a woman with a British passport. It has to be the girls' mother.'

'Is Miriam British?'

'No, she's Irish. At least she was Irish when I met her. When she left, she moved to London. It is ten years ago. She probably changed her passport. It's easy enough for Irish people who were born, or whose parents were born, before 1948 to get a British passport. And she has lived there for the last ten years. It couldn't have been hard.'

'What are you asking me?'

'Should I tell Ali and Mer?'

Leonora considered for a moment. 'Truth is usually best, Karl. If you don't tell them now, they will find out later. You could wait until the morning. I doubt they are sleeping much at all, but it will only add to their worries.'

'Thank you,' he said.

\*\*\*

'I don't think there will be any news for the next few hours. We must all get as much sleep as possible,' Karl said, coming back into the living-room. He hugged both girls. They stood in the middle of the room with their arms wrapped around each other. 'So much easier if we could pray,' Ali said. 'I would find it better if I thought there was a god watching out for Cassie tonight.'

'Do you remember the hymns we learned when we were children?' Mer asked. 'In Ireland, in the convent?'

'I remember particular lines and words,' Ali said. 'Embedded in my brain I suppose. Some are from the psalms, some from songs. I don't know which is which any more, but I find myself thinking about them. The Lord is my shepherd. Credo in Unum Deum.'

'I find myself thinking of the sea. I think Cassie is thinking of the sea,' Mer said.

'Dancing in the waves?' Ali said with a small, and somewhat wry, smile. 'Yes.'

They went upstairs together holding hands. 'We'll get her back,' Ali said. 'It's the feeling of helplessness, the feeling that there's nothing we can do. It's odd, but for the first time I can see why you were so desperate to rescue me from Maurice. I don't think I could see that clearly before, but now I can.'

'You once told me that sisters are forever,' Mer said. 'And it's true. The bond...'

Ali nodded. 'We need to sleep now, for Cassie's sake if not for our own. She is tough, tougher than either you or me, but she's going to need us when she comes home. Like I needed you. Like I need you.'

Downstairs, Karl was finally alone with Anneke, Bernd and his parents. 'There's something I have to tell you,' he said. 'I didn't want to say it in front of Ali and Mer. It's difficult... unbelievable I guess.'

'What is it?' his mother asked.

'The man from the Ministry, Herr Brunner, asked if he we have a relative named Miriam Peters. Apparently she is on the plane.'

'Miriam?' His parents looked at him and then at each other.

'That's the name of my ex-wife,' Karl said briefly to Bernd. Bernd now seemed so much a part of the family that he felt he could not exclude him from this conversation. He also knew that Bernd would be a support for Mer if and when he had to share this news. And he knew that Leonora was right and that he would have to tell them in the morning.

'Cassie... Greece...' his mother pondered aloud. 'Did she find Miriam and then this somehow unfolded?'

'Why would she go looking for Miriam? Did she know where she was living?' his father asked.

'I have abolutely no idea. I can't remember when she last mentioned her. It never occurred to me...'

'Have you had any contact with her?'

'After we divorced I sent her photos of the girls once or twice. I did it through the lawyers. I don't think she came looking; I think Cassie did that.'

'But why? Why didn't she tell you? Why would she go looking?'

They sat silently for a moment before Karl added, 'I think it's probably natural that she went looking for Miriam. I wish to god she hadn't, but I have to accept it.'

'It was kind of you to send photographs,' his father said, still thinking about Karl's previous comment.

'I think I agreed because on some level I... I don't know. I loved her. I love our girls. She gave me these girls, quite literally as it turned out. She handed them to me when she left. Had she asked to see them when they were younger I would have considered it. She didn't leave because of them. I am quite sure that she left because our marriage didn't fulfil her. I'm sure that she must still love them or else she wouldn't have asked to see their photographs. It makes no difference anyway. What is done is done. I am going to tell Ali and Mer in the morning that she is probably on that plane. I decided to hold off tonight on the off chance that they might get some sleep.'

# CASSIE'S TALE

But it was Armageddon and I was back on my feet with the gun at my temple again and my knees buckling.

'Don't let them kill me, Mum. I don't want to die.'

I wanted to be brave and face this moment. I had told myself over and over that it was coming and that I would be strong, that I would not die screaming to live, that I would let the Minotaur do what he must and tear me limb from limb. But my courage had left me and I was a puppet again, dangling in his arms and then I heard my mother's voice through the drumming in my ears and I was pulled back from the high drop to the ground as they waited for the refuelling that was not going to happen.

My mother said 'Take me.'

These two words echo and will echo through the caverns of my mind. Take me, take me, take me...

And the Minotaur pulled back from the doorway, and I his shield, his puppet, moved back with him out of the line of fire and he flung me back into the plane and pulled my mother in front of him. He shouted something and then I heard the gunshot and, in the crystal clear silence as the pounding in my head stopped for the first time, I heard something fall, a whoosh of silent air, and a thud as my mother's body hit the ground. I crawled on my hands and knees to try to get back up the aisle but a man, a passenger on our ferryboat, pulled me from the floor and into a seat beside him.

'Stay quiet,' he whispered. 'Just stay quiet, and when it starts get down.' I had no idea what he meant. Nothing could start. It had finished. I had found my mother and now she was gone. Gone, gone, gone again. But not to a houseboat on Camden Lock, gone to stony earth this time. That thud. That mother. All was finished.

But he was right. That man, who pulled me from the carpeted floor with its little cat's eyes, was right. There was an explosion at the back of the plane and smoke and we hit the floor. We cowered as sheep being led to the slaughter. The four horsemen of the Apocalypse rode in. The fields of Megiddo were laid waste.

I missed that bit of the bloodbath as I lay beneath the man who had rescued me. Smoke, a blast, or blast a smoke, who knows. Gunshot. I had never heard that before that day but I knew what it was. I knew it intimately and immediately. Something wet poured down the plane and washed my face. The blood of the lamb, I thought. But no, it was the blood of the Minotaur; his face was close to mine in the aisle when the smoke cleared. I looked into his dying eyes and I knew that there were more things in the heavens and on this godforsaken earth than I would ever understand.

His dying eyes looked the same as his living eyes. Our eyes met and then they dulled. One of us died.

We would leave Megiddo. We would wander the earth looking for a safe place, but there are no safe places.

In the next hour we were put on another plane. My mother's body was lifted and wrapped in a sheet and put on that plane, too. Someone washed my face but I could still smell and taste the man who had killed my mother. Demeter, I thought. Demeter. A mother's love. As Hades cleft the earth and pulled Persephone into the underworld, so had Demeter rescued me. She had pulled me from the pomegranates to the Garden of Eden, given me fruit and I had eaten. I had taken. I had survived. But at what cost? What price was paid?

The horsemen gave us water and food. They returned our passports. They spoke with each of us and told us how we were on our way to Rome. We would be brought to hospital and then to our embassies. We were safe.

The children were crying. Crying is good. It is a reaction, an expression of grief or relief. I would like to have cried but I was completely numb. I had no memory of how tears were formed. The man who had pulled me from the aisle and then thrust me down between the seats when the plane was stormed was saying something, but I couldn't hear or understand him. He took a handkerchief from his pocket and he wiped the blood of the Minotaur from my forehead and my cheeks. He got some water and he wiped my face again. 'We're flying to Rome,' he said. I didn't know what he meant. I had my passport in one pocket, my mother's perfume in another stuffed in with my wallet. I had money, some anyway, and my rail ticket, valid for a while longer. I would go home.

Then my mind closed down. I could feel it closing like steel shutters and it blocked off one bit after another until I could not remember my name or what I was supposed to be doing. The plane landed in the early dawn and I had no idea where we were or who I was or what was happening. We were ushered from our seats and out the doorway to descend the steps of Pegasus and I paused for a second and I looked at the sky and it was blue like yesterday's sky was blue, and the air was hot but the light was different. I waited to feel the cold barrel of the gun on my temple.

I stood there until a man in uniform came up the steps and took my hand and led me down and I wondered again where I was.

# CHAPTER EIGHTEEN

Morning arrived, and with it came the phone call to say that the passengers had been rescued and were on a flight to Rome. The television showed terrifying images in the dark of someone being shot in the doorway of the plane and the body plummeting to the ground. 'That wasn't Cassie,' Ali said. 'It wasn't Cassie,' she repeated desperately.

'No, it wasn't Cassie,' Karl said.

'One fatality among the passengers, all the hijackers dead...' the newsreader said as the picture moved to Rome and the arrival of the plane and the passengers being brought out. There was Cassie, looking surprised as she stopped and stared at the sky. This video clip would be used on the news in the coming days when Cassie disappeared. But at that moment, with no notion of what was already unfolding and that Cassie was already on the run, Karl mentally prepared to fly to Rome to fetch her.

Herr Brunner from the Ministry, who now felt like a bosom friend of the family, was rejoicing with them on the phone. Karl would be met at the airport and brought to the Embassy in Rome where Cassie would be escorted as soon as she was released from hospital. They were reassured that physically she was unhurt. The dead hostage had been identified.

In the midst of his relief, as the girls hugged each other and Oma came and put her arms around him, Karl told them the news.

'Sit down, girls,' he said. Bernd came and put his hand on Mer's shoulder. He had guessed immediately from Karl's voice, and indeed had already had suspicions when he saw the images of the hostages being swapped in that strange and violent moment in the doorway.

'Your mother,' Karl began. He could hardly find the words and was sorry now he had not told them the previous night that Miriam was on the plane. 'Your mother... she was on the plane. Somehow she traded places with Cassie... she is the hostage who died.'

They sat and looked at him in bewilderment.

'How...?' asked Ali.

'But...' said Mer.

'Yes,' said Karl. 'I... I heard last night that she was on the plane... I...'

'She's dead...' said Ali. A question or a statement, it was unclear.

'She took Cassie's place, and Cassie is safe,' Karl said. 'She gave us back Cassie.'

'Why was Miriam on the plane? How did that happen?' Mer was shouting. 'How did she get there?!'

Ali stood shaking in the centre of the room. 'How?' she kept saying over and over.

'We're not sure,' Karl said, coming and putting his arm around her. 'We don't know. We think that Cassie may have gone and found her.'

'But why? Did Cassie ever say she was going to do that?'

'No,' Karl led her to a chair and sat her in it. He felt he should have known, felt he should have done something to stop Cassie, but the truth was it had never occurred to him that she might have formed a plan to find her mother.

Mer now was weeping quietly on the sofa. Tears of relief mixed with tears of disbelief and grief. 'She must have loved us after all,' she said when she could speak.

'A mother's love,' Oma said coming to sit with her. 'A mother's love,' she repeated.

But Mer knew that the past had opened up again, come back to haunt them. All they had done to replace their loss from years earlier was back again. Images that she had replaced with the stories she wrote, the new life they had built, the comfort they had recreated in Germany slipped away and she and Ali were young girls again facing the unbelievable and the agonising loss that they would always carry.

'We should go with you to Rome,' Ali said quietly to Karl. 'We need to be there with Cassie.'

Karl nodded. 'Yes. Go and pack. I'll organise two more tickets. There'll be a car here shortly to bring us to Stuttgart. Pack lightly. We should be back tomorrow, or the day after.'

Their elation was subdued by shock as they stood in their rooms and collected what they needed.

***

They were on board a plane to Rome a few hours later. The flight seemed slow, but eventually they arrived and were met by a somewhat bewildered man from the embassy who had the unenviable task of telling them that Cassie had definitely got off the plane and had boarded the bus but had not been seen since.

'But how could this happen?' Karl asked.

'We don't know. She definitely got off the plane.'

'Yes, we know. We saw her on the television,' Mer said.

'The hostages were brought to various hospitals in the city. There are no real injuries among the passengers; dehydration and shock are the only problems. One dead, as you know, and I'm very sorry. I understand you were divorced, but I'm sorry for you all.'

'But Cassie...' Mer said.

'We have someone going around each of the hospitals talking to the other passengers. Some have already left and have gone to their embassies. We have found a man who was actually with Cassie when the plane was stormed and he will talk to you. He's at the Irish embassy. We're going to go there now.'

They were cordially received at the embassy, the Irish ambassador and his wife greeting them and offering commiserations. 'Please come in. Will you have tea or coffee? We had one passenger on the plane as you know, Tom Dunne. He is inside waiting, hoping to get on a plane tonight directly to Dublin.'

Tom Dunne stood up when they came into the room. They shook hands and sat down and hung on his every word.

'I'm afraid I can't tell you very much,' he said. He was in his late twenties or early thirties, tall and dark with an intelligent and kind face that seemed unnaturally pale. 'I've been told that Cassie has disappeared. She was in a state of shock when it was over. We all were, but she probably the most. Her ordeal had been worse than ours. I was sitting one row from the front on the other side of the plane to her seat, and she had been kept at gunpoint for most of the journey. When she was thrown down the aisle and swapped with her mother, she tried to get back to the door and I stopped her. I pulled her into the seat beside me. When the plane was stormed I pushed her to the floor and we stayed there till it was over. As you know, we were put on another plane and I stayed with her. We arrived in Rome and she was put in a different bus, or maybe an ambulance, I'm not sure. I lost her then and I didn't see her again. I'm afraid I'm not being of much use.'

'First of all, thank you for helping her.' Karl said.

'She was incredibly brave,' Tom said.

'Is there anything else you can tell us?' Mer asked.

'She was shocked. We all were. That's my overriding memory. There had been pandemonium when the plane was stormed, and afterwards a sense of disbelief, which was almost greater than the sense of relief. Even on the last flight, back here to Rome, I kept thinking none of this is really happening. When they gave us back our passports and checked who everyone was and that we were all accounted for, I had the feeling that she didn't really know what was happening. But that wasn't surprising, as none of us did. I still can't believe that I'm alive. No doubt she felt the same.'

'Did she say anything?'

'Nothing. They gave us hot drinks and food. She had the blood of one of the hijackers on her face and clothes. I wiped it off. There were a lot of people crying. I spoke to her. I tried to encourage her to eat something. She drank whatever drink they gave her. I told the man who was looking after us that she was very shaken. He said she would be cared for once we landed. I tried to talk to her several times, but I felt she couldn't hear me or wasn't listening. I suggested she slept. She kept looking at me. When we landed I told them again that I felt something was wrong. Nothing was right. I mean something else. I came down the steps before her and I realised she had stopped at the top. I told them that she was in shock, and that she had been held at gunpoint for most of the flights, and then someone went up to help her. That was the last I saw of her.'

They sat there digesting his words. Karl broke the silence first. 'Thank you for what you did, both for protecting her when her mother was killed, and for your kindness to her during that last flight. We should leave you to your own recovery, but I wonder if we could take your contact details just in case...'

'Of course. I don't think there is anything I can add though.'

They stood to leave, and while Karl thanked the ambassador and his wife, Tom approached Ali and gave her his address.

'You live in Monkstown?' Ali said. 'That's a coincidence. We lived there too when we were children, at Seapoint.'

'I swam there as a child.'

Karl came over and put his arm around Ali's shoulders.

'Tom lives near Seapoint,' Ali said passing her father the address.

'Bit of a coincidence,' Tom said.

She gazed at him, wondering about the events that had brought both him and her sister to be on that ill-fated flight.

'What are you going to do now?' he asked.

'We'll stay here until we find her. She can't have got far,' Ali said.

'I have to leave shortly,' he said. 'My parents have been out of their minds... well, you know, the way you have been feeling. I have to get home to see them, otherwise I would stay and help. Can we keep in touch?'

She nodded. 'Yes,' she said. 'Do you still swim at Seapoint?'

He smiled. 'Yes, regularly.'

They left then, Karl and Mer coming to shake Tom's hand. 'Thank you again for the part you have played in all of this,' Karl said.

'A safe journey home,' Mer said to him.

They went back to the German embassy, and a hotel was found for them nearby. 'I don't think I can sleep,' Mer said. 'I feel we should be out on the streets looking for Cassie. She must be somewhere not too far away.'

'I'll drive us around for a bit if you like. A statement has been released to the press and the police are looking for her. We'll find her. It's just a question of time.'

They drove around the streets for over an hour until Karl said, 'I feel this is pointless. We need sleep. Tomorrow's another day.'

***

And so began a whole new episode in their lives as they started the search for Cassie. The papers the following day were full of the siege and the release of the hostages. They carried a grainy picture of Cassie standing in the door of the plane with a gun to her head, and another one of her standing at the top of the steps looking up at the sky. The article explained that she was missing and was probably in shock.

Events unfolded slowly as no trace of Cassie was found. In England the police went to the houseboat, which was now empty. Elsa did not return. In Greece the police were asked to see if they could find her as Karl felt there was the possibility that maybe Miriam and Cassie had been with her there. There was no trace of her. Photographs of Cassie were put up on walls in Rome with a reward offered for information leading to her return. They searched night and day for nearly two weeks until one evening Karl said to Ali and Mer, 'She may not want to be found. She may need time to deal with what has happened...'

'We can't give up,' Mer said.

'We'll never give up,' Ali said.

'We're not giving up. We need to reconsider...'

They went to the embassy, where they were advised to go home. 'We check the hospitals every day. We are in constant contact with the police. You ought to go home.'

'I think one of us should stay,' Mer said. 'I can defer for another year. Under the circumstances I am sure they will let me. I can stay here and write and look for her. It doesn't matter to me where I write.'

'But you have Bernd waiting for you,' Ali said. Bernd had come to Rome and had helped for a week and then had gone back home. 'Perhaps I should stay. There's an American College here where I could do my Masters. My Italian isn't good enough yet to do it in the university.'

'No, Ali,' Karl said. 'I don't want to inhibit you in any way, but you have been through so much and you are still vulnerable. I think you should be with the family for a while longer.'

Ali smiled at him, a wry, sad smile. 'Papa,' she said. 'I've moved on. I didn't think that I could, I didn't think I had the strength, but what happened over the last few weeks has changed all of that. My focus is different. I know it's less than two months since I left... Maurice,' she struggled to say his name, it stuck in her throat. 'But it seems so much longer. There is such a space between that part of my life and now. I look back and I can't believe I was that person, or that I couldn't see that I had to leave him. Distance has changed the perspective and, while I feel totally exhausted by what has happened to Cassie and this search for her, I am so far removed from the ridiculous situation I got myself into.'

'Ridiculous?' Karl said. 'Not the word I would have chosen, but I'm glad you see it differently now.'

They went back to Germany, a strained and sad journey, where Oma met them at their home. She had stayed there in case Cassie had somehow turned up, while Opa had returned to the farm. Bernd was there waiting for Mer, and she clung to him in silence. They walked by the river. 'It's unbearable,' she eventually said. 'I think of Cassie so young and so frightened, a gun to her head, being thrown around that plane, of her being there when our mother was murdered, and I can't begin to imagine the fear and the sense of powerlessness. I keep wondering if she is hiding somewhere like a wounded animal, and then I think that maybe she doesn't know who she is. They said she was in a state of shock. What if she is still in that state of shock and is living on the streets...'

'I know,' Bernd said. 'I know.'

'I'll never stop looking for her,' Mer said.

'I know that, too,' Bernd said.

# CASSIE'S TALE

They took us on buses from the plane to the terminal where ambulances, soldiers and police were waiting. I slipped away either there or at the hospital, I still don't remember. I ran through the streets trying to find somewhere I recognised. I saw the station and the trains and I knew a train would bring me somewhere so I produced my ticket and boarded it. Was it that day? Or was it the next? Or days later? I don't know.

I seem to remember sleeping under a bridge by a river. Once I saw a picture of me on newspaper billboard. I hid. I boarded a train. I bought a drink and I may have slept. We moved from country to country. I saw mountains and hills and fields and small towns. I bought food on the train and at some point I got off and took another one.

All places, all people, all are linked. Sometimes we see the link. Sometimes it eludes us.

The train stopped in Strasbourg. I knew that name. That city. The statue of justice with her scales. There was something I had to do here. Something I could not remember. I found the cathedral. I stood outside hoping I would remember. So many people. I could not remember.

A wise or a foolish virgin; I did not know which.

# CHAPTER NINETEEN

D o you ever feel we are extraordinarily unlucky?' Ali asked Mer.
'How do you mean?

'Do you really want me to list the bad luck in our lives? You had
cancer as a baby and then got that vein thing later, our mother left us,
I married a complete bastard, Cassie was on a hijacked plane and then
disappeared... our mother was murdered...'

Mer looked surprised. 'No,' she said eventually. 'I don't think it's
anything other than chance. You are forgetting about all the good
things. I survived cancer and I live very well with the other problem.
You were in love for a little while. I am in love now. We've had
wonderful times in our lives, wonderful memories, and we have hope.
We can't live life examining the past, not our past anyway.'

'Why are you always so positive?' Ali asked.

'The world has never been a safe place,' Mer said. 'We have no
reason to think it ever will be. That doesn't mean that we can't hope it
will be, and that we can't hope that everything will be all right, but we
don't recognise it when it is. We're not grateful enough for the good
things. It's awful right now, with Cassie missing I mean... but it will be
all right. We'll find her, I just know we will. She found our mother.
Granted, it didn't work out very well...'

'That's the understatement of the year. I wish Cassie had never
found her. I can't imagine why she went looking for her.'

'Don't you feel anything for her, our mother I mean?'

'No. Yes. Maybe. It's not clear. I sometimes think that I stayed with
Maurice because of her.'

'How do you mean?'

'I didn't want to be the kind of person who ran away. And before
you say anything, I do see now that there is no real comparison. I don't

for one moment believe that Papa was cruel to her. And I don't know why she ran off and left us. Papa once told me that she left us for someone else. It was an explanation of sorts at least, though I hated her for loving someone else more than Papa and us.'

'I didn't know that. I didn't know he had told you that. I sometimes wondered,' Mer said thoughtfully. 'I suppose it doesn't matter any more anyway.'

'I felt sick all over again when it turned out that someone was Elsa. The whole thing is sickening.'

'Does it matter that it was Elsa?' Mer asked.

'Maybe not. I don't know. I think I should have known it was Elsa, but for some reason I didn't. I had an image of her running off with some man, a knight in shining armour, fairy tale stuff. It left us abandoned, bereft, and I tried not to think about her new life. In some ways it's all easier now that she is dead. But it's so sad. I feel so sad. Like we were strange accidents of birth. Our parents happened to meet. We happened to be born. I keep thinking how glad I am that I had no children with Maurice. If I had, I would have been repeating that pattern because surely I would have left him earlier? Surely I would have wanted to protect my child and I would have got us out of there? And then, I think that maybe if I had had a child with him, maybe he would have been different.'

'Do you really believe that?'

'No. I can't say I do. But I do think about it. It keeps coming up in my mind. I was so desperate not to be like Miriam. So desperate to create a good place where I could live, and yet in my own way I did repeat what she did.'

'No, you didn't,' Mer said. 'Ali, you didn't. You made a mistake. You fell in love and he turned out to be very much the wrong man.'

'But is that not that what our mother did? Did she not fall for the first man who came her way, and she married him and later realised it was all wrong for her?'

'I have no idea. Maybe he was all right for her for a certain period of time, and then she just couldn't handle things. Don't you remember how she used to go on about wanting to be a hippy? Wasn't it odd that she did not want to be called Mum or Mummy?'

'I used to like that about her,' Ali said. 'I felt she was very modern and it made us different from other children. Special, maybe. Later I realised I just wanted to be like other children. The normal family.'

'Whatever that is,' Mer said. 'I don't think there's any such thing. I think behind the closed doors of other people's houses there are the same disturbances happening. I don't mean the same as behind our closed doors, I mean other disturbances. Things we never hear about. Arguments, unhappiness, lack of communication.'

Ali looked at her. 'You never fail to surprise me, Mer,' she said. 'Growing up, you were always so naive and vulnerable. I thought your illnesses had made you that way.'

'I wasn't vulnerable,' Mer said.

'Maybe it's the wrong word. But I know I had a need to protect you. And yet, here we are all these years later, and you are more in control than any of us. At least that's the way it seems. I got things so wrong. Cassie… well, Cassie got into an even bigger mess...'

'But aren't these things that just happen? We make choices when we can, and sometimes those choices are right. You happened to choose wrong, but you have the chance to try again. Cassie will too. I suppose it's not surprising that she went looking for Miriam. It's just awful the way that turned out. But if Cassie had not been on that plane, it would be some other family going through what we are going through. That's life. It happens to be us.'

'Nothing is clear, is it?'

'Yes and no. But there is closure; for us and our mother, we have finally found closure. And when we find Cassie, we will find out more about our mother and why she left.'

'What if we don't find Cassie?'

Mer grimaced. 'We have to. It's as simple as that. We will keep on looking for her and waiting for her, and eventually we'll find her.'

'What if she has been murdered or something and we never find out?'

'Don't say that, Ali. We have to live with hope.'

Their roles had changed, and they both knew it. Ali had been picking up the pieces of her own life when the hijacking occurred, and the unfolding events had both distracted her and given her a sense of resolve. Mer had grown more slowly from strength to strength, and while she was as devastated as her sister, she had more support. She had been in a stronger place when Cassie's plane had been hijacked, and that gave her more strength now.

'I wonder how Papa is getting on,' Ali said.

***

Karl had left the previous evening to stay overnight with his parents, and then to meet with the lawyer his father had retained. The lawyer was dealing with Ali's divorce. Opa had already been to see him and had set the proceedings in motion. The lawyer had contacted Maurice a week or so earlier, and said they were coming to see him, and suggested he had a lawyer there too.

By the time Karl arrived at his parents' farm, however, circumstances had changed.

His father was waiting for him, and their original plans to have dinner out, an early night and the visit to Maurice the following day had undergone a transformation of the kind Karl would never have expected.

'I got a call from the Calliers' lawyer about an hour ago,' Opa said to him. 'It seems there was an accident of some sort. Maurice is dead, he was hit by a bus and was killed instantaneously.'

'What? When?'

'Some days ago I think.'

'Why didn't his parents contact us?'

'They're probably in shock. And I suppose because we made no contact with them once Ali left Maurice they saw no reason.'

Karl mulled this over in his mind. 'What happens now?'

'We are to go to Maurice's parents' home tomorrow with our lawyer, as arranged. They will have their lawyer there.'

'Should I come too?' Oma had asked Opa earlier.

'No, Karl needs to deal with this. I think he feels that he let Ali down, and this is one actual thing he can do for her.'

'This will be fine,' Karl's father now said to him.

'Did he die leaving a will?'

'I have no idea.'

'I will do the talking,' the lawyer said the following morning when they met in Strasbourg and drove from the city out into the countryside to the Calliers' mansion set at the end of a long, straight driveway, where even the trees seemed unbending in the breeze.

The lawyer was disbelieving when Karl admitted he had never met Maurice's parents. 'They were kept away from us for some reason, and yes, I should have insisted, but I didn't want to interfere in Ali's life. I wanted access to it, but I didn't know how to do that without hurting her.'

He described how he had looked at the photographs of Ali lying in the hospital bed and read the medical report. 'You should have insisted on pursuing this with the police,' the lawyer said.

'Ali was too afraid,' Karl had explained. For some reason this too now sounded lame, and he felt again that he had let her down.

Standing outside Maurice's parents' home, Karl thought how much he disliked confrontation, and he could only hope that the lawyer was right and that this could be handled quickly and quietly. Cassie's absence was eating into him and he just wanted to get through this so that he could return to the girls and continue the search.

The lawyer knocked on the door. A maid answered and showed them in.

They had stood in the hallway until a man appeared and introduced himself as the lawyer for the Calliers.

The two lawyers appeared to know each other and they greeted each other cordially.

'Let's go into the dining-room and you can meet Mr and Mrs Callier,' he said as he ushered them across the marble hallway and into a room at one side.

Maurice's parents stood as they entered the room.

'These are strange and sad circumstances for us to be meeting,' Karl said as they shook hands. 'On behalf of my family, I am sorry for your loss.'

It seemed almost beyond his comprehension that he had travelled the previous day to fight for a divorce for his daughter, looking for small settlement to help her start her new life, and now they were sitting dealing with Maurice's death, wondering what implications that death was going to involve.

'They were already separated,' the Calliers' lawyer said, 'and we would contest that Maurice's will, in which he left everything to his wife, should now be null and void.'

'I think not,' Ali's lawyer said. 'She was still his wife in the eyes of the law, and of course I am sure you would not want these to go into public record.' He pulled out the photographs and the medical records from Ali's stay in the hospital.

A stunned silence followed as both of Maurice's parents looked at the documents. Maurice's mother lifted one of the photographs and then looked at Karl in sadness before standing, pushing aside her chair, turning and walking out of the room. Karl knew from the slump and slight shake of her shoulders that she was weeping.

Maurice's father read and re-read the report before replacing it and the photos in the file and pushing it back across the table. 'There will be no contest to the will,' he said after a long silence.

Sitting across the dining table, Karl felt a moment's compassion for these people who had lost their son, but it was removed, distant from his reality. His daughter had been bullied and beaten by their son. He sat silently and contemplated, not for the first time, what this would mean for Ali. Not divorced, but widowed and wealthy. Would that be easier for her? He had no idea.

They left with more than they had ever expected.

When they stood in the hallway, Maurice's mother rejoined them for a few moments.

'I am sorry for your loss,' Karl said again.

'I too am sorry,' she said. He thought or maybe hoped that she was referring to what her son had done to his daughter. He could not be sure.

Walking down the steps to the car he wondered how any parent could actually protect their children. Everything seemed terribly random to him. His father touched his arm in the car. 'At least we can now concentrate on Cassie without having to face a court hearing,' he said.

\*\*\*

Karl came home from Strasbourg. 'Ali, we need to talk.'

She was dreading this. She could not begin to imagine what it was like for him going to pick up the remnants of her marriage. There had been shame before, but it was now enhanced. He would finally meet her parents-in-law to settle a divorce; he who had asked so often over those years to meet the people who had produced her husband. She felt many things, but shame was to the fore. He had been so kind to her about her marriage and her abandonment of her own family, and she knew it. 'It's all right,' he had said to her. Not once, but a thousand times.

'Should I not face this myself?' she had asked. And he had said no. And she, not just traumatised by the untimely end to her marriage, but also by the far worse events that had subsequently happened with Cassie on the plane, had sat and stared at him. 'Papa, is this not asking too much...?'

She had the feeling he was pleased he could do something positive for her.

She had spent that day thinking of what it must be like for him to go there to fight on her behalf. She had no idea what he would encounter, and when he came home and said they must talk, she felt a terrible sense of fear. His face was so still, almost as if he were looking through her, and she was terrified what he might say. She feared, most of all, that he had met Maurice and that he had told her father that she was a bad wife; that somehow all the blame would land on her. There was nothing to prepare her for his words.

'Mer, come and sit with Ali,' he said. Mer, surprised, came and sat with Ali on the sofa in the living-room. She remembered sitting just so, but with Cassie, one day a long time ago in their house at Seapoint.

She slipped her arm around Ali's shoulders. They both sat mute.

Karl walked to the window and then back. 'Ali,' he said. 'Look, I don't even know where to begin with this... Let me just say it. It appears there was an accident some time after you left, and Maurice was hit by a bus. He was killed. He died.'

Ali and Mer sat and looked at him, and suddenly Ali began to laugh. The laugh started low and then it rose. From an ordinary laugh it became hysterical. She laughed and laughed. 'Of all the things I thought you might say, that was not one of them. Dead? Maurice?'

'We were in Rome when it happened,' Karl said.

Ali stopped laughing as though she could suddenly understand what he was saying. Maurice was dead. Gone. The relief was enormous. There would be no divorce proceedings, no papers to sign, it was over. A line had been put under that chapter of her life.

'Are you all right?' Mer asked her. She had been startled at Ali's laughter, now she could see it was just a reaction.

'Is it my fault?' Ali asked.

'Your fault?'

'If I had not left him, maybe he would not have been just where he was at that moment...'

'That's nonsense,' Karl said. 'Accidents happen. It's done. There are a few things we have to talk about.'

Ali looked at him and sighed. She felt she should be crying but there were no tears. She need never see Maurice again; *would* never see him. It was over.

'What kind of things?'

'Well, for starters, it appeared he had just bought a new car. A black Porsche. It's yours.'

'I don't want it,' Ali said.

'Wouldn't it be nice for you to have a car again?'

She smiled. 'Yes. But I'd like to have a little pale blue Volkswagen.'

'Shall I arrange for the Porsche to be sold?' Karl asked.

She nodded.

He would tell her about the fortune later.

As she lay in bed that night, the sense of relief was still overwhelming. She did not wish Maurice dead, but knowing now that it was really all over, she felt something akin to euphoria. She did not want to feel like that. Euphoria was not a good feeling as she knew that the opposite would come in later. She feared coming down from that feeling and did not want to feel despair again. She lay there sleepless, telling herself to be relieved that that period of her life was really over; that there really was no going back; that Maurice would never appear on the doorstep looking for her, and that she would never accidentally encounter him somewhere on the street.

# CASSIE'S TALE

The wheels on the bus... A bus, I thought as I stood there in Strasbourg outside the Cathedral. I would get on a bus.

I walked away and headed for the canal. I saw a man.

Someone else's Minotaur.

He stood at the edge of the pavement looking at his expensive golden watch. His arrogant handsome face. His cold eyes. I approached him. I stood in front of him. I looked at him. He looked at me. For a second his eyes widened in surprise, but there was no steel barrel of a gun on my brow, and I stepped forwards to confront this particular monster. And as I stepped forward, he stepped back off the pavement, missed his footing and fell. The bus did not miss him. The wheels on the bus went round and round and then they stopped.

I walked away.

Somewhere on the edge of the city I hitched a lift in a lorry where I dozed. I saw the driver's nose twitch and I knew that I smelled putrid. We drove for hours. I pretended to sleep. I crawled into the back of the lorry when he stopped to fill his tank. He got back in, and finding me gone he sprayed the cabin. I heard the whoosh of the spray and knew he was trying to get rid of the stench. Ulysses encountered that stench. Philoctetes I think. He was wounded and stank so badly they had to leave him behind. I slept then. I felt the lorry drive on to a ferry and I felt the swell of the waves and I wondered if I was nearly home. I knew my home was at the sea. It was about the only thing I did remember.

We arrived somewhere and once again the lorry revved up and we drove ashore. I heard my driver talk through the window with someone in the dark. 'My last trip,' he said. 'I drop the lorry off tomorrow, and then home. My wife and I are moving to Australia. A fresh start. She's packed and ready. We leave immediately. Good bye England.'

'And g'day Australia? Well, good luck.'

'Thank you. I can't wait.'

England. Not where I had intended. I climbed out of the lorry when he stopped shortly afterwards, and I walked until I found a beach. It was too dark to see if it was the right beach, my beach, and I was very cold. I walked to the waters' edge and I stripped off my clothes and I swam in the dark before dressing again, my clothes pulling uncomfortably against my wet salty skin. I threw my passport into the sea. I no longer had any use for it. It meant nothing. I had no name now. It had gone back to the waves.

It was so cold.

I was so cold.

I lay down on the pebbly sand and I fell asleep, and as I closed my eyes I knew I was back in the Underworld and I called for Demeter.

Beaches are different. This was not the right beach; maybe not even the right country. I just knew it was not Seapoint. All beaches encounter the sea; the waves wash in and throw up the pebbles and the shells and the tiny grains of sand ground down forever and ever. Ground down. Mum, Momma, Mama, Mother, I seek for a name. Miriam. Demeter. Demeter. She saved her daughter. She found Persephone. She brought her back to earth.

She saved me. I remember the electric shock from the strip of carpet down the aisle of the plane. My grazed knees burned as they skidded on it. My hands grasped at nothingness. She had said, 'take me.' And the Minotaur did.

He took her.

He took Demeter and she never got to look into the bottom of Pandora's box.

Or maybe she had. Maybe once long ago she looked into that box and out flew all the things she could not handle. I don't think she was a strong person. I don't think she knew how to evaluate. She gave me her perfume. I sprayed it on my wrists and I breathed it in, day after day, week after week. It was my last link. In Greece she had let Medusa lead her. 'We're going to dinner.' 'We're going to the Acropolis.' 'We're taking a boat.' 'We're going to the bar...' Oh, Medusa and the Gorgons.

Demeter followed her. She did what Medusa wanted. I tagged along, always thinking it will get better, she will notice me, she will know I need something. Demeter whispered, 'When we get back to London, we'll talk properly then.' I waited and waited.

I saw her as someone I did not know nor understand.

Then there was a moment on an island when I said, 'I'm going to swim. Are you coming, Mum?' And there was a look in her eyes. She looked at Medusa. She looked at me. She was trapped.

I smiled. 'I'll meet you both later,' I said, 'at the bar.' I let her off the hook. She let me let her off the hook.

Later she let me off the hook in the doorway of the plane.

I was too young to remember clearly when she left. I was eight years old. Yes, that day was etched into my mind, but in a vague and blurry way. Before she left, when I was a little girl, we played at the beach, we swam on warm and cold days. I played in the garden. Sometimes I sat on her knee. But not often. I don't remember our connection. Our home functioned but she was not at the helm. I think we thought she was. But she was weak. I saw it that day when I said I would meet her at the bar. There was relief in her eyes. Medusa ruled. Perhaps Papa had ruled before that. Perhaps she needed that but thought she needed freedom. Perhaps she found freedom of a sort with Medusa, that the burdens of being with Papa were too heavy. Three burdens, Ali, Mer and me.

I swam in clear blue water on that Greek island beach, keeping an eye on my towel and clothes on the beach. They had gone and left me and I knew then that there was no going back. I wanted my sisters there. I wanted to swim with them. I wanted us to rise from the sea as Venuses. I found a shell and held it to my ear and there was an echo of waves reverberating eternally. I stayed on the beach until darkness fell and I knew that no one would look for me, that no one would find me; I waited until the stars fell from the skies and I was tired and I walked back to the village, bypassing the bar where Demeter and Medusa were drinking Retsina or Ouzo, or probably both, and I found our tiny hotel and I went to bed.

I wished that night, and not for the first time, that I had not bought that rail ticket and that I had stayed in Tübingen and found a summer job, that I could walk along the riverbank and dream, swing in the tree in the garden behind the house, and in the evening sit with Mer and draw and paint pictures to go with her stories, smell the Hefekuchen rising...

I wished. I wished a thousand things, and most of all I wished that I was not on that island waiting for something to happen that could never happen.

That island, that beach, that swim changed.

It became another beach, cold with stones cutting into my skin. So thin. My skin. So horrifyingly thin. To live. To die. The cast of the dice. I stood in the doorway of the plane and saw the earth beneath, and Demeter said, 'take me,' and then I was on the carpet in the aisle. She must have known.

She must have felt that it was the end. I know, I know with all my heart and soul that she gave herself for me. A man... some man... he pulled me into the seat beside him. 'When it starts, get down...' When it ends, get up. Do all the things you are supposed to do, and the world is your oyster. I had held that shell to my ear. I had tried so hard to be ... what? A daughter? A sister? A schoolgirl? A human being? I had looked inhumanity in the face and I had seen betrayal on all levels.

The stones on the cold beach cut into my flesh. The skin on my wrists was thin. I found a rusty razor blade on the beach, eaten by tide and salt, and I slashed the hair from my head. Blonde tufts lay on the sand. The wind lifted them and carried them back to the sea. I shivered in the morning light. And then I closed down the last shutter. I shuttered the shutters, and I put the lid back on Pandora's accursed box.

# CHAPTER TWENTY

Time passed. The slow ticking of the clock on the mantelpiece marked it out, the seconds and minutes that dragged and stretched painfully into weeks and months. A long slow year passed. Eight thousand, seven hundred and sixty hours, as Ali said.

Mer's first book had been purchased by an Italian publisher and was being translated. Mer's agent had arranged a meeting with her publisher at Mer's request. She and Ali flew to Rome where Ali had gone to the embassy to check in with them in person. This had become a regular routine. As expected there was no news, but it gave them the feeling that they were doing something and that they were keeping Cassie's name alive and out there.

There was a photograph of Cassie in the embassy and Ali touched it with her fingertips. As long as there were photographs up on walls or appearing in the media there was still hope. She was met with kindness, hospitality, a cup of coffee, a short conversation, but there had been no developments. She could not help thinking that the patience and understanding she was receiving might not last if she and Mer turned up every other month for the rest of their lives looking for help. For how long would they be prepared to put up with these two forlorn sisters inquiring about their missing sister while knowing there was no progress? Their father phoned the embassy in Rome every Monday evening and the Ministry in Bonn every Friday.

Ali felt exhausted when she left the embassy. She told herself it was not a wasted journey. As long as people knew they were still looking, that surely that raised the chances of finding Cassie. She had discussed raising the value of the award for anyone with information leading to the finding of her sister. Her contact in the embassy seemed reticent, and she had the feeling that they didn't want to be inundated with responses as they had been in the earlier days. She agreed to give her address as the contact.

She walked slowly down the street thinking, as she always did, about what other avenue they could pursue.

Meanwhile, Mer was meeting with her new publisher. 'Ah, Merope, at last.' She was greeted with open arms and kisses on both cheeks and shown through the publishing house and introduced around. 'Welcome on board,' she was told, over and over. She smiled at everyone and shook hands, pleased at the reception she was getting, though impatient to get through it as she could not wait to sit down with her publisher and discuss details. She had a plan and she needed to sell it.

Just as Ali had coffee in the embassy in a quiet office, Mer too sat in due course with her editor on a plush red chair in a conference room. There were copies of the contracts on the table, a pen at the ready. Coffee was served and Mer sat back and looked at the woman who was looking after her, a chic and smartly dressed woman who seemed anxious to get the required signatures.

'We are delighted you came to visit us,' her editor said. 'It's not often that an author we are translating comes to see us.'

'I'm here on a mission,' Mer said. 'As you know I wrote this book and the next one that you are buying. My younger sister Cassie did the artwork for both, though I will be signing the contracts for the pair of us.'

'Ah, yes, Cassie, such a talented artist...'

'Yes,' Mer said. 'I know that my agent has told you that Cassie is missing. She has been for twelve months now.'

'I do indeed know. I remember the whole hijacking incident all too clearly. I recall reading that she had disappeared afterwards. There has been no news?'

'No. Nothing. She was last seen getting off a plane here in Rome, and since then not a thing. My father and my older sister Ali and I are doing everything we can to keep her profile in the public eye. Now, I know it is impossible to tell how well this book will do, but your initial print run is ten-thousand copies, or so my agent tells me. I want to ask you if you will put Cassie's picture on it. I know you can't put it on the front cover which is where I would like it,' Mer said with a small smile. 'But would you put it on the back cover? Would you say that the artist is missing? If you sell ten-thousand copies, then at least that many people will see it. It's a children's book, so is most likely to be bought by parents, doubling the number who see it immediately. Children are naturally curious. They will see the picture...'

'I understand. I really do. Let me think for a moment. In fact, I think I should consult with a colleague as this would not be our usual style at all. But there is a way around everything. Do drink your coffee and I will be back to you shortly.'

Mer sat there eyeing the contracts and sipping her coffee. At least they were considering it, she thought. That was something. She knew from her agent that this kind of request would normally be brushed aside, but the publisher seemed to have compassion and undertanding.

She came back with a man and they sat down with Mer.

'Look, we would like to help you, but there are a number of issues. Cassie may be found before this goes to print; I'm sure you've thought of that.'

'Of course. It's what we hope for every single day,' Mer said.

'So, we cannot put on it that she is missing, because if she's back by then it will be too late to change the cover. Also, if we put her photo on the book without explaining why, then we would need to put yours too. It's a question of symmetry. All of this may well be resolved shortly.'

'But if it isn't...' Mer said.

'We understand. Let's do it this way. We put Cassie's picture on the back, and yours inside the back cover. That way we have a semblance of balance assuming Cassie has already been found. And when the book comes out we will throw some kind of a party in one of the larger bookshops and get publicity for the book...'

'And for Cassie if she has not been found by then...'

'Yes. We will make sure that the publicity includes her disappearance. Merope, you mustn't give up hope.'

'I haven't and I never will. I think each day that it will be today that she returns. Right now my older sister is in the German embassy here in Rome. We try to come back every few weeks, every chance we get, and each day we think it may be today... but just in case it's not, that's why I was asking for this bit of publicity for Cassie.'

'Don't worry. You'll get it. If she hasn't been found by then, it will throw her back into the public eye.'

'Thank you. I'm grateful.'

'Have your books been translated into other languages?'

'Just into English. They were bought before Cassie disappeared and unfortunately have gone into print. I say unfortunately because it happened before I thought of this idea... Cassie's photograph I mean.'

'It's not often we hear of an author regretting a publication. But I'm sure other translation rights will be sold, and you can get her picture on the books. The fact that we are doing it will give you leverage. Now, let's get these contracts re-drafted and signed, and then may we take you out to lunch?'

'Thank you,' Mer said, 'but I've to meet my sister. We're going to stick pictures of Cassie all along the river on walls and trees and down in the major tourist spots. It's what we do each time we come here.'

'I understand.'

***

Those few days passed quickly with no results, and they returned home, their feet sore and their hearts as heavy as the day that Cassie disappeared although they tried, unsuccessfully, to hide this emotion from each other.

'I feel more positive,' Ali said. 'At least we know that something big will happen when the book is published. You did well, Mer.'

'We both did,' Mer said. 'Now, when is the next time you are free to go back to Rome? I'll book our flights tomorrow.'

'I was thinking…' Ali said slowly.

'Yes?'

'Just suppose Cassie didn't stay in Rome, or even in Italy. I know we've gone over about this before, but let's talk about it again. Just supposing she went somewhere else, where do you think she would go?'

'Here I think,' Mer said.

'Okay, but she didn't come here. Where else do you think she might go?'

'Seapoint? Our old home in Dublin? Do you think she could have got there?'

'I don't know, but when I think about her I always connect her with the sea.'

'Not with sliding down banisters and swinging in trees?' Mer asked.

'No, I think about her in a particular place and I wonder if she might have gone to Dublin.'

'I can't imagine how she could have, but it's not impossible. Everyone felt that she must be in Italy. Do you want to go to Dublin then and I will get Bernd to come back with me to Rome? He had wanted to come this time.'

'You should have said. We could all have gone.'

'Well, first of all these trips are costing so much money, money that you inherited from Maurice… and secondly there are some things I need to do with you. Bernd and I have our time together. You and I looking together has seemed the right thing up until now. But you're right. We have nothing to lose by looking further afield.'

While they were unpacking and sorting out their clothing for the laundry, she called in to Mer. 'I feel much better when we have a plan in place,' she said.

'I do too. It gives us something to focus on, and I think that's what we need more than anything right now.'

'One of us should give Papa a call and tell him we're back. You or me?'

'It's your turn I think.'

They both hated the phone call in question, dreading hearing his hopeful voice, and then the slump in it when there was no news.

'I find myself saying silly things like "no news is good news" and clichés like that, and it irks me. It's not the way I usually talk,' Mer had said some time earlier on the return from a previous trip searching the streets of Rome.

'I know what you mean.' They both found it so difficult carrying their father as well as themselves, and had decided to take it in turns, or whichever of them felt stronger on the day in question would make the phone call. They could have waited until he got home from work, and had done that the first few times, until they realised that when he came in the door he actually hoped that Cassie was with them.

Ali went downstairs to phone their father, postponing it for another few minutes as she looked through the mail on the hall table. One envelope, addressed to her, was postmarked Dublin with an Irish stamp. What a coincidence, she thought, as she and Mer had just been talking about going there. She put it aside, assuming it was from one of her childhood friends who every so often sent her a card or a short letter, although she only sporadically replied, and now that she thought about it, she realised that she had not replied in quite some time.

She phoned their father, reassuring him that they were safely back, that the embassy was still keeping its feelers in place, checking with the police and with hospitals.

'There are some positive things to tell you,' she said. 'No news, nothing like that, but Mer and I have a plan afoot.'

'Good,' he said, but she could hear the despondency in his voice. 'I'll be home in an hour.'

'Maybe we should go out for dinner tonight?' Ali suggested.

'If you like,' he said.

Hanging up the phone, Ali turned around to find Mer standing in the doorway looking at her.

'Everything okay?' Mer asked.

Ali shrugged. 'You know.'

'I do,' Mer said. 'Maybe I should have called him instead of you. And you're right about dinner. We need to go out, even if we've both had enough of bars and restaurants from the last week. We'll go out. We'll put a positive spin on events.'

'It's just easier to talk to you than to him. I know exactly the place you're in, how you're feeling. In fact we don't even need to talk, we just look at each other and know. We can cover it up, but we both know. But with Papa it's different. I keep trying to put myself in his shoes and I just see unending despair and desperation, which is what we're feeling too. Oh, I don't know how to express any of this.'

'I know,' Mer said. 'But we have a new plan. Cassie's photo will be on the book. You are going to check in Dublin. Speaking of which, have you given that trip further thought?'

'Yes. I'm going to contact a radio station. I need an agent,' Ali said, 'like you have.'

'Well, I'll call my agent and see if she has any contacts in Dublin that you can use while you are there,' Mer said, determination in her voice. 'And you have to take my camera with you as I would love some photos of the sea and Howth.'

'Consider it done,' Ali said, as she opened the letter from Ireland.

*Dear Ali,*

*I think of you often and wonder how you, your sister and father are doing. I also wonder if you have had any news at all about Cassie. It has been a long year and I should have written to you earlier. I had meant to, but the time never seemed right.*

*From time to time I have contacted the German Embassy here to see if there has been any news. They are not very forthcoming, but the answer appears to be no.*

*I would so like to hear how you are and if there is anything I can do.*

*You are in my thoughts. My brother and my parents send you their kindest regards.*

*Affectionately,*

*Tom Dunne*

Ali passed the letter to Mer. 'What a timing coincidence,' she said. 'It's from that Irishman we met in the embassy in Rome last year.'

'That's lovely,' Mer said, having read the letter and passing it back.

'I wonder why he wrote now. It seems a very long time since we met him.'

'He's probably had a difficult year too. It's hard to think of how other people have handled this time, but obviously he is thinking of us. It's nice that he wrote. You should see him when you are in Dublin,' Mer suggested.

'I'm not sure. It was the briefest of meetings that day in Rome.'

'Well, don't exclude it as a possibility,' Mer said.

\*\*\*

Three weeks later, Ali flew to Dublin. Her flight was late and she only arrived just in time at the radio station. She was nervous as she introduced herself in reception and was rushed down a corridor to the interview room. As she sat down behind her microphone, she forced herself to push aside the jittery feeling she had and to concentrate on the purpose of her being there.

'Today we have Ali Peters with us,' the presenter said. 'Ali has just flown in from Germany to be with us and she is here with a mission. I'll let her tell you her story.'

'Thank you,' Ali said. 'Yes, a mission describes it perfectly. I have two sisters and they were both born here in Dublin. Many of your listeners will remember the hijacking last summer of the flight from Athens to London. My youngest sister Cassie was on that plane. I know that photographs of her standing in front of the hijacker reached the newspapers around the world, and later when the hijacking ended and the passengers were flown to Rome, my sister Cassie disappeared. That is a year ago now and we still don't know where she is.'

'Do you have reason to think she might be in Dublin?'

'No. No hard facts I'm afraid. It's just that we have tried everything else we can think of, concentrating on Italy as it seemed that she must be there. But on our most recent trip to Rome, I started to think about where I would go if I were running. You see, we know that she was severely shocked by what happened. Our mother was killed in her place on the plane, and we imagine that she was traumatised by this.'

'Yes, indeed, that would be understandable. I am very sorry about your mother's death; a terrible thing for you all to have to handle. Do you know any more about what happened after your mother was shot?'

'Thank you. All we really know about that moment was that the hijacker was holding Cassie in front of him as he had done on previous landings and refuelling. We were told that our mother said *take me.*' Ali gulped. It was so difficult to talk about, but for Cassie's sake she would do it.

'I can't begin to imagine your emotions...'

'I'm fine,' Ali said. 'Our prime concern now is for our sister.' Concentrate, she told herself. 'There are two links to Dublin,' she continued. 'Our mother was from Dublin, and also we were raised at Seapoint and spent all our waking hours down at the beach. Our house overlooked the sea. Cassie lived there until she was eight. I know the strength of the links that we, as sisters, feel towards that place. My other sister and I both think, or maybe we just hope, that possibly Cassie has tried to find her way back there. Bearing in mind Cassie was in a state of shock, the hijacking, our mother being killed, and then who knows... She got off that plane in Rome and disappeared. The newspapers here have been kind enough to run her picture and an article on her disappearance in both today's and tomorrow's papers, and we're hoping that maybe someone might recognise her.'

'Your sister is eighteen now?'

'Yes, she was seventeen when it happened, she will be nineteen shortly; she's tall, slim, blonde, with curly hair. She was a bubbly, happy person who was just growing into herself when she disappeared. And all we want is to find her, to know that she is safe.'

'Ali Peters, thank you for talking to us today. I've just heard that the television studio next door have invited you on to a programme that airs in an hour's time, so you will be able to show your sister's picture on it. And listeners, check the show, check the papers and maybe you will recognise the missing Cassie Peters. Remember, she survived that horrendous hijacking last summer, and her family want her back.'

'Thank you,' Ali said.

They shook hands as she left the studio. 'Good luck,' he said to her. She nodded and made her way across to the television studio.

Once again she braced herself, unsure of what to expect. It transpired that she was going to be interviewed for the news and the piece would be aired on both the six o'clock and the nine o'clock news. It was a two-minute slot, and Cassie's picture was shown both before and after the interview. She repeated what she said on the radio, this time concluding by saying, 'If anyone has any information about my sister Cassie Peters, please would they call me. I'm staying in Jury's Hotel in Ballsbridge and I can be contacted there until Monday.'

The interviewer said, 'Thank you, Ali Peters. Don't forget, if you have seen Cassie Peters please contact us here at the studio or call the police. All information will be passed to the Peters family.'

The microphone was turned off. 'We'll cut that bit about contacting you in Jury's Hotel. You don't want every crank badgering you all night and all weekend.'

'Thank you,' Ali said. 'I didn't think. I'm really glad this was being pre-recorded, if that's the word.'

'Don't worry. That piece was good, and the photograph of Cassie will be shown at least twice. I wish you good luck. We'll be following the story, hopefully to a successful conclusion.'

Ali made her way to the hotel and checked in. She felt exhausted. She knew that she should eat, but she was too tired and she went to her room. She did not unpack. She put her case on the baggage stand, turned on the television and lay down on the bed. She slept through the interview and woke at about ten that night to hear the phone ringing.

Groggily, she reached out and answered it. 'Hello?' she said.

'Miss Peters, we have a call for you from a Mr Dunne. Shall I put it through?'

'Yes, yes please,' she said. There was a click on the line.

'Ali, this is Tom Dunne,' he said. 'We met in Rome...'

'Yes of course. I know who you are. I got your letter... I... How... how are you?'

'I'm fine,' he said. 'I had a problem finding out where you were. I saw you on the news earlier and I rang the station. I had to convince them of who I was. They had interviewed me when I came home after the hijacking, so eventually the penny dropped and they realised the connection. They gave me your hotel. I'm calling because it occurred to me that if this is your first trip back to Ireland since we were children, maybe you don't know anyone, and maybe I could take you out to dinner.'

'Now?' Ali asked, realising that she was still hungry, but that it must be very late.

'Well, I had been thinking about tomorrow evening, but if you haven't had dinner...'

'Well, have you had dinner?'

'There's a place in your hotel that stays open most of the night. It's called the Coffee Dock. I'll be there in twenty minutes. Is that all right?'

'Yes,' Ali said. 'Thank you.'

She felt slightly bewildered and wondered if he had some information about Cassie. He would have said it, she thought, as she got off the bed and went to wash her face and hands and to comb her hair. Glancing in the mirror she thought she looked awful, tired, drained... she couldn't find a word strong enough. She thought back to the girl she had been aged sixteen, and even to the woman she had been the previous summer. She had progressed from a relatively happy teenager in a new bikini to a woman on the verge of divorce ten years later. She did not think of herself as a widow, but as someone whose marriage had ended before her husband's death.

That day in the Irish Embassy in Rome, when she, her father and Mer met Tom, she had felt a spark of some sort. It had surprised her at the time as she was recovering from Maurice and had assumed she was inured from such feelings. She had of course pushed it aside, but occaionally she did think about it. It had surprised her that she was capable of connecting with someone, but it had been so fleeting that later she was unsure how real it had been. But in the course of the intervening months, as Cassie's disappearance became prolonged, she convinced herself that she had imagined it.

Twenty minutes later she was down in the Coffee Dock. Tom was already there. He greeted her with a hug. 'It's good to see you,' he said. 'And before you ask if I have any news about Cassie, I don't. I just thought you might like some company.'

She nodded. 'Yes. Thank you. I would.'

He insisted on buying her dinner although he had eaten already, and he got them both a glass of wine. They sat opposite each other.

'This is embarrassing, eating in front of you like this.'

'Not at all. I will pick at your chips and drink my wine.'

There were some silences during that one-sided meal, and Ali would look up and see him gazing at her.

'You've been through the wars,' he remarked.

'Do I look that bad?' she said, knowing full well that she did.

'No, of course not. I think you look wonderful. I was just commenting on the fact that this last year must have been draining. You look just the way I remember you from last summer, that surreal day in the Irish embassy in Rome when you, your sister and father walked in. I had thought that unreal feeling a lot on the plane; the feeling that what was happening could not be happening. And then in the embassy that day, you walked in and...'

'And?'

'I don't know,' he said. 'I just felt something.'

So he had felt it too, she had not imagined it; it had been real. She found him suave, funny and flirtatious, and she found herself laughing again.

'I haven't laughed in ages,' she said.

'Time to change that,' he commented. 'Great laugh there, Ali, great smile. More of the same please.'

From anyone else she thought that might sound trite, but it did not from him. She was grateful for the company, glad to have food and to share some time, grateful too that she did not have to explain herself to Tom. He knew the ordeal her family was going through, and he had experienced what Cassie had. For some reason this gave her reassurance. It seemed to mean that fewer explanations were required. They talked easily with each other, sometimes a little shyly when they referred to their childhood days at Seapoint, knowing that somehow they must have been there at the same time.

'Are you married?' she asked, hoping that did not sound as forward as she thought it might.

'No, I never married,' he laughed. 'Did you?'

'Yes. I did. Too young and to the wrong man.'

'Want to talk about it?'

'No. It's not on the agenda,' she said.

'The agenda?'

'I mean... I don't know what I mean. I think I mean I don't want to talk about it because we're having a nice time, and...'

'That's fine. Another time. I would like to hear it.'

'Would you? It's a sorry story.'

'Now, tomorrow, do you have plans?'

'No. I've done what I came to do. I thought I might go to Seapoint, have a walk, take some photographs for my sister Mer.'

'Let me walk you down memory lane then,' he said. 'You're tired. You should have another drink, it'll help you sleep, and I'll collect you in the morning.'

'Great. Thank you.' For some reason her heart was pounding. She shook her head in disbelief. This could not be happening, this feeling of connection, even excitement, of being alive again. She thought she was done with all that. And with the feeling of happiness and pleasure that she so briefly felt came a feeling of guilt. How dare she feel like that with Cassie still missing?

'Don't look like that,' Tom said. 'You know you're allowed to feel happy. When Cassie comes back she will be better for knowing that you had happy times. I know I would want that for my brother. And yes, I do think about that, about what you're going through, and if it were reversed, if I were the one missing, I would like to think that my brother, while looking for me, managed to enjoy himself at least some of the time.'

She nodded. He had read her thoughts. It was not surprising really. He was the last to see Cassie, to have spoken to her, to have wiped the blood from her face. In his own way he must be haunted by that.

'Now finish your drink,' Tom said. 'You're going to bed. We're going to have a good time together tomorrow. I'm going to meet you for breakfast here at ten. You need to sleep. We'll forget that last drink, unless you want to take one up to your room with you?'

'No. I'm ready for bed now,' she said. 'Tom... thank you.'

He brought her to the elevator, kissed her on the cheek and said 'sleep well.'

***

Ali did sleep well. It took her a while to unwind as so much had happened during the day. She went over the interviews in her head, wondering if anything would come of them. In her heart she did not think that anything would, but there was always the hope. She did not let herself think long about the hope, it was always too painful and yet it always came back to that, hope. She thought about Tom contacting her and coming to the hotel, about sitting looking at him and liking what she saw and trying to relate it to the man she had so briefly met in the embassy.

It seemed strange to her that the connection was as simple as it appeared. Tom seemed to feel the same. She smiled as she thought of things he had said. She was glad he had contacted her by letter before she came to Dublin, and even more pleased that he had made contact when he saw her on the news. It seemed churlish of her now not to have replied to his letter. Churlish? Too strong a word, she thought. She simply had not had the energy to reply to it.

And then she was asleep, and she, who had not dreamed that she could remember since shortly after she had married, dreamed once again. It was a strange dream with snow falling on a summer's day, of snakes in a zoo, of a rock they called the Hillier when they were children, and of Cassie slowly, slowly pushing that rock up a beach that was on an incline. It might have been a disturbing dream, but when she woke in the morning she had the feeling that Cassie was alive. It was the first thing she thought of when awakening, a knowledge that somewhere out there, outside the hotel, outside in the world, Cassie really was alive. So strong was the feeling that she thought of phoning Mer, but then remembered she was in Rome with Bernd for the weekend, sticking up posters in the now all too familiar spots.

She got up and showered and met Tom for breakfast.

'Do you get tired of people asking you how you are?' he asked as they sat down.

'Yes,' she said with a smile. Once again he knew how she felt.

'After I got back from Athens last year, people kept asking me that question. How are you, Tom? How are you doing? The worst of it was that I felt they did not want to know that I thought I was going out of my mind. They seemed to want to hear about the drama of it all with no understanding that for me it wasn't drama; it was trauma. The immediacy of what had happened had been so intense and I needed to put distance between then and the afterwards.'

'So what did you say to people?'

'First I said, 'I'm fine, I'm doing fine, thanks'. Of course this was a lie. Let's eat, I'll tell you more about that shortly.'

She watched him during breakfast, wondering how he had dealt with what had happened.

As they walked to his car to drive to Seapoint, he began talking about it again.

'Survivors carry guilt. I've read about it,' he said.

'Guilt?'

'Yes. You go over and over things, thinking if only I had done this or that; if only I had overpowered one of the hijackers, used him as a shield instead of what had happened...'

'Are you being serious?' Ali was horrified.

'Yes, totally. And yes, I know the whole plane would probably have exploded with multiple deaths instead of one. But that's the way the mind goes. I'm quite sure I'm not the only person to think like that. All of them must have felt it, the pilot, the co-pilot, the cabin crew, the men on the plane; the women too... For all I know, even the children. There is an endless, exhausting feeling that maybe I could have done something. And then there is always the realisation that if I had, the outcome would have been different. I played it like a film in my mind. I couldn't sleep for a long time afterwards, and when I did, the nightmares...'

'I'm sorry,' Ali said.

'Not as sorry as I am. I also go over and over the final landing in Rome, and think that maybe I should have taken your sister under my wing...'

'But you had saved her on the plane. You covered her on the floor...'

'Yes. Oh, yes, I did everything right. Logically I have nothing to blame myself for. Everyone on that plane was a potential victim. And we were powerless. And yes, I did help Cassie. But I still feel guilt. Everyone was in a state of shock. The children were crying. People were shaking. I don't know who was in the worst state, and it doesn't matter because I can't do anything more about that now. But Cassie was the one who had been through the worst ordeal. She was almost shot, and her mother died. Your mother... sorry. Your mother, too. And I think about that, and how your mother managed to take her place in those final seconds, and I think I should have done that. I should have said "take me". Only I didn't. I sat there in my seat terrified just like every other passenger on that plane.'

'Have you any reason to think that the hijacker who swapped Cassie with my mother would have taken you instead?'

'No. None. I know that. In fact, he probably wouldn't have. He might well have just shot me right then.'

They arrived at Seapoint and he parked the car. They walked down the pathway where Cassie had fallen all those years ago, and Ali touched the hedge that came over the wall and pulled off one of the buds. They did not talk as they walked down to the Martello tower. He took her arm as they walked around it and onto the slipways. The tide was half out, half in. She could not tell which way it was going. Once she would have known. It was a nice enough day with a blue sky reflected in the sea, puffy clouds in the sky, warm but not too hot. They stopped walking and she stood and stared at the sea. The top of the Hillier appeared above the water. It did not look as big or as majestic as she remembered it from childhood. They went and sat down side by side on the slipway, shoes off, legs dangling over the edge above the rocks, the sea swirling beneath them moving the fronds and weed on the rocks, around and around, back and forth, the black bubbles on the seaweed lifting and dropping in the endless movement of tide and time.

'I had thought...' Tom continued his thoughts of earlier as if unaware there had been a good ten-minute silence. 'Hoped, not thought. I had hoped that during those long hours on the plane that somehow Cassie's personal hijacker, and that's how he seemed, would have bonded with her. I kept thinking isn't that what happens? And that he wouldn't be able to kill her because of this bond. I knew, I think everyone on the plane knew, except for the children of course, that there was going to be no happy ending.'

'Yes, we knew that, too,' Ali said.

'I kept thinking that whatever happens next was going to happen very fast and that we, the passengers, must be ready to drop to the floor. I knew that instinctively. And when the hijacker lifted Cassie again and brought her to the door of the plane, I thought, I really believed that somehow he would be shot and the plane stormed. I knew it was all about to happen. And then it didn't. The whole thing changed. She was thrown on the floor and the hijacker took your mother...'

'You don't have to do this,' Ali said. 'It's all right. You really don't...'

'I read it all wrong. And that's where the guilt comes in.'

'But what did you read wrong? You did nothing wrong. They swapped places, my sister and my mother, and what unfolded was out of everyone's control.'

'I know. I just wanted to tell you.' He put his arm around her. 'May I put my arm around you?' he asked.

She leaned against him. She knew he was so caught up in his thoughts that his movement and his words had just happened in reverse order.

'Have you... got over it? For want of better words...' she asked.

'Mostly. I just wish that the outcome was different. I wish that you had Cassie back where she belongs. That is probably the only real thing that I could have changed. When I work through all the guilt for surviving, and realised, as I mostly do, that I could not change the course of the actual hijacking, I then think, well Tom, you could have saved Cassie.'

'My family feels that you did save Cassie. What happened after that just happened. Who knows what state Cassie was in, what was happening in her mind? You've described terrible emotions. Hers must have been a thousand times worse. Our mother died instead of her... and other things...'

'What other things?'

'I don't know if you know that our mother left us when Cassie was eight, do you?'

'No. I didn't.'

'Yes, well... long story, but she went to live in England and we went to live in Germany. And somehow last summer Cassie went and found her. At least, that's what we assume happened. Flight records have been investigated and it appears that Cassie must have met up with our mother in London and took a flight with her to Athens. They spent a couple of weeks in Greece and then they flew back together. And you know the rest. So you see Cassie must have been through quite a lot in the weeks before the hijacking, getting to know our mother, and then losing her like that.'

'I see.'

'I wonder does that make it worse.'

'How do you mean?'

'Well, if she had our mother with her all those growing-up years, she would have lost someone she knew as a stable foundation in her life. Would that be worse than losing someone she had already lost as a child?'

Tom shook his head. 'There is no answer to that.'

'I know. But *my* mind won't stop going over and over things like that. Tom, you said that you mostly have got over it, over the feelings of guilt, over the whole event. How did you do that?'

'Ironically, it was through talking. Eventually I realised I had to stop saying I was fine, and to talk it out. And I did, with my family, my parents and my brother. They listened, just like you listen. The more I talked, the less I ran and re-ran the film of how it all might have been, the less I found myself helpless on that plane. Living inside your head is a terrible thing.'

'That I know,' Ali said.

'Let's walk,' he said. 'We'll walk along the seafront to Dun Laoghaire. Will you have dinner with me this evening? We could drop in on my parents either before or after. I'd like them to meet you. They live near here. If you would like? You don't have to...'

'I'd love to,' she said.

They smiled at each other, and he helped her up from their seat by the water's edge. They walked to Dun Laoghaire, and somewhere along the way he kissed her.

*** 

'I should go home tomorrow,' Ali said. It was the following day and she and Tom were standing in her hotel room.

'Could you not stay just one more day?' he said.

'I want to. You know that. But I should go back.'

'How can this be happening?' he said, pulling her into his arms. 'We've just found each other. I felt it last year that day we met, and then later I told myself it was just a reaction to shock. I don't want to let you go.'

'I'm doing my Master's at the moment, and I give tutorials to undergraduates, and I have a number of them this coming week,' Ali said. 'I can't cancel them. But...'

'But?'

'Could you, would you come to Germany next weekend, or... as soon as you can?'

'Yes, of course I will. Try and keep me away.'

They looked at each other with the profound sense of disbelief that had enveloped them both over the previous two days. To have come all this way and not to find what she was searching for was no more than Ali expected. Of course she had hopes that some news of Cassie might emerge, but, as yet, none had. To have met Tom and to have resurrected feelings of love and affection as she had once felt for Maurice, of really beginning to care for someone was beyond any hope she might ever have had. She had thought it would be a long time, if ever, before she could feel again.

He pulled her gently onto the bed and wrapped his arms around her. 'We're both tired from talking and walking,' he said.

She leaned into him and nodded. They were both exhausted from talking but there was still so much to say and to hear.

'Do you have the feeling that we might have met before?' Ali asked.

He nodded. 'Yes,' he said. 'I feel like I know you already, and I have no idea why.'

'I still haven't told you what happened to me,' she said slowly, 'but in a sense Cassie saved me. Only in a sense, because I did get away by myself, but Cassie had pieced together what was happening. It was worse than she imagined but Mer told me that one of the last things that Cassie said was that she was going to come and find me, and not leave until she did. It's all a bit muddled, and it's also stuff that I don't like thinking about, let alone talking about. I will tell you, but not right now. But I need you to understand that until Cassie is found, I really can't sit back and properly enjoy other things.'

'You can tell me when you are ready,' Tom said. 'There's no rush. I will see about getting a flight to Germany next weekend. Now, we should kiss again. It has been at least an hour since the last kiss, and considering that I'm going to have to wait a whole week...'

# CASSIE'S TALE

Around and around the wheels of the train, the wheels on the bus, the wings on the plane, the turn of the earth, the rising and setting of the sun, the washing of waves over my mind. Around and around.

I found nothingness. Silent days. Quiet room. A place to sleep that was neither hard nor stony. Confined perhaps. Perhaps too confined. Designed to keep me in and the monster out. The Minotaur. In my nightmares he finds his way in, the cold barrel of the gun on the dripping sweat of my brow. Deep, deep I went and closed the gates and doors behind me.

During the day there is the calm, futile nothingness of the hands of the clock moving slowly. Meaningless until nightfall and the lights are turned off. They leave a light for me. Sometimes I sleep. Sometimes I don't. They come and talk to me. They walk with me.

Memory flickers.

I remember. I remember. The laughter of children. The crying of children. The heat of summer days. Here I look out the window at the seasons changing. When winter comes, the land is cold and frozen and nothing grows. I know it is the time that Persephone has returned to the Underworld, and Demeter, forlorn, awaits her return.

I am allowed to walk in the grounds but someone always comes with me. They talk and talk to me. I have nothing to say. There are no words. I wear the clothes they give me. I eat the food they feed me. I watch the clouds wisping, floating, speeding across the sky. Sometimes I see the trail of smoke from a jet plane overhead, and then I close my eyes and try not to remember the light on the wing of the plane, of a girl standing in a doorway, of the ferryman, Charon, with the painful grimace on his face. The living put a coin in the mouth of the dead as payment for their journey. The Keres were the death spirits. They hovered on the battlefields and ripped the souls from the dead and brought them to the ferryman. I once read that when Pandora opened her accursed box, it was the Keres who were released. I wonder am I one of them, one of the sisters of Fate.

In my sleep it is not a white-dressed nurse or a doctor who follows me down the River Styx. It is the Minotaur. He calls me by my name. Persephone. Everything is so muddled again.

I am the nameless one.

Oh the heart that mocked me and the hand that fed.

I am the sacrifice that went wrong.

# CHAPTER TWENTY ONE

Months passed and the seasons changed again and again, and a normal morning dawned in the Peters' house in Tübingen. Karl Peters rose early, showered and dressed. He no longer looked in the mirror for more than a few seconds as he brushed his hair. He could not bear the face he saw. His hair was grey, the lines on his face deep, with a depth of unchanging sadness in his eyes that no matter what he did would not go away.

Sometimes he thought of the day in Rome when he had been asked to identify his ex-wife as there was no one else to undertake this task. It must have been the day after Cassie disappeared in the airport. He remembered the smell in the hospital morgue, the white sheet covering the waxy body he had once coveted, the closed eyes, the bullet wound, the bruising. He had reached out and touched her hair and then he had nodded. The identification was complete. There was no one to claim her. A funeral service was arranged and he, Ali and Mer had sat in the front row of a tiny chapel and listened to the words of perpetuity. An Irish priest had read the words *Ashes to ashes, dust to dust.* She was cremated later that day, and at some point he was given an urn that bore her ashes. He put it aside in his hotel room, uncertain what he should do with it.

It was Mer who had said to him over a year later when they were home in Tübingen, 'Papa, I was thinking maybe we should let Miriam's ashes go into the river.'

He was puzzled. 'What river?'

'Well, the Neckar. I mean, she was once happy there. You said that you and she met on the towpath. Would that not be a good place to let her go?'

He nodded. 'I had wondered if I should get the ashes to England, seeing as that is where she lived for so long.'

'All water meets somewhere, all rivers join seas; it would be easier here, and it would also mean that if we wanted to think about her, we could go down to the river and know where we had put her. Tom is coming this weekend to be with Ali, and it might be a good time.'

\*\*\*

They did just that, early one morning shortly after sunrise. It was the fourth weekend that Tom Dunne had flown in from Dublin, as he now regularly did to spend time with Ali or on the start of a journey to accompany her to Rome. Ali and Mer now took it in turns during holidays and long weekends to fly there to try to keep Cassie's profile alive.

They were a small group, Karl and his daughters, Tom holding Ali's hand, Bernd with his arm around Mer, and Leonora standing beside them, as Miriam's ashes went with the river in the early dawn before the oarsmen arrived.

Karl remembered Ali saying as they stood on the towpath, 'I feel like an actor in a play, playing a role and a bit unsure if I have learned the lines correctly.'

He knew what she meant. He felt he had no real reason to be disposing of Miriam's ashes; that it was not his role, but that he was there for the girls and for the absent Cassie. He could not bear to think about Cassie, but he could not stop thinking about her. She was everywhere. In the house, he sometimes thought he could hear her laugh. In her room, touching some of her things late at night before he went to bed, he would sit on a chair and stare at her pillow and imagine her blonde, tousled curls sprayed on the white cotton. He missed her untidiness and the schoolbag thrown on the hall floor and thought of the amount of times he had fallen over it, and now he longed to fall over it again.

'More like a Greek chorus,' Mer was saying, bringing him back to the towpath and away from his thoughts. 'The only problem is that we don't understand what has happened and so can't explain it.'

'Does anyone want to say anything?' Karl asked.

They shook their heads.

'Then, may she be at peace,' he said, putting the lid back on the empty urn, and turning he walked back along the path and placed the urn in a bin.

He wanted to feel something but there was nothing there except for the terrible fears for Cassie. He often tried to tell himself that she was deliberately staying away, hiding maybe, unable to face them after Miriam's death on the plane. He feared she might blame herself for that. He imagined that she might feel, since she had been the one who went to look for her mother, that she had brought about this tragedy. Of course he was not absolutely certain that she had gone to find Miriam, but he could find no other explanation for what had happened. They might have just bumped into each other in Greece, although on the scale of probabilities, this seemed less likely.

He had, of course, long since spoken to her friend Anna, who was supposedly going to accompany her on her train trip, and Anna had denied any knowledge of such plans. He often thought how little people know each other. He had known Miriam, and then found he did not know her at all, but maybe that was different, he thought. It was probably not that surprising that Cassie had headed off by herself. After all, teenagers did things, and were secretive; it was part of growing up. That, of course, made him think about Ali. He was grateful that her marriage and that particular phase of her life were over, but saddened that it had ever happened.

When Ali told him that a friend was coming to visit from Dublin, he remembered forcing himself to be polite, terrified that some new horror was about to befall her.

He liked her Tom Dunne though, liked him in a way he had not expected. He had no clear memory of him from their meeting in the embassy in Rome that terrible day when Cassie had disappeared. He was reassured, if surprised, to find he was the man who had helped Cassie on the plane, that he too had lived through the hijacking. He thought he would feel overly protective of Ali for the rest of her life, and now he found he was not worrying about her any more, or at least not at this moment. He liked the way Ali's beautiful face lit up in a smile when Tom was there.

'Karl,' Leonora was touching his arm, always gentle and always there. He was moved by her dawn attendance at this strange charade on the river bank, glad that she was there, and glad too that Ali and Mer each had someone to support them.

'Yes,' he said, pulling himself back to the present.

'I wonder if we should go back to my place. It's too early to find anywhere open for breakfast, and I took the liberty of getting in food yesterday just in case you felt like it.'

'The girls...' he said.

'All of us,' she said. 'You and me, Ali and Tom, Mer and Bernd.'

'Thank you.'

'Are you sure you want to leave the urn in that refuse bin?' she asked.

'What? Oh, yes. It's empty,' he replied. 'It's all done now.'

She nodded.

He remembered breakfast in her apartment that morning, the smell of coffee brewing, pastries being reheated in the oven, small-talk covering emotions that could not be expressed. Miriam was finally gone. In itself that would have been a relief were it not for Cassie. Everything came back to Cassie, just as everything did over the long slow months that followed.

***

But on that ordinary morning two years after Cassie's disappearance, he looked into her bedroom on the way downstairs, just as he always did. He drank coffee in the kitchen, and then cycled to the university. He picked up a newspaper on the way. Locking his bicycle at one of the bicycle rails and undoing the clips on his trouser legs, he looked up to see Leonora Meyer approaching him. She looked at his face as she did most mornings and registered no change. There was tiredness in his eyes. She reached out her hand and touched him. 'Karl, come and have breakfast with me,' she said. He nodded and they walked together into the building.

'Karl, would you like to have dinner with me tonight?'

'Dinner?' he said. He seemed surprised. He was used to their coffees, their breakfasts, their lunches.

'You know, I cook, you come over, we have a drink and then we eat,' she said. There was no irony in her voice, only concern.

'I usually go straight home,' he said. 'In case there is some news.'

'Karl, I know. But I was thinking, maybe one evening off. You come over to me. If there were any news, you would hear quickly enough. We would make sure they have my phone number.'

Karl looked bemused. 'I suppose they do have your number. Mer anyway. Yes. Yes. Why not?'

And, realising that he might sound uninterested in having dinner with her, in having a break from the repetitive tedium of the waiting days, he said, 'Sorry, Leonora. I would love to have dinner with you.'

***

Back at home, Ali and Mer showered and dressed and met in the kitchen. They hugged each other briefly as they did most mornings. 'You make coffee, I'll get the cereal,' Ali said. They busied themselves in the kitchen.

'What time do you have to leave?' Mer asked.

'Late start for me today,' Ali said. 'I'm giving a tutorial at eleven. Two students who are afraid of failing exams; I'm their last hope. How about you, what are you doing today?'

'Nothing exceptional,' Mer said. 'I'm going to the library, meeting Bernd for lunch, and writing... that's the plan.'

'It's a nice day,' Ali said looking out into the garden. They were both silent for a moment, Cassie was there in their thoughts. They had once said to each other that every time they spoke about the weather or the seasons, Cassie seemed to be very close to them as they both wondered was she experiencing the same feeling of sun or wind or rain on her skin.

'Juice?' Mer asked.

'Please.'

After breakfast they tidied the kitchen and Ali wiped the table. The phone rang.

'You or me?' Mer asked as she put the milk in the fridge.

'Me,' Ali said going into the other room.

She answered the phone. 'Yes, this is Ali. Oh, Herr Brunner...'

In the kitchen, Mer stopped what she was doing. Her heart started pounding and she made for the living-room door. Ali was sitting on the sofa, her face completely white, holding the phone as if she did not know what it was. Mer moved quickly and took the phone from her. 'Hello,' she said. 'This is Merope Peters. Herr Brunner, is that you? What has happened? Has something happened?'

She listened silently as he repeated what he had just told Ali. 'A girl has been found in a hospital in England. We think she may be Cassie. I don't want to get your hopes up, but there is a very good possibility...'

Mer closed her eyes and told herself to breathe. 'Why do you think it's Cassie?' she asked.

'It's a tenuous link,' Herr Brunner said. 'But it is the first time that something likely has happened. This girl has been in the hospital for almost two years. She has never spoken. They believe she has amnesia.

But someone in the hospital made the link yesterday afternoon and contacted our embassy in London. Someone from the embassy went down last night. He can't be sure, and they have just contacted us.'

'We'll go there now,' Mer said. 'I can't think clearly.'

'I understand that. I don't want to get your hopes up in case this is not Cassie. But I think there is more than a good chance that it is.'

'We should go alone,' Mer said. 'I mean, we ought not to tell our father until we know for sure. I don't think he can take much more...'

'Again, I understand. If you can get yourselves to London, I will have someone meet you and bring you to the hospital.'

'Can you organise the flights for us?' Mer asked hopefully. 'We'll be ready in a half hour, and then we'll take the train to Stuttgart. Is there a flight from there?'

'I'll call you back. Get yourselves ready, passports and whatever else you need. I'll be back to you in about twenty minutes.'

Ali was crying on the sofa. 'Ali,' Mer said. 'There's no time to cry. We can cry later. We've to move fast now. You've to cancel that tutorial. I'll write a note for Papa. I'll tell him we'll call later, just in case he gets home before we have the chance to talk to him. I need to phone Bernd.' She handed the phone to Ali, who was staring at her.

'Ali, please, you must cancel your tutorial. Herr Brunner is going to phone us back and we need the line free. Then get your passport and an overnight bag. We need to be ready to leave in thirty minutes.'

Suddenly jolted into action, Ali did as she was told. The tutorial was cancelled. Mer wrote a note and left it on the kitchen table. She was unable to contact Bernd and she raced upstairs to put a bag together while she thought what to do. She did not want Bernd worrying. In desperation she came back down and phoned his mother. 'Frau Meyer,' she said as she was connected to his mother's office in the university. 'It's Merope Peters.'

'Oh, I just had breakfast with your father,' Frau Meyer's voice was warm, and then concerned. 'Is everything all right?'

Mer explained that she needed to leave a message for Bernd and had no time to spare. She hesitated and then decided to bring Frau Meyer into her confidence. 'So, you see,' she said, having explained about the phone call from the Ministry, 'we don't want to get Papa's hopes up in case this is not Cassie.'

'I understand,' Frau Meyer said. 'Don't worry. I won't say anything, and I will find Bernd. God speed, Merope. But please phone me as soon as you know.'

Mer thanked her and hung up.

Three hours later they were on a flight for London. Occasionally they looked at each other but neither sister could find anything to say. They held hands from time to time; they stared out the window at the clouds beneath; sometimes their hands shook; sometimes hope surged in their hearts and then was pushed aside in fear. 'Supposing it is,' they each thought, then replaced it with 'supposing it is not'.

Ali kept thinking of quotes about hope. It springs eternal in the human breast, she thought. She hated hope filling her like that, knowing that it would die and there would be an empty feeling afterwards. She thought of a quote from Nietzsche, '*In reality hope is the worst of all evils, because it prolongs man's torments.*' And that was what she was feeling, totally tormented. She wanted the plane to fly faster, for the inevitable to be faced so that she could begin all over again.

'My thoughts are driving me mad,' she whispered to Mer.

Mer faced her. 'We can't live without hope,' she said. 'Just hold on. It won't be long now.'

'And if it isn't Cassie?' Ali said.

'Then we will face that when it happens.'

'You're so stoical,' Ali said.

'No, I'm not. I think that we take it in turns to rise and fall.'

The plane arrived on time and they were met once again by an official from the embassy. He was young with an enthusiastic face and he shook their hands. 'This is the most exciting thing that has happened to me since I joined the diplomatic service.' Their pale, nervous faces looked hopefully at him. 'I went down last night to the hospital,' he said. 'The girl there is about the right height. If it is your sister, she's much thinner than in the photographs we have in the embassy. She's about the right age, but I couldn't be sure. Come,' he said. 'I have the car in the car park, and the hospital is only about fifty minutes from here.'

'Did you speak to her?' Mer asked, trying to keep pace with his long strides.

'I did, but she was unresponsive. I couldn't tell if she understood what I was saying, although the doctor said that he thought her eyes flickered when I spoke to her in German. Obviously they have only spoken to her in English. They had no reason to do otherwise.'

'Her English is fluent though,' Ali said.

He loaded their bags into the car, and they sat quietly as he negotiated his way out and onto the road. The sky was overcast and hinted at rain.

# CASSIE'S TALE

They came, my sisters, my nymph star sisters, sylphs in the midday sun. They took Demeter's place and they searched the earth and the skies, but it was a long time before they thought to journey to the Underworld.

Their faces loomed in and out as I lay on my bed, and the flickers of memory began to connect. The flickers became larger and longer, and my sisters held my hands. I wanted to cry, but I had used up my tears. I wanted to scream, but I had lost my voice. I wanted to remember, and not to remember, because there was safety in the dark places, skirting the corners of the labyrinth. As long as I hid, the Minotaur would not find me.

Down the River Styx they come, Alcyone and Merope, their boat pausing beside me, their hands wraithlike as they reach out to me. They whisper my name over and over, and I remember. Faces become clear in my mind, all the faces I had obliterated. Medusa, Demeter, the Minotaur. I must sleep; in the depth of sleep, even though there are nightmares, it is better than being awake.

I close my eyes. 'Sleep,' the nymphs say. 'Sleep now, little Cass, we will not let you go.'

They call from their constellation.

They want me to join them.

How can I tell them the sacrifice went wrong, that their mother is dead?

# CHAPTER TWENTY TWO

Mer stroked Cassie's hand and waited until her breathing was even and it was clear her sister was asleep. She stood then and faced Ali. They stared at each other in silence, before joining the doctor and the nurse in the corridor outside. Mer reached for a tissue in her bag and wiped her eyes.

'Are you all right?' the nurse asked. 'Would you like to sit down?'

Mer shook her head. 'Thank you. I'm fine. The tears are just tears of relief. We've been looking for her for such a long time.'

The doctor nodded. 'Perhaps you would like to join me in my office so we can talk,' he said.

'We'd like to take our sister home,' Ali said.

'I understand,' he said, 'but before that happens we do need to talk. She's in a fragile state...'

'We've been searching for almost two years,' Mer said. 'We have to take her home. She will be safe with us. We will care for her.'

'It's not that simple,' the doctor said. 'Come.' He led them down the corridor, the nurse in tow, and into a room at the end. 'Please sit,' he said, gesturing to the chairs in front of a desk. 'Until yesterday, we didn't even have a name for her.'

'Her name is Cassie Peters,' Ali said. 'She's our little sister. She will be twenty this year.'

The doctor opened a file on his desk and started writing. 'Where was she born?' he asked.

'In Dublin, on August 23rd 1964,' Ali replied. 'Look, I don't see why we can't just take her home with us.'

'In due course you can. But first of all we need to know what happened to reduce her to the state she is in, and you need to know what has happened since she arrived here. Let's talk, and then let's work out what is best for her.'

Mer was wiping tears from her eyes again.

'We should phone our father. He doesn't know. We thought it better to wait until we were sure.'

'Phone him now,' the doctor said pushing the telephone across his desk.

'You or me?' Mer asked Ali.

'I'll do it,' Ali said, reaching for the phone and dialling the number.

'Can you ask him to tell Bernd and Frau Meyer as well?' Mer said. There were tears still coursing down her face.

'Doctor,' the nurse said. 'I wonder if I should organise some tea.'

'Thank you, Nurse,' he said. 'That's a good idea. You are in shock,' he said to Mer. 'It's perfectly normal.'

'I just can't believe we have really found her. We were looking in the wrong place. All this time...'

'Let me fill you in,' the doctor said. 'For our part, well, Cassie, as we can now call her, was brought here nearly two years ago. She was found at the side of the road by a passing police car. She was clearly very troubled, non-responsive, frightened. Someone, perhaps even she, we don't know, had hacked off her hair. There were no other signs of assault, sexual or otherwise. She has been here since then. No one came to identify her, although it was in the local papers at the time. The only time she participates is in our art therapy class, and that is how we finally made a connection. Her drawings are very good, very specific, very detailed. One of the nurses bought an English translation of a book of Greek myths for a niece or nephew, and she was looking through it, and the drawings in it reminded her of Cassie's art. She brought it to me and we contacted the German Embassy here in London and asked if the name Cassie Peters, the name on the book, meant anything to them. Your name,' he said to Mer, 'and Cassie's are on the front cover, and inside there is a short biography and it said you live in Germany. The embassy told us that she had disappeared two years ago after a hijacking, and they sent someone down last night.'

'We got the phone call this morning,' Mer said. 'We were on the first flight we could catch.'

The nurse came back carrying a tray with tea and biscuits.

'Have a cup of tea,' the doctor said. 'Then we will go back to Cassie.'

'I'm sure she recognised us,' Mer said.

'I think so too,' the doctor replied. 'One of the nurses is sitting with her to be there when she wakens. She will have a lot to deal with as she comes to terms with things. I have no doubt that she was suffering from complete amnesia and her mind now has to adjust. She may not remember everything. This is going to take time. And time for both of you, too. You've been on quite a journey.'

'It wasn't too bad,' Ali said. 'An early start this morning...'

'I didn't mean that journey,' the doctor said.

Mer took Ali's hand in hers. 'We're going to be all right now,' she said.

'I have no doubt,' the doctor said.

*\*\**

Karl arrived on the following day. He was still in a state of disbelief. So much time had elapsed and so much anguish had been endured. He found Ali sitting on a bench outside the hospital. She looked up in relief when she saw him getting out of the taxi. 'Papa,' she said, running over to him.

'Is it really Cassie?' he said.

'Yes, it really is.' He held her in his arms.

'It's over now,' she said. 'All that waiting and worrying. She has recognised us, but hasn't yet spoken. Mer is sitting with her now. She keeps falling asleep – Cassie I mean. We're taking it in turns. We've spoken to the doctor.'

She told him then how Cassie was found and brought to the hospital, and was only identified when the nurse bought a translation of Mer's first book and recognised her drawings.

'Is Mer coping?'

'Mer always copes,' Ali said. 'That's the one sound thing, the one sure thing we can rely on. I'm out here shaking and Mer is in there comforting Cassie.'

'Don't put yourself down,' he said. 'You've been through your own wars, and have survived. You cope just as well.'

'No, Papa, I don't. I always thought I was the strong one, the leader, the eldest child, but I failed on so many levels.'

'I don't think you failed at all,' he said. 'And I won't have you say that you did. You picked up the pieces because that is what we have to do and you did it. Now, let's go in.'

Cassie was awake when they arrived at her room. She looked at them as they came into the room. She gazed with her large, blue eyes.

'Come, Papa, come and talk to her. Look, Cassie, it's Papa,' Mer said.

She watched her father walk across to Cassie's bed, and how he bent down and lifted his daughter into his arms and cradled her like a baby.

Turning, she left the room and walked down the corridor. She needed air. She stopped in the main hallway as though uncertain which way to go. Her eyes were drawn to a picture hanging on the wall to the right of the main door. She stopped in disbelief. An icy cold shiver ran down her spine.

It was the picture of a nun, her nun from her Irish hospital, the nun from the strange anaesthesia dreams from long ago.

A nurse appeared beside her.

'Hello, Mer,' the nurse said. She and Ali were already well known in the hospital, part of a rejoicing and a celebration that all the staff felt at the discovery of who their lost patient really was. 'Is everything all right?'

'Who is that?' Mer asked pointing at the picture.

'She's the nun who founded this hospital. She wanted it to be a sanctuary for the lost,' the nurse smiled.

'The lost?'

'People with problems.'

'Was this picture here yesterday?' Mer asked. 'I don't remember seeing it.'

'No. It wasn't. We just had the vestibule painted and her portrait was found in one of the storerooms, and it was decided to place it here.'

Mer nodded. The eyes of the nun seemed to look at her. The ageless face, compassionate and warm from her dream world, looked down at her.

*What is lost has been found,* she thought.

# CASSIE'S TALE

They come again, my beloved sisters, the sylphs from the dawn of my time, and this time my father accompanies them. They stand or sit, and watch and talk. I can hear their voices and their words. I remember them as soon as I see them, Mer's gentle voice cajoling me back from the dark. I sleep and wake and sleep again. Each time the voices pulling me back.

I am not sure if I want to come back. I had a choice. I have a choice. I lie with my eyes closed, sometimes listening, sometimes not.

'We need you with us,' Mer whispers. 'We need you to come back to us.' She tells me a thousand stories, stories of looking for me, of Ali and a man called Tom Dunne who spent his spare time in Rome with her searching the streets and sticking up posters, of how Ali was rescued from the cold-eyed Maurice, and how they will never give up on me. There is some memory of Maurice, but that is not for now.

I think they should give up. I am worthless, a nothing that sought out my mother and she died because of me. If I speak they will want answers and I have none to give. I have nothing to say about anything. But they want me back. Their persistence is overwhelming. I squeeze Mer's hand so that she will know I can hear her and that I can understand but that I'm not yet ready.

There is so much memory and so much absence of memory. The links are not clear. I know the river Neckar, the river Styx, Camden Lock, the ever-moving sea at Seapoint... I know they are interlinked. I know that all people from the beginning of time connect and re-connect. I know the randomness of every thing. Every single thing overlaps and then spaces out so that I cannot see the connection. I keep losing the connection.

I know I have a choice. I can stay here in this safe place. I can keep the shutters closed and keep memory at bay. Or I can open my eyes and face the unsafe world outside where battles rage and insignificant people die on dusty landing strips, where the Keres come and rip the souls from the dead and feast on their blood. I listen to Mer talking about Ali and how she had to be coerced not to go back to Maurice, how our father prepared to face Maurice's parents and to demand an end to the brutality she had encountered, and the strange freedom of finding that Maurice had been hit by a bus, while Ali was safely at home in the gingerbread house.

The story draws me in.

I feel fault there too at not having spelled out earlier what I thought was happening in Ali's life, but Mer is putting a different spin on the tale. She seems to be thanking me for telling her that day in the railway station as I set off on my journey into the Underworld. She thanks me for seeing what had happened and for redirecting the course of Ali's history. She says Ali is finding happiness again, that she will find it now that I have been found.

She tells me how she and Ali have spent every spare minute searching the streets for me. How they never gave up. How they would never give up. She tells me how she and Bernd could now walk together in the evening at the river and how she will no longer cry at my absence, but that she needs me present in the present. She tells me that our mother died on an airplane and how she was cremated and her ashes scattered down the flowing Neckar River. She says that Miriam is at peace and we can let the past go. She says I am needed in the present and the future. She tells me how our books, yes, she says 'our books' have been translated and how I was found because of that. She says there are two more books written but that she is holding out for me as her illustrator and that she needs me back. No one can paint the darkness as I can.

She tells me how our mother left a will, and the house at Seapoint is ours. She says we will go back there and dance on the beach.

The pomegranate seeds, once sweet, are now bitter. The cleft in the earth is widening. There is room for me to climb back. She tells me of the sun outside and the rain, the feel of light on skin and the comfort of the human body heating in the day's warmth, of work to be done, fulfilment to be found, the joy of a kiss, of love and passion, and that all of these things are mine, I just have to come back out.

She tells me how she and Bernd had put their lives on hold but could move on once I returned. That I would move on with them. They would look after me all my life. All their lives. That Ali would never let go. She said there was nothing left in Pandora's Box save hope. She says that hope is ours. That we will never give up.

No Demeter to free me, but sisters and a father and their love.

Sometimes, I think today, that is enough.

*The jungle rooted in his shatter'd hearth,*
*The serpent coil'd about his broken shaft,*
*The scorpion crawling over naked skulls;* —
*I saw the tiger in the ruin'd fane*
*Spring from his fallen God, but trace of thee*
*I saw not; and far on, and, following out*
*A league of labyrinthine darkness, came*
*On three gray heads beneath a gleaming rift.*
*"Where"? and I heard one voice from all the three*
*"We know not, for we spin the lives of men,*
*And not of Gods, and know not why we spin!*
*There is a Fate beyond us."*

*From 'Demeter and Persephone' by Lord Alfred Tennyson*

# ACKNOWLEDGMENTS

I am grateful for the love and support of my children Steffen and Sophie Higel.

Thank you to all my cousins, for then and now, particularly Pamela McCourt Francescone, Deirdre McCourt and Orson Francescone.

I thank my pillars, Diana O'hUid, Ann Sheppard, Denise Harnett, Jean Sutton, Monica Kennedy, Orla Brennan and Perdita Quinlan: there are times you make me feel like the Acropolis.

Thank you to Caroline Montgomery.

Thank you to everyone at New Island for all their work and support.

Thank you to Val Fox who asks the right questions, to Bernie Lodewijks for reading and to Archie and Mary Green, who salvaged everything when the drains overflowed.

I thank my siblings Fergal and Lucy Stanley for being part of the memories of Seapoint.